Shane Hegarty

KMOUTH

WORLDS EXPLODE

CHAOS DESCENDS

DARKMOUTH

CHAOS DESCENDS

SHANE HEGARTY

Illustrated by James de la Rue

HarperCollins *Children's Books*

First published in hardback in Great Britain by HarperCollins *Children's Books* in 2016
HarperCollins *Children's Books* is a division of HarperCollins*Publishers* Ltd,
1 London Bridge Street, London, SE1 9GF

The HarperCollins website address is: www.harpercollins.co.uk

1

Printed and bound in England by Clays Ltd, St Ives plc

MIX
Paper from
responsible sources

FSC C007454

FSC™ is a non-profit international organisation established to promote
the responsible management of the world's forests. Products carrying the
FSC label are independently certified to assure consumers that they come
from forests that are managed to meet the social, economic and
ecological needs of present and future generations,
and other controlled sources.

Find out more about HarperCollins and the environment at
www.harpercollins.co.uk/green

For Caoimhe

Vile Moun
THE INFES

GIANTRIA'S CASTLE

Dead Forest

PREVIOUSLY IN DARKMOUTH

Ten months after returning from the Infested Side, Finn still had to be careful where he sneezed.

If he sneezed in the kitchen, the microwave went *ting*.

If he coughed too hard, the television changed channels.

One night he snored so loudly it woke him with a terrible start and the sound of thunder in his ears. He sat upright, calming his breath, convinced he had caused something, somewhere to explode.

Things had, after all, exploded before. *Everything* had exploded. Gateways. Caves. Worlds. People. Finn.

While trying to find his father, Hugo, he had accidentally thrown himself, Emmie and Estravon the Assessor into the Infested Side. There Finn had discovered that he had the ability to *ignite* – to explode with devastating power, sending out a wave of energy that laid waste to everything around him. Although he had found this out only once he had exploded.

He had been further astonished to find it left him in one piece. More or less. A scar across his chest reminded him of what had happened. As did the occasionally problematic sneezing fit.

So much else had happened on the Infested Side. He had walked with the enemy, blown a giant hole between worlds, found his long-missing grandfather, Niall Blacktongue, become involved in a Legend rebellion and, to the loudest complaints of all, ruined Estravon's best trousers.

He'd done all of this having landed in the right *world*, but three decades too early to find his father. It meant he could add time travel to the list of things he hadn't meant to do.

Yet, despite this, his father had been rescued and the Legends had been defeated at Darkmouth's Cave at the Beginning of the World.

Ten months on, and that same energy occasionally welled inside him, unexpected, uncontrolled, but otherwise all was quiet in Darkmouth.

Finn sat in his classroom, paying little attention to the teacher, looking instead at the empty chair where Emmie used to sit. With her father, Steve, she had been sent to spy on Finn, but had ended up sharing these adventures with him. When all that was done, she'd had to return to the city with her dad.

Life was quieter without Emmie. He missed her. Not that he'd admit that to her.

Finn stared out of the school window for a while. There wasn't much to see. No Legends. No gateways. Darkmouth had not been attacked by a single Legend since and was becoming just like any other town. His family was in danger of becoming just like every other. And even the Savage twins sitting here in his class, two bad attitudes and one chewed ear between them, had stopped bothering him and instead treated him with as little interest as they did the rest of the kids.

The collapsed section of the cliffs, where the gateway to the Infested Side had been opened and then dramatically closed, was covered now with tall green grass, bringing a sense of new growth following destruction. The people of Darkmouth wondered if their town might join those others around the world that used to be plagued by Legends, but which were now free from that blight for the first time in a thousand years.

Finn's birthday was approaching. His thirteenth. A big

one, especially for an apprentice Legend Hunter like him: it was the age at which he could finally become Complete. That was something Finn had always dreaded. But, as he gazed out of the school window, he let his mind dwell on dangerous questions. Would he now live an ordinary life, free of the responsibility of being a Legend Hunter? Was the war actually over? Was it *this* from now on in? No destiny. No prophecies. Just life. Ordinary, everyday, Legend-free, unexciting life.

He might have dwelled on these questions some more except he had to sneeze.

"Bless you, Finn," said his teacher.

Finn quietly blew through his cheeks, relieved he hadn't set off the school bell.

What he didn't realise was that three rooms away the sprinkler system had burst into life, drenching twenty-five panicked kids, one surprised teacher and two very twitchy class hamsters.

I

The hotel room was quiet and still, untouched for years by anything but the light that sliced through the torn curtain. Its sheets bleached of colour, a bed stood in the corner. It had not been slept in for a very long time. Over the sink, a thin green line of slime hung from the tap. A chair sat at an awkward angle by the wall; a snuffling silverfish carved a track across its layer of dust.

A thump rattled the room, shook the dust, sent the silverfish scurrying for safety.

There was another louder thud, from the other side of the closed door. With one final crunch, and an accompanying grunt, the door swung inwards, crashing against the corner of a small writing table. In the darkness stood the silhouette of a very large man, his green eyes lit by the strip of daylight, a kilt settling about his knees.

Once he had assessed the room for a few seconds, the

man bent and entered. Beneath a cracked brown leather jacket, the hem of his kilt danced about hairy legs and his metal sporran clanked under the weight of the seven knives slotted along the top of it. He drew a whistling breath through his whiskers, ran his finger along the writing table's dust.

A tiny spider pushed through the grime on his fingertip and leaped towards the carpet.

"This room is perfect," said the man.

He was Douglas, from the Scottish Isle of Teeth. He came from an ancient family of Legend Hunters, whose deeds still echoed through the annals. But Douglas's deeds did not echo. He was unlucky enough to have been born into an age when Legends bothered only one town and one Legend Hunter family. It meant that he was a Half-Hunter, with the blood of a Legend Hunter, but no Legends to fight.

Instead, Douglas was a pastry chef. This way, he at least got to use knives at work.

Every day, Douglas longed to spill the blood of the Infested Side's Legends, to prove himself in battle and earn his place in a line of great warriors. But right now, in this room, he had only one very important question.

"What time is breakfast served?"

A stooped woman shuffled in from the dimly lit hallway, carrying an extremely fluffy yellow towel and some shampoo in tiny plastic bottles. She pushed past Douglas and placed them roughly on the bed. This was Mrs Cross, the hotel's owner, and her name was an appropriate one.

"We haven't had guests in this place for thirty years," she complained, "and as soon as I open again you lot demand a slap-up feed served to you as soon as you wake. Isn't it enough that I brought shower caps?"

She dropped a crumpled plastic hairnet onto the towel.

The Half-Hunter glared at her, decades of pent-up frustration simmering behind his eyes.

"Breakfast is from seven until eight thirty every morning," Mrs Cross sighed. She shuffled back out of the room, grumbling as she went. "If you're even a minute late, you can suck on the towel for all I care."

She pulled the creaking door behind her, until it stopped ajar on the rucked carpet.

Alone in the room, Douglas stood at the bed and, one by one, pulled the knives from his sporran. A short blade. A fat one. Bone-handled. Wooden-handled. Serrated. Smooth. A delicate one that was very useful for cutting apple pies.

He lined them up in a neat row next to the towel, then rummaged further in his sporran and placed a toothbrush alongside the knives.

Behind him, he heard the creak of a floorboard.

"Ah, porter," Douglas said, not looking around, but fishing in his sporran for something else. "You must ha' brought m'bag. You can put it in the corner there."

Douglas pulled a comb from his sporran and added it to the bed's line-up. Behind him, the unseen porter didn't move.

"I said to put it over in the corner. Oh, you'll be wanting a tip, I suppose?" Douglas turned while searching for change. "I coulda just carried the bag up m'self—"

In the shadows of the room, a figure was taking shape, pouring from a floating mouth as if formed by a scream. It filled out between feet and head. What might once have been hair was now a writhing mass of oozing tar. What might once have been a face was now a shifting landscape of scars in which sat eyes fiery with blood. What might once have been human was something even more horrible.

"Is that *you?*" asked Douglas, pushing up his leather sleeves in anticipation of trouble.

In the shadows, the figure remained. Silent. Watchful. Eyes ablaze.

"They said you were dead," said Douglas, the edge of his mouth curling in anticipation of a fight. "But ne'er mind, because it's gonna be a pleasure to send you back to whatever hell you've come from."

The figure held out charred hands, as if in a show of peace. Beneath the depthless black of its hair, those pupils were fixed islands on coursing rivers of blood.

Douglas ducked and grabbed a carving knife, spun while swinging the blade at the figure before him.

The weapon passed uselessly through the phantom.

The horrifying apparition waited until it could see the realisation cross Douglas's face, a look that said: *All the pastry knives in the world wouldnae be enough for this fight.*

Then the phantom struck.

In a brief, desperate bid for safety, Douglas gripped the curtain, tore it from the window, so that a burst of light shocked the room.

The curtain did not help.

Douglas was gone.

2

Outside, ignorant of the terrible events in the hotel room, Darkmouth was busy with shoppers, giddy kids and the source of their excitement: Half-Hunters pulling suitcases behind them, pushing large boxes ahead of them, arriving in steady numbers, trying not to poke passers-by with the ceremonial swords that hung from their waists.

Coming down the centre of the road, ignoring the oncoming traffic, the honking of horns and shouts of protest, were two Half-Hunters in grey leather trousers and red padded jackets. They carried a huge banner, sagging along the ground between them. On it, between two dancing Minotaurs, was large lettering that read:

CONGRATULATIONS 'FINN THE DEFIANT' LEGEND HUNTER AT LAST!

3

Finn could hear his own breath. Worse, he could smell it. Stale. Hot. Filling the helmet so that it made his nose twitch and his eyes water.

"My visor's steaming up and—" A long wooden sword hit him hard on the side of the head. "Ah, come on!" Finn protested, through a ringing ear and murky vision.

The sword clattered him on the other side of the skull.

Through the fogged-up visor, Finn saw his father thrust forward from the long white space of the training room, his feet light on the soft mats that covered the floor. Finn dodged quickly and spun away.

"You can't keep running," said Hugo, turning to face him. In the sleek reflection of his dad's helmet, Finn saw his own visor-covered face, the sides of his helmet daubed with red streaks of paint meant to imitate blood.

His father moved in with a skilful swish of a blade aimed at Finn's nose. Finn just about reacted in time

21

to block it, but his father loomed over him, pressing down slowly, surely, so that Finn's knees began to buckle beneath him. "Sooner or later," said Hugo sternly, "you're going to have to fight back."

"I hate to admit this," said Finn, sinking under the pressure of the sword, his back beginning to bend precariously over his legs, "but you're right."

He dropped suddenly, almost limboing away from his father as Hugo stumbled forward at the sudden removal of the body that had been holding him up.

Finn hit his father in the hinge of one leg. Hugo dropped to one knee and Finn released a tiny laugh of satisfaction. He immediately regretted this celebration for two reasons.

First, the smell of this morning's boiled egg filled his helmet.

Second, his father hit back.

The tremor from Hugo's blow worked its way through Finn's armour, a rattle that reached his shoulders and shook the golden ropes of the epaulettes that hung on his shoulders.

To catch his breath, Finn pulled the helmet from his head. Gathering himself, Finn glared at the mirror that ran the length of the wall, saw himself in the new fighting suit he'd spent recent months working on. Making your

own fighting suit was the Legend Hunter tradition. It was also necessary in Finn's case, since the last one had been destroyed on the Infested Side.

This new one was made of dull steel, shiny leather, overlapping straps. The fat buckle on his belt was moulded into a wide biting mouth. There was a somewhat unconvincing painting of a Minotaur's horns and gaping mouth across his chest. And the quivering epaulettes had been added because this was a fighting suit he'd made not just for future battles he hoped to avoid, but also a graduation ceremony he knew he couldn't. Unfortunately.

"Do we really have to have such a big ceremony?" he hissed.

"Of course," his father responded, low. "People have come from all over the world to see this."

"No pressure at all," said Finn. "It'll be good to become a Legend Hunter after everything, I suppose. But maybe it could have been just a family occasion."

"Serves you right for surviving the Infested Side, battling legends, rescuing me, saving Darkmouth and being generally heroic," said his father.

"I'll know better next time," said Finn, a grin curling the edge of his mouth.

Hugo jabbed his weapon forward, and Finn realised too

late that it was simply a diversion, something to push him off balance. He made to parry the blow, but his father was already behind him, and before Finn could even react, had wrapped his arms round his chest, hauling him up so that his legs kicked at the air.

Finn felt the breath forced from his lungs, yet remained as calm as he could, refusing to let the crush panic him. He knew this was a test.

"I'm nearly thirteen," he spluttered, arms jammed down his sides, but his right hand flicking a clasp on his fighting suit. "I'm too old for tickles."

The whole outfit peeled open like a banana, and Finn slid down through it, free from his father's grip.

Jumping away, he again saw himself in the mirror, and this time regretted wearing a vest and old sports shorts. His boots were still on his feet, and his legs disappeared into them like bamboo in a plant pot.

Hugo threw the empty fighting suit in a heap on the floor, a smile creeping across his face. "The Goodman Manoeuvre," he said. "Excellent."

Finn glanced at the mirror again. "Um... I need to take a break," he said suddenly, panic and embarrassment flushing through him.

"We're only just getting started," responded his father,

coiling himself into a highly intimidating pose, a mass of metal over muscle ready to bear down on Finn.

"No, Dad, we need to stop now," insisted Finn.

"In two days you'll become a teenager," his father pressed, his voice low, as if someone was listening.

"I know, but—"

"Tomorrow you have your Completion Ceremony and become a true Legend Hunter."

"I haven't forgotten—"

"The first new Legend Hunter in many years," continued his father. "We need to have these manoeuvres nailed down for the event or they mightn't let you go through with it."

"But—"

"And they will cancel it. Trust me. That's the reason Billy the Loser got his name." He wound up to attack again. "Well, one of the reasons anyway."

"No, that's not the problem," Finn said, leaning forward while whispering. "It's my shorts. I've torn them."

His father relaxed from his cobra pose, lifted the visor on his helmet and peered round Finn's back where, sure enough, the top layer of his shorts was splitting and threatening to reveal the stripy boxers beneath.

Hugo stood tall, seemed to think about it for a

moment, before turning to the mirror. Finn looked at it too and again got a glimpse of how weak he appeared beside his father. Then his father flipped the visor down, and immediately resumed his attack stance. "Come on," he said. "No one can see it."

In despair, Finn's eyes opened wider than the split in his shorts. "What? Of course they can see it!"

"They can't," Hugo insisted.

Petulant, Finn stepped to a switch on the wall.

"Don't," said his father.

Finn pressed the switch anyway.

From a point at the mirror's dead centre, the reflection cleared, like condensation evaporating from a window, until the full length of the wall became completely see-through. On the other side, two rows of seats were revealed, packed with a couple of dozen people. Some in a variety of fighting suits. Some in just ordinary suits. One wore an all-in-one bodysuit of shimmering blue scales. There was even a family there, a mother and father watching in wide-eyed delight, while their teenage son gazed on with a look of such boredom it would be a wonder if his face ever found the muscles to smile again.

"Half the Half-Hunter population is watching me," said Finn, pointing at the audience behind the glass.

They had won tickets in a raffle: the chance to see the apprentice train before the Completion Ceremony.

"It's tradition," Hugo said. "They get to see you."

"Yes, but I don't want them to see *everything*," said Finn, jabbing his thumb at the tear in the back of his shorts before heading for the door.

Hugo pulled the helmet from his head. "Should we take a break at this point?"

On the other side of the mirror, the Half-Hunter in blue scales shoved a handful of popcorn into his mouth.

"Yes," sighed Hugo. "Let's take a break."

W
ith a shake of his head, humiliation complete, Finn marched up the corridor, past the paintings of all those Legend Hunters who had gone before him, ignoring the judgemental glare of his famously unhappy great-grandfather, Gerald the Disappointed. The further up the corridor he went, the older the portraits became, until the earliest paintings had faded into faces made unrecognisable by peeling paint. It was a constant reminder of how long Finn's family had been Darkmouth's Legend Hunters.

He reached the hallway, where a narrow door brought him into the stark contrast of a house as ordinary as any other in Darkmouth. Apart from one thing: all the people at the windows. Outside were the Half-Hunters who hadn't won tickets to see him train. The flash of cameras. The dark flicker of silhouettes crossing the garden.

"It'll all be over soon," said Finn's mother, Clara, as

she arrived from the living room on her way to the stairs. "But not soon enough. Hold on, you're wearing shorts." She looked through the door to the Long Hall, where Half-Hunters were gathering their things to leave. "Your father's fault, right? Did training not go well?"

Finn bit his lip.

"Just remind yourself it won't be like this for ever," Clara said, putting an arm round his shoulder. "I've done that pretty much every day since I married into this family."

Outside, Finn heard the murmur of those loitering Half-Hunters, watched the shapes cross the door, saw one grow larger and darker until it poked a nose through the letterbox.

"Hello. Let me in," said a voice desperately. A man's voice. "Please, there is about to be a terrible disaster."

He sounded French. Or Swedish. Or maybe Korean. Finn wasn't great with accents.

"Please," said the Half-Hunter. "I need help."

Finn sighed, closed his eyes in a long blink to compose himself, while Clara carefully opened the door. A Half-Hunter was dancing about on the doorstep, wearing some kind of black, naval-type uniform, complete with coloured strips on his left breast and chunky red and black cufflinks.

"Thank you," he said as he burst in. "Where's the toilet?"

Clara nodded towards a door under the stairs, and the Half-Hunter dashed straight for it.

There was another knock on the door. "Toilet's already full," said Finn.

"Do you need me to unblock it?" asked Emmie, pushing her head round the door.

"That's not what I…" said Finn, flustered. "Hi, Emmie. You're here."

"I wouldn't have missed your big ceremony for anything," she beamed. "You know you've a split in those shorts?"

Finn felt himself blush. "Good. Not my shorts. I mean, it's good you're back."

"Just for the ceremony," she said. "Unless something goes terribly wrong again in Darkmouth. I've my fingers crossed for that."

"I'll do my best," he smiled, while hoping nothing whatsoever would go terribly wrong.

"Hey, Finn, Clara," said Emmie's father, Steve, walking in after her. "You know there are a lot of people out there taking pictures of your garden wall."

"I signed an autograph," said Emmie, excited.

"No one wanted mine," said Steve, failing to pretend that this hadn't bothered him a bit. "I guess no one cares about the guy who rescues you every time you need it."

Hugo arrived from the Long Hall. "We're all about to need rescuing from the tourists following me up from the training room."

"I'm always available to bail you out," said Steve. "Unless it's an issue with the toilet."

Hugo looked puzzled. They heard the toilet flush. The door opened. The now much calmer intruder emerged, drying his hands on his trousers before giving an exaggerated swipe of relief across his forehead. Realising he'd hit the Legend Hunter jackpot, he thrust out a hand to shake Finn's, who took it reluctantly and squirmed at how damp it still was.

"Oh boy," said the excited Half-Hunter. "I am Nils, from the Norwegian Blighted Village of Splattafest, and you are all here. In Darkmouth. Together. Are those flowers poisonous?" He inspected a bunch on a small table.

"No," said Clara.

"But those coat hooks shoot deadly darts, yes?"

"I'll just get that door for you," said Hugo. "It's been

lovely to meet you, but…"

"We are all looking forward to the great Completion," said Nils. "Especially what they plan to do with the dozen golden monkeys. Something to do with the six hundred scorpions, I think."

"OK, it's about to get crowded in here," said Hugo, looking back at the group of raffle winners coming up the Long Hall.

"I made special souvenir cufflinks—" Nils said, but he was cut off as Clara politely ushered him out. As she did, the front door gently swung open to reveal a queue of maybe half a dozen Half-Hunters.

"I need the toilet as well," said the one at the front, dancing on the spot for added effect.

"Oh yeah, me too," said the next.

"I'm bursting," said the third.

Either side of Finn, there were Half-Hunters crowding into the house. He looked at Emmie. "I need rescuing."

"Rescuing you is my speciality," she smiled. "Let's get out of here. Although you should probably put on some trousers first."

5

"Do you still get the stink?" Emmie asked Finn, and offered him a sweet from a brown paper bag.

They were sitting on a low step at Darkmouth's largest monument, a grey, grimy obelisk with a white plaque whose words were so worn no one knew any more why it had been put there. There was warmth in the day, and blue sky mixed with bubbling cloud. Finn had his hoodie pulled tight over his head as a disguise against the Half-Hunters swarming the town.

"Do you mean the smell of the Infested Side?" Finn replied. "Like rotting vegetables that were already stuffed with old cheese?" He dug in the brown paper bag.

"I'd say it smells more like a fish wearing yesterday's socks," said Emmie, chewing on something that was gradually turning her tongue blue.

Finn crunched down on a red sweet, letting the sugar

fizz through his mouth. "It's been worse for my dad," he said. "Because the serpents hid him among Legends so smelly that no one else would go near them, that stench lasted ages afterwards. He had to burn his clothes. And then he had to burn the bonfire he'd burned those clothes on."

"At least there's been no Legends since," said Emmie.

"Yeah," said Finn.

"Just normal stuff, like school and whatever."

"Yeah. Just normal stuff."

They each rummaged in the paper bag open between them, popped a sweet in their mouth and sat quiet for a little while longer.

"It's boring, isn't it?" Emmie exclaimed eventually.

"*So* boring," said Finn with a burst of relief at being able to share. "I never thought I'd say it. Never. But it's just that after everything we went through…"

"Legends. Crystals. Serpents," said Emmie.

"Gateways. Shapeshifters," said Finn.

"And everything we saw there."

"Stuff no one has seen," said Finn. "At the time, I thought I never wanted to see a gateway again, didn't want to meet another Legend. I just wanted to go on as normal. But— "

"Normal is boring, right?"

Finn gave her a guilty look. "Kind of. I mean, me and Dad still train a lot, but now I've nothing to use the moves on."

"Welcome to my life," said Emmie.

"He doesn't like to show it, but I think Dad's bored too," said Finn. "He spent weeks on the Infested Side and, even though all that time he just sat there, waiting to escape, it was still like nothing anybody had done before. Well, nobody except Niall Blacktongue, but no one likes to talk about that."

"At least people know he *went* to the Infested Side," said Emmie. "I'm back at school in the city and no one there has a clue what I did. They just think I was away for a while with my dad's work, but they have no idea what he really does."

"What did you tell them?"

Shapeshifter

"That he's a travelling DJ."

"*What?*" laughed Finn.

"I didn't know what else to say," she said. "And it sounded kind of cool."

"DJ Steve."

"Hmm. Maybe not so cool."

Finn threw a green sweet into his mouth.

"Anyway," Emmie said, "you must be all set for the Completion Ceremony, right? It'll be a big deal. The whole Legend Hunter world is going to be watching."

Discomfort immediately contorted Finn's face.

"Sorry," Emmie said. "I didn't mean to upset you."

"No," he grimaced. "Be careful of those green stripy sweets. They're really sour."

She laughed at that. He swallowed the offending sweet with an anguished wince.

"Oh, I wish they'd go away," said Finn, nodding towards a couple of Half-Hunters across the street, irritating locals by taking pictures of every hole in a wall.

"Maybe we can sign another autograph."

Finn grimaced at the thought. "Or maybe we can get out of here before they spot us," he said, pushing himself up and heading away from the obelisk.

They darted round a corner, across a couple of narrow

alleys with walls that rose high over them and were topped with whatever sharp objects might keep a Legend out. But here and there were gaps, where nails or broken glass had fallen free and not yet been replaced by whoever lived behind the walls. There had been no Legends in a while. The people of Darkmouth were growing a little too used to that.

Down a cobbled lane, Finn and Emmie encountered a couple of Half-Hunters in fur coats rushing excitedly to the spot where Mr Glad's shop used to be. It had been gutted by fire on the night Mr Glad had turned on Hugo, nearly destroying the town as a result. That was almost a year ago now, but to Finn it was beginning to feel like a lifetime away. It was certainly long enough that the shop had since been rebuilt as a hairdresser's. Those Half-Hunters in furs would leave not with pictures of the lair of an infamous traitor, but of *Snippy Snips*.

"Down here," Finn suggested, and the two of them slunk along an adjoining laneway, in and out of the town's maze of streets, until they squeezed through a gap and on to the strand close to the slumped remnants of the cliffs. Surrounded by busy Half-Hunters in boiler suits, a scaffold was rising from the ground. It was a stage, still just a half-formed skeleton of steel rods, with huge rectangular pieces of floor leaning against them ready to be put in place.

"Is that it?" Emmie asked.

Finn nodded. This was the place where, the following night, he would become Complete. No matter how incomplete he felt.

"Is that a cannon up there?" said Emmie, looking closer.

"Apparently so," confirmed Finn.

"And over there, in those tubes?"

"Fireworks," said Finn, not even looking at them.

"That'll be enough of a racket to, like, wake the dead," said Emmie.

"I wouldn't mind a bit of Legend Hunting," said Finn. "It's just becoming a Legend Hunter in front of everyone that I'm not so keen on."

That triggered something in Finn, and he reached in under his hoodie to withdraw a silver chain. On the end was a cylindrical locket, an ornate swirling pattern on its case surrounding a small window that revealed sparkling scarlet dust within. "Do you still have yours?" he asked.

Emmie pulled out an identical locket from beneath her jacket. Inside was dust and sand, the last pulverised remains of the crystals they'd found in the cave before it was destroyed. Finn's dad had presented one to each of them, as a reminder of what they'd been through together. "It was nice of your dad to give us these," she said.

"I know," said Finn. "For my last birthday he got me a box of spanners. But I think his time on the Infested Side has mellowed him a bit. He's softer on me too. Some of the time."

"Even my dad wears his locket," said Emmie. "Although he says it itches a bit."

"It does itch," admitted Finn, rubbing at the front of his neck.

"It's better to be itchy than dead," Emmie smiled. "Or worse."

"Yeah. Suppose." Finn pushed the locket inside his clothes, tilted his head back to shake out the last sticky shards of sweets from the paper bag. A couple of them fell into his nostrils, irritating his nose. He sneezed.

Down the road, away from the strand, they heard the screech of a car, the growl of an engine.

"Since the Infested Side, my sneezes can, you know, set things off. My parents look at me funny if I get annoyed about anything, like I might blow up the kitchen," Finn said. The car engine grew louder. "But this is a new one."

The growling grew nearer, and a moment later a large

black block of a car hurriedly took the corner.

"It's Dad," said Finn.

The car pulled up in front of them. The tinted window on the passenger side whirred down and Hugo leaned towards them.

"Get in," he said urgently. "Something's happened at the hotel."

6

Finn, Emmie and Hugo stood at the entrance to the hotel room. Dust still swam in the air from where the door had been roughly pushed open.

But the dust was not what they were looking at.

"I should never have reopened this place," the hotel owner said, pushing in between them. Mrs Cross held a fluffy yellow towel, or at least half of one, torn raggedly. "But I was begged to. Pushed into it. Convinced it'd only be a few days and they'd be no bother. But it's been only bother from the start. All I've had is complaints since your lot started arriving here. The beds are too soft. The pillows too feathery. The shampoo smells too fruity. And now *this*."

From downstairs came the *ting* of the reception bell. She ignored it. Instead, she pointed at something very strange in the air.

Finn's father stepped forward to examine it. On the

far side of the room, just to the side of a narrow window, about two metres off the ground but fixed and unmoving, was a scar in the air. Three gouges, as if great cracked nails had clawed at empty space.

Ting, ting went the reception bell downstairs.

Hugo walked round the phenomenon, his face registering a measure of surprise. He motioned Finn over to him.

As Finn approached, he examined the marks without touching them, saw how they were almost puckered, with edges raised and uneven like roughly stitched skin. As he passed, the angle narrowed until the marks disappeared entirely. When standing behind them, they were completely invisible. There was nothing at all to see except for Mrs Cross's deeply annoyed face staring back. Her displeasure was almost strong enough to burn its own hole in the air.

Finn and Hugo moved back round to the front of the room until they could again examine the strange markings from the front.

"Now what am I going to do?" the hotel owner asked them. "I can't exactly rent out this room, can I? I've been in this trade for sixty years and I can tell you this: no one wants a room with ghostly scratch marks imprinted in the ether."

Ting. Ting. Ting.

"Oh, give it a rest," she shouted out of the door.

"You must tell no one," Hugo said to her.

Mrs Cross gasped. "And what do you suggest I do? Just leave it here for guests to hang their hat on?"

"You *could* tell the Half-Hunters," said Hugo, "but only if you want to turn this room into the greatest tourist attraction in Darkmouth. You think they're bothering you now? Wait until you show them this."

Ting. Ting. Ting. Tingtingting.

"Pack it in!" she yelled from the doorway. "Right, Hugo. I'll be quiet for now. But if that thing doesn't fade you will get the bill for a single room, with breakfast, occupied from today until the end of eternity." She left the room to clomp down the short corridor towards the stairs and the tinging bell in reception. "What do you lot want *now*?"

"What's that on the carpet?" asked Emmie.

Bootprints were burned into the floor and surrounded by a sulphuric shadow. It seemed apparent that whoever had been standing in them had been in this spot whenever whatever happened took place.

Hugo crouched to examine the print. "They're Hunter boots all right. Standard issue. Except they're made in Scotland." He caught Finn and Emmie's reaction to his detective skills. "OK, so I already knew it was a Scotsman who took this room. These were the boots of a Half-Hunter called Douglas. And I have a very nasty feeling that he was standing in them when these marks were made."

Knives, a toothbrush and a comb were laid out neatly on the bed. Hugo stood again, and the three of them faced the marks branded in the air, glancing at what may or may not have been the remains of Douglas of the Isle of Teeth.

Hugo blew hard through his cheeks. "We can tell no one either," he said.

"OK," said Finn.

"Yep," agreed Emmie.

Hugo fixed his attention on Emmie. "Understand?"

She looked offended. "Just because I spied on Finn once doesn't mean I'm always spying. It was ages ago and

I didn't even want to anyway. I'm not going to tell anyone about this."

"Would the Half-Hunters not be able to help, though?" Finn asked.

Hugo moved slowly towards the grimy window, looked out on to the street. Finn and Emmie joined him. Together they watched a Half-Hunter strut down the street, wearing a long chain-mail skirt and samurai sword. He was being followed by a group of small, excitable children and occasionally he would delight them by turning and growling in pantomime fashion.

"Gis a go of your sword, mister," they heard a kid say to him.

"I would like to," replied the Half-Hunter, "but the last child I gave it to is still being glued back together."

The children squealed with delight at that, and kept tailing him as he moved on.

Hugo nodded towards the man down on the street. "That is a fellow called Kenzo. He's come all the way from Japan just for the ceremony. His Legend Hunter family goes back 1,500 years, and he's the second generation that's had nothing to do but use their swords to cut sandwiches. And it's only a wooden sword anyway."

Kenzo was holding a scrap of paper, seemingly

checking house numbers against it.

"You know what Kenzo does now? He's a children's entertainer," Hugo continued. "Birthday parties. That sort of thing. That fighting suit looks impressive, but it's had more chocolate biscuit cake on it than blood."

"You don't think they'd be up to it?" asked Finn.

"Not only would they not be up to it, this isn't their Blighted Village," said Hugo. "It's ours. Which means this is our problem. That's the tradition. That's the Legend Hunter law. That's the way it's going to be. So, we tell no one. Not even Steve, Emmie. And for now, Finn, we won't mention this to your mam either. She's unhappy enough with all this fuss as it is."

With queasy horror, Finn realised that a greasy blur on the window was a palm print, large and firm. Was this Douglas's last desperate act as he tried to escape? Finn stood back, turned away from it as he had an idea. "You don't think this has anything to do with... Well, you know who?"

"Doubt it," said Hugo. "Wouldn't make sense."

"You know who *who*?" asked Emmie, baffled.

"Finn, have you told Emmie about him yet?" asked Hugo.

"No," said Finn.

"Told me what?" asked Emmie.

"If we tell you, you're not to speak to *anyone* about it," Hugo insisted.

"I keep saying I won't," she answered, irritated. "And I don't even know what it is I'm not supposed to tell anyone about anyway."

"Do you know where to find him?" Hugo asked Finn.

"Same place he always is, I'd say," answered Finn.

"Same place *who* is?" asked Emmie.

"I didn't really say much earlier, because I wasn't sure I was allowed," said Finn bashfully. "But there is at least one Legend loose in Darkmouth. Want to see him?"

7

They found Broonie the Hogboon right where Finn expected to. In a small patch of soil and plants, divided into squares hardly bigger than a double bed, hemmed in by high walls on three sides, and a tall wire fence on the fourth. This was the local allotment, where people came to grow vegetables and fruit – and where the only living Hogboon in Darkmouth came to feast.

"Why has he got his head stuck in that beehive thing?" whispered Emmie as they lurked behind the fence.

"It's a wormery," explained Finn.

"A *whatery*?"

"A wormery. The gardeners use them to make compost. Although, to be honest, I overheard someone saying that the compost hasn't been great of late. And smells a bit funny. *Plus* the wormery doesn't have many worms in it. I didn't want to tell them I could guess why."

Broonie's slurping was quite pronounced, his green

legs dangling where he had pulled his skinny frame up to stick his head in.

"He eats the worms?" said Emmie.

"Lots of them," said Finn. "Even though he complains about the taste."

Broonie didn't seem to notice them, just twitched a floppy ear as he continued to eat.

"I thought the Council of Twelve ordered you to desiccate him until they could decide what to do with him," said Emmie.

"That was the order," said Finn. "But it wasn't his fault he ended up here. He just got shoved in through the gateway really. He didn't want anything to do with any war."

"You let him out!" she exclaimed.

"Shush," said Finn. "We don't allow him out all the time. Just once a week. For twenty-four hours only. The rest of the time he spends in the house. Complaining about everything."

Broonie paused in his banquet. Belched loudly. Resumed eating.

"The Council of Twelve gave Broonie back to us, but only once he'd been desiccated," said Finn. "They didn't want him running loose, causing trouble. He's still just a Legend as far as they're concerned, not to be trusted. The

Desiccation was horrible. There were shouts and screams and, well, a lot of cursing. Hogboons know a lot of curses. And, when it was all over, they gave him to us in a jar."

"But you brought him back," said Emmie.

"Reanimating him was even more horrible. And there was even more cursing. But Dad felt we owed Broonie something given he sided with the resistance over on the Infested Side. Or, at least, got kind of stuck with the resistance. And then got stuck with us."

Broonie stood upright. A long slurp suggested he was sucking in a worm. His right ear revolved towards them.

"You know I can hear the two of you," he said, without turning. "As if I couldn't smell you before you even arrived."

Finn gently pushed through the gap in the wire from behind which they had been watching Broonie, holding it open for Emmie to follow. He crept up to the Hogboon.

"Hey, Broonie!" Emmie shouted as she skipped ahead.

"Quiet," begged Finn. "We don't want the Half-Hunters knowing he's here."

"Look who it is," Broonie said to Emmie as if she was another trial sent to test him. "Come to see the poor creature in his prison, have you?"

"My dad said I should check on you," Finn said to the sullen Hogboon. "You know, to make sure you're OK."

"To see if I'd escaped again," sneered Broonie.

"You've escaped before?" asked Emmie, examining the Legend's green skin, droopy ears and droopier nostrils.

"I tried to," said Broonie. "I got something worse than Desiccation for my troubles. I got a strict talking-to from that grunting Legend Hunter Hugo, and a promise that if I ever tried it again I'd be thrown into a jar and put at the very back of the highest shelf so that no one would ever find me again."

A car drove by, and they all ducked. Except for Broonie,

who was short enough as it was. And petulant enough.

"How would they know if you just ran for the hills?" asked Emmie, once they were sure the car was gone.

Broonie pulled a locket from the rags at his neck. "Because of this."

"Oh look, you've one just like ours," said Emmie.

"It's not like yours at all. Yours isn't welded on to your neck, is it? It's not locked tightly in place," said Broonie. "And it isn't being used to track your every move, like this is."

"Oh, that's very clever," said Emmie.

"It's very sore," corrected Broonie.

Another car went by. Again Broonie stayed upright as if in protest.

"What's that dirt on you?" Emmie asked, after the bright lights had passed on. "It's like you slept in a skip."

Neither Finn nor Broonie said anything, and Emmie realised why.

"You slept in a skip?"

"It makes him feel at home," explained Finn.

"What's the worst that could happen to me?" Broonie asked, but had no interest in waiting for a reply. "Nothing. Because the worst thing has already happened. Being here. Trapped in this world, with its people and smells and smells of people and its utter lack of scaldgrubs. These earthworms are passable, but they don't taste nearly as putrid as I would like."

Finn opened his mouth to say something, but Broonie raised a green, knuckly finger to let it be known he hadn't yet finished ranting.

"And as if that's not bad enough," added the Hogboon, "I have no freedom. And the little bit of life I do have is bound entirely by the clock here, when I must return as planned to be subjected to a lengthy period of torture in your house."

"Torture?" asked Emmie.

"My dad listens to country music when he's working in the library," explained Finn.

"It makes my earwax bleed," snorted Broonie.

"Make sure to be on time, Broonie," said Finn, sorry to bring it up. "You were a few minutes late last time and Dad was ready to put you in a biscuit tin for all eternity."

"I don't know if I care any more, such is the anguish of my life here," said Broonie, dismissive.

"You're so funny, Broonie," said Emmie.

Broonie grunted, then thrust his face in the hole at the top of the wormery and began chomping again. Finn and Emmie lingered briefly before backing away and leaving through the gap in the fence.

Evening was drawing in. As Finn and Emmie crossed a couple of alleyways that ran off the strand, Finn thought he saw something move in the twilight. He stopped and peered towards it.

"What is it, Finn?" asked Emmie.

"I'm not sure," he said. "Do you remember when we were on the Infested Side and felt we were being watched by Legends?"

"Which we were. By a lot of them."

"I just have that sense again. As if there's somebody out there."

They waited, watched. There was nothing but settling darkness.

"This is why I love Darkmouth," said Emmie. "Always something odd going on." She shoved him in the shoulder playfully and ran off. "Race you!"

Finn hesitated just a moment, then followed, belting after her.

Across the lane, a succession of shadows skittered across the dim alleyway.

8

Kenzo the Japanese Half-Hunter rang the rusted doorbell on the house, hummed its cheery tune as he waited.

The letterbox opened, fingers propping it open from inside, and a man's voice asked gruffly, "What?"

"Excuse me," said Kenzo as politely as he could, and yet loud enough to speak over the rattle of his metal skirt as he stepped back. "Your sign says this is a bed and breakfast?"

"Go away," said the man. "We're shut. We're always shut. And we're especially shut now."

Kenzo bent down level with the letterbox, and could see nothing but those splayed fingers and a single bloodshot eye. "I require only bed. No breakfast. In fact, a floor will do fine—"

A walking stick thrust through the letterbox, forcing Kenzo to retreat sharply. Its owner waggled it from side to

side in a manner that was not likely to cause any damage, but still managed to very neatly get across the message that no Half-Hunters were wanted here. And, in case it didn't, the man in the house shouted, "Shoo!" for extra effect.

Kenzo had spent what now felt like half a lifetime travelling to Darkmouth, and the other half wandering about the town. He had long wished that he would one day get to visit this, the only true Blighted Village left on Earth. It was not quite turning out how he had imagined.

He could ask the other Half-Hunters for help, but that would require, well, asking for help. And he didn't like to do that. A true Legend Hunter should not require assistance. They must be self-sufficient. Quick-witted. And, every now and again, a bit uncomfortable wherever they lay their head.

So, Kenzo left, deciding to make his way towards where the houses crowded in on the rocky beach. He heard voices ahead of him in the fading light. A boy. Then a girl. She was laughing, and he could make out two small figures breaking into a sprint up a laneway that led back to the main street of Darkmouth.

Away up the strand, he could see the scaffold being set up for the Completion Ceremony, what would be a stage for the big event. Even now, as it grew late, there was life, lights, busy Half-Hunters, tasked with setting up the platform, preparing to work through the night. Shivering as the chilly breeze moved across the stones, Kenzo saw the skeleton of an old boat, upturned and washed up on the beach, its hull rotten but holding on to enough wood to offer some shelter for the night.

The crescent of the moon had been blanketed by cloud. There was a flicker of lightning. No thunder followed.

The wreck's hull had rotted away so that it looked like a giant's ribcage half buried in the beach. Kenzo stooped to enter it, then smoothed out the shingle at his feet, pulled the coat from his shoulders and placed it across the flattened spot. He lay down. Kenzo would stay here tonight. It was not perfect, but he was always one to keep his spirits up. He would treat this as an adventure. It was the best he could do.

Something stirred in his bag. Kenzo sat upright and undid its rope to reach in with both hands. He gently removed a white rabbit, and immediately began snuggling at its soft neck with his nose, shushing it to keep it calm. He took a head of lettuce from his pocket and let the rabbit eat it while it sat on his chest.

"Good Nibbles," Kenzo said. "Nice Nibbles." His fluffy

pal was the big star of his magic tricks at children's parties.

There was the scrunch of stone. Something was moving around the wreck.

"Hello?" he said. "Who is there?"

The stones scrunched again, footsteps forcing the beach aside.

"Hello?"

A presence moved in front of him, darkening the decaying wreck, disappearing again. Kenzo leaped to his feet, sending the rabbit hopping to the ground while he scrabbled for his sword, which was wooden because no parent wants a real samurai sword at a kids' party.

"Come out and show yourself."

The shadow moved behind him. He turned and arced the sword until it quivered at the nose of his stalker.

A little boy gasped, his eyes wide with shock and fear. Behind him, two other kids gasped with fright.

Kenzo exhaled, withdrew the weapon.

"You must stop following me," he said, but the children were already running away, scrambling across the stony beach, carried by the fright of nearly losing a nose.

A little stunned, Kenzo watched them leave, shaking his head in bemusement before returning to his temporary bed, where Nibbles was already resting.

Scrunch.

Kenzo sighed, tired of these intrusions.

Scccrunch.

"Please, children," he muttered, "I must get my rest."

Kenzo stood again, but this time found himself under a tall shadow. The shadow of a shadow. A shifting shape that emerged from the air, pulled from a scream, the edges coalescing in a swirl. Its hair was like thin snakes writhing from its head, the eyes pinwheels of red, and the distorted mouth carrying a malevolence that could cut a person in two.

Kenzo swung his sword at the intruder, catching it in the side. But the ghost's molecules moved away, letting the blunt blade pass through.

The phantom reached out, touched Kenzo's chest.

The last thing Kenzo saw before he disappeared was the very person he had come to Darkmouth to celebrate. It was Finn. Approaching the wreck.

Their eyes met.

Then Kenzo was full of stars.

9

To Finn it was as if the Half-Hunter had been sliced by light from neck to belly, the light dancing for a moment before spreading out in each direction and swallowing the man.

The victim's stare burned on to Finn's mind. Eyes wide. Fear vivid. And then nothing. Just a vague yellow smudge carried across the air slowly. And, in the sand where he had stood, scorch marks around bootprints.

Lingering, a face that was mutated and mutating, a figure rearranging itself in the breeze. But Finn recognised who this was instantly. Even if he couldn't believe it.

"*Tick, tock,*" said the phantom before scattering into nothingness in the grey light of evening.

Emmie scrunched on to the scene. "What's going on, Finn?" she asked. "Why did you come over here?"

Finn gawped dumbly, hardly able to explain. "I thought I saw something, like a light dropping from the sky, and

came over to look. But when I got here…"

He stood aside to let her see the scratches in the air.

He showed her the scorched bootprints.

"That's Kenzo," he said. "The Japanese Half-Hunter. *Was* Kenzo. He was swallowed or something."

"It's like those marks at the hotel," Emmie said, eyes wide in amazement.

"But that's not the scariest thing," said Finn.

"It's not?"

"No. I *saw* what swallowed him," Finn said. "It was Mr Glad. He's back. He killed Kenzo."

LIECHTENSTEIN:
TWO MONTHS EARLIER

TWO WORLDS ~ ONE VICTOR

*T*he headquarters of the Council of Twelve was on a side street, in the small capital city at the heart of the tiny Alpine country of Liechtenstein. There was no sign above the door, no plaque on the wall, no hint at all that this was the nerve centre of the Legend Hunter world except for a missing chunk of the third floor caused when someone pressed the wrong button on the wrong weapon many years ago.

Inside was a warren of corridors and staircases, criss-crossing at odd points, or leading to dead ends. There were large doors to small rooms and small doors to large rooms and at least one door that for some reason opened to nowhere but a fatal six-storey drop to the pavement outside.

On the seventh floor – which could be reached only by first taking an elevator to the ninth floor – there was a small room with a plaque on the door describing it as the Office of Lost Arts.

Inside that room sat a fellow by the name of Lucien, one

of the great many assistants to the Council of Twelve. One early afternoon, he was pondering what was generally the most serious decision of his working day – whether to have a sandwich or a salad for his lunch – when a small canister arrived through the communications tubes that networked the building and landed with a fwhop on his desk.

Lucien adjusted his oversized glasses, which immediately slid back down the bridge of his small nose. He twisted open the container and unfurled the pages inside. These were notes from the Council of Twelve and they detailed a tale of heroism and survival so extraordinary, and an invasion so fierce, that it was almost unprecedented in the annals of the Legend Hunters.

It told the story of mere children, Finn and Emmie, of the last active Legend Hunter, Hugo the Great, of Estravon the Assessor. Of gateways and lost Legend Hunters. Of time travel and a beach battle.

The message further instructed Lucien to read up on it, check all the reports and to write a report about those reports. And then he would be expected to report back on whether there was anything further to report.

He was ordered to do all this without delay.

Naturally, Lucien went for lunch first. Later, munching on a salad sandwich, he licked a finger, turned the pages, peered at a blurry photograph of Darkmouth's beach post-battle, which showed a carpet of desiccated Legends half buried under collapsed earth. He marvelled quietly at this scene.

What Finn, Emmie, Estravon and Hugo had achieved simply by returning from the Infested Side was unprecedented. Here was a small group of people – a Legend Hunter, an Assessor, two children – who had done not just something extraordinary, but almost unbelievable.

They had gone to a stale and ruined world full of creatures hellbent on destroying humans. A place where, it was said, even the soil tried to kill you. And they had lived to tell a story that would echo through the generations.

As he pushed a rogue piece of lettuce into his mouth, Lucien felt a twinge of envy towards those Half-Hunters who had been there for the battle. He had a bolt of longing for the adventure experienced by mere children, especially that boy Finn who had now gone through two gateways in his lifetime and come back alive each time.

Lucien was here in Liechtenstein, twiddling his thumbs, shuffling through bits of paper, finding occasional excitement from seeing how far he could tip his chair back on two legs before he fell over.

Meanwhile, Darkmouth was the last battlefront in a long war against Legends. And it was home to a true hero. There was no doubt about Finn's heroism. No doubt whatsoever.

Unless you thought about it.

Which Lucien began to do.

10

Finn sat on the edge of his bed, his toes wriggling in giant claw slippers he'd got for Christmas, knuckles pressed hard into his stinging eyes as he tried to rub away the images of the night before. As morning sun slanted through the blinds, his mind was still unable to comprehend the reappearance of a man he thought long gone, but who was back. Just not in a form Finn recognised. He'd called his father immediately and together with Emmie they'd spent the late hours examining a scene none of them could fully understand.

As if that wasn't enough to worry about, he was waking to a momentous couple of days. The Completion Ceremony would take place tonight. He would be thirteen tomorrow. It had been building to this his whole life.

But, right now, something else was beginning to dominate his senses.

Pancakes. He could smell pancakes.

He stood and put his head out of the bedroom door.

"Something's going on," said Clara, passing him on her way to the stairs. "Something is always going on."

Finn didn't know what she knew, and thought it best not to offer any information. He didn't like holding things back from his mother, but neither did he want to be responsible for blurting out that a couple of Half-Hunters had been disintegrated by the returning phantom of Mr Glad. That kind of thing would spoil anyone's morning.

He followed his mother, trudging downstairs and realising he could hear a couple of voices in the kitchen already.

"Do you want more pickles with that?" he heard his father asking.

"Mmmm-mmmm," he heard Broonie agree, his mouth clearly full, presumably with pancakes and pickles. This was highly unusual.

Clara reappeared in the hallway, grabbing her keys. "I know this is a big day for you, Finn. But I really need to get out before that breakfast is over."

Finn didn't know what she was talking about. "Mam, why is Dad making Broonie pancakes?"

"Last meal of a condemned man," said Clara, throwing on her jacket and heading for the front door.

"A condemned Hogboon actually. Your dad's looking after things before the Completion tonight. Anyway, it's going to be a crazy day for you. For us. So I'm going to go to work and find something more relaxing to do for a while. Maybe look at pictures of rotting teeth or something."

He could hear Broonie slurping while Hugo asked him if he would like more moss on his pancakes. Clara sighed and left.

Finn went into the kitchen, the shuffling of his huge slippers announcing him.

"Hey, Finn," his dad said, with a cheeriness so forced Finn knew it could only be building up to something bad.

Finn gave him a wary look. Broonie raised a knobbly hand in acknowledgement, unable to speak because his mouth was so full of pancakes, moss and something that looked like a fat twig. Or a skinny slug. Finn couldn't be sure.

"I was just explaining to Broonie about what happened last night," said Hugo.

"Nasty business," said Broonie, specks of food spraying from his mouth. "That scoundrel Mr Glad is back. Doesn't bode well."

"No," said Finn, unsure about what was going on here.

Hugo spooned some more moss on to Broonie's plate. "I've had to tell the Council of Twelve about this," he said to Finn. "We've got some ghostly version of Mr Glad disappearing Half-Hunters into thin air, and he said those words…"

"*Tick, tock*," said Finn, still watching Broonie slurp up his treat.

"*Tick, tock* is not good. *Tick, tock* sounds like something's about to go off. The Twelve were on their way to your ceremony anyway, so there's no point in trying to keep this to ourselves any longer."

Finn had hoped for a bit more reassurance than this. That his father was stumped was not a good sign.

"The ceremony is definitely going ahead then…?" asked Finn, torn between a desire to be made a Legend Hunter and the hope it might be done without too much fuss.

"I'd expect so," said Hugo, matter of fact, while fishing about in a drawer in search of something. "Even if things are going badly, the Council of Twelve likes a spectacular event. In fact, I was just telling Broonie what a big day it is for you."

"I'll stay out of your way," said Broonie, licking his lips clean of squished pickles.

"And I was *reminding* Broonie," continued Hugo in a pointed tone, "that lots of special guests are due in Darkmouth. The Council of Twelve. More Half-Hunters. The golden monkeys."

"Ah no, are they really doing the golden monkey thing?" groaned Finn.

"They won't get so much as a whiff of this old Hogboon," said Broonie, giving his armpit a quick sniff. "No need to worry on that score."

Hugo turned, and Finn saw that he had a roll of electrical tape and a pair of scissors in his hand. Broonie realised this too and stopped mid-munch, looked at each of them. "Pancakes," he said as if just figuring out a vital clue in a great mystery. "*Pancakes.* I should have known when you gave me pancakes!"

"Do we need to do this?" Finn asked his dad.

"We do, I'm afraid," said Hugo.

"The pancakes weren't even that great, to be truthful," hissed Broonie. "Not enough eggshell pieces for my liking."

"Do we have to tie him up?" Finn asked.

"No," said Hugo, "but only if he'll… you know what… willingly."

Broonie's drooping eyelids opened wide as he

understood fully what was going on. "Oh, it's desiccated I'm to be? Maybe *you* should try getting shrunk some day!" he screamed at them. "I promise you it's a treat beyond delight!"

"The Twelve think you're *already* desiccated," said Hugo. "If they see you like this, they'll make sure to do it themselves, and they won't be as gentle as us."

"I was being sarcastic, you do realise that?" said Broonie. "It's not a treat. *Or* a delight."

"Let's all agree it's not pleasant," continued Hugo. "But we have bigger problems at the moment."

"So I must pay the price for your problems."

Finn sighed and shrank a little. It was too early in the day for this. It would always be the wrong time of day for it. "We'll make it quick," he promised.

"It'll only be quick for you," complained Broonie. "For me, it is a slow, cruel trip towards oblivion. After all I've done for you."

"You're right," said Hugo. "You helped Finn defeat a rampant Minotaur. But, let's be honest here, we've saved your life too. You could easily be back with the Council of Twelve being questioned and examined—"

"And prodded," added Broonie. "There was lots of prodding."

"No one wants to hurt you, Broonie," said Finn, genuinely upset by all of this.

"Really?" asked Broonie.

"Really," said Hugo. "I promise we'll reanimate you when this is over, give you a big chisel and you can go out there and eat all the old, hard chewing gum you can dig off the pavement." Hugo held out a hand. "So what do you say?"

Broonie eyeballed him in return, assessing the offer for a few seconds before making his decision. "You know," he said, "you humans really do have the most appalling eyebrows."

Then he ran.

Four minutes and twenty-six seconds later, and after the loss of a couple of pieces of crockery, Broonie was wrapped in tape and protesting as loudly as his gagged mouth would allow.

"We'll get him to the library. You're going to have to grab his feet," said Hugo.

"Why do I have to grab his feet?" protested Finn. "They're vile."

"*Hhhggmmm!*" Broonie complained. "*Hhhhgggmmmm mm!*"

They lifted the Hogboon like a roll of carpet to a spot

on the kitchen floor between the bin and the washing machine.

"You watch him while I grab a Desiccator and get this thing over and done with," said Hugo and nipped out of the door towards the Long Hall before Finn could protest.

"*Hhhggghhkkmmm!*"

"I know," said Finn, hating every moment of this. "I'm sorry."

"*Hhhgggmmmm,*" added Broonie, then "*kkhhhhhhukkkk,*" as if choking a bit.

The Hogboon seemed in genuine distress now, all trussed up like that, with the locket clamped tight in his neck. "*Kkkgggggggggggurrrrrrrkkk.*" He writhed on the floor, thrust his head back, struggling for breath. It was awful to see.

Finn couldn't stand it any longer and bent down to pull a corner of the tape from Broonie's mouth. The Hogboon gasped a breath. "My neck," he rasped. "The clasp. Too tight. Can't breathe."

The doorbell rang. *Bing bong.*

"Dad!" Finn called out of the door into the hall. "Can you get that?"

"Help," gasped Broonie, a spray of spittle leaping from his lips.

"I'll loosen it," Finn said. "But just a bit." He fumbled with the lock on the very back of the necklace. What code? He tried the house's alarm code and sure enough the lock loosened and Finn could let the clasp out a bit, to the evident relief of Broonie who gulped in breath as if it was his last chance.

The bell rang again, urgent now. *Bing bong. Bing bong.*

"OK!" Finn shouted at the door. "I'm coming. Stay here, Broonie. There's no point in trying to wriggle anywhere."

Pressing the tape across Broonie's mouth again, he ran from the kitchen, opened the door.

Emmie stood on the doorstep.

"They're coming," she announced urgently, pushing past Finn.

"Who's coming?" asked Finn.

"What's going on?" enquired Hugo, appearing in the hall with a Desiccator barrel in one hand, its canister in the other. A breeze tickled each of them, air whooshing through the house as if a door or window was open elsewhere. Hugo looked at the open door of the kitchen. "Where's Broonie?" he asked, walking towards it.

Finn tensed immediately, and followed Emmie to the kitchen. They each peered under one of Hugo's armpits as he stood, shaking his head, the restrained fury clear in every hard breath through his nostrils.

On the floor was a pair of scissors and shorn electrical tape. But no Broonie. Over the sink, a small window was open to the yard out the back, and the walled alleyways leading into Darkmouth.

"Fantastic," said Hugo.

"He was choking, Dad," explained Finn, feeling the world sink away beneath him.

"I presume he went through a whole routine, did he?" said Hugo, and began to imitate a choking Hogboon. "*Kkkggggggggggurrrrrrrkkk*. Help me. *Kkkgggggurrrrkk*.*"

"No, it wasn't like that," said Finn, even though it had been exactly like that.

Hugo turned, pushed past Finn and Emmie to get to the Long Hall, quickly returning with a scanner: a chubby box with a screen that winked into view, displaying a hand-drawn map of Darkmouth. A blue dot appeared. This was the tracking device in Broonie's locket. He was already moving at pace from the house.

Hugo clicked the Desiccator, arming it. There was a meek wheeze from its canister, the sound of its fluid engaging for action.

"This is getting serious," said Hugo. "Mr Glad has killed two Half-Hunters. More may die. He's up to something, even if we don't know what it is yet. So we'll go and bring Broonie back, but this time we'll do it without any messing around, without playing nice. We'll track him like we would any Legend. Hunt him down. Shrink him. Bring him back. Then we'll start dealing with this situation properly."

"Are we going to tell the Twelve he's loose?" asked Finn.

"I'll think about it," answered Hugo.

"Oh yeah," said Emmie, "that's what I came to tell you."

"Hello," said a voice. "Anyone home?" Steve stuck his head round the door. "Hey, Hugo. You'd better have the kettle on."

"Ah, it's just you," said Hugo.

"And me too, delighted to finally be back in Darkmouth," said Estravon the Assessor, appearing from behind Steve, his hair black, slick and combed so neatly it looked like he may have measured each individual strand to make sure they were all the same length. He stepped into the house, his long legs encased in a blue suit with a velvety sheen. He wore a bright red tie.

"Good morning, Hugo, Finn, Emmie. Doing some training already?" Estravon asked, spotting the Desiccator. He looked at his watch. "Anyway, that's all the time allocated for small talk; we must get on with business."

He stood aside to reveal a group of people behind him. They were ancient men and women in colourful robes and heavy chains, and each had their own drably suited assistant just a step behind their right shoulder.

Hugo's face fell.

Estravon thrust his chin out, and announced proudly, "Allow me to introduce the Council of Twelve."

12

"What a day this is," exclaimed Estravon, running a hand down his fine suit, and unable to restrain his enthusiasm as the Council of Twelve and their assistants settled in the library. Surrounded by the armour and relics of generations of Legend Hunters, and by shelves filled with the desiccated remains of countless Legends, the new arrivals sat and slumped on the various kitchen chairs and even a sofa that had been dragged down the Long Hall to the library.

Hugo and Finn sat behind the main desk. Emmie was half sunk into a beanbag to their right. There had been no seats left.

Finn's father was distracted by the scanner tucked away between their feet and the blue blob that was Broonie skipping through Darkmouth in a somewhat haphazard pattern. And a conspiratorial glance between them

back in the main house had been all that was needed for the three of them to agree that they were better off not mentioning this small but important detail right now.

"Yes, what a day," repeated Estravon, looking towards Finn and Hugo. "The Completion of a new Legend Hunter. After which, Hugo shall become a member of the Council of Twelve. And here they all are in Darkmouth for this historic occasion."

However, Estravon dropped his voice and grew sombre at this moment. "Actually, not *all* of the Twelve are here. As everyone will be aware, Zero the First has been unable to attend due to a long-standing appointment with his doctor which, unfortunately, turned into a more permanent appointment with a cemetery."

Everyone in the room bowed their heads for a moment in memory of the recently departed Zero the First. While they did this, Finn took his chance to examine the Council of Twelve.

They were about as old as any people Finn had ever seen. They wore robes, every one a different colour, but all heavy enough that they appeared almost weighed down by them. One woman wore a yellow garment that, on second glance, might actually have been a very old, grimy white. On her shoulders was a scaly green trim.

A man sported a faded red robe with spiked epaulettes, another a deep purple one with an orange fur collar.

Around their necks were chains festooned with medallions – the very bottom of these engraved with a number. One of the great privileges of becoming a member of the Council of Twelve was that, having worked for so long to earn their Legend Hunter name, they then traded it in for a mere number between 1 and 12. Hugo the Great would become Hugo the Twelfth, but only once Finn became Complete.

Every other medallion on the chain was decorated with carvings of their families' triumphs or their own personal battles. Because while they were slow now, and obviously reliant on the assistants who stood attentive behind each of them, with their grey suits and empty expressions, the Twelve were old enough to have known a time when Blighted Villages were invaded regularly, when the world was in constant need of protection. As very much younger men and women, they had fought those battles themselves, felled Legends.

Now one elder in a silver robe was battling sleep. And losing.

The moment of silence was over and Estravon waved his hand in the direction of one of the Twelve. "Allow me first to present the most noble Cedric the Ninth." With that simple introduction, Estravon sat.

Cedric rose. The medallions resting on his red robes bore images of serpents and sea creatures, and one panel showed what must have been a younger version of him striking down a giant. Now the thin skin of his neck just about held up his large tottering head. And he coughed, like an engine trying to start.

His assistant, blond and tall with a blank face, moved to help him, but Cedric waved him away as if he did not want to be seen to be weak. Finally, after one last hack and a thump to his chest, he got the words out.

Serpent

"Is it true you saw Mr Glad?"

Finn looked to his father, whose nod told him he could answer freely.

"I saw him," confirmed Finn. "But not him. He was there, but kind of wasn't, if you know what I mean."

He could see that they didn't know what he meant at all.

"Did he run away?" asked Cedric.

"No," said Finn. "He just sort of vanished. Or drifted away."

"And the marks in the air," interjected the yellow-robed woman, grey hair piled on her head like rocks and a great scar running from the centre of her forehead around her eye and ending at the cleft of her chin. "What did they look like?"

Estravon stood. "Allow me to introduce Aurora the Third." He sat down again.

Finn grabbed a piece of paper and a pen from his father's desk, and walked round to the front of it.

He sketched the marks from the hotel room and the beach, then held them up.

"Claw marks?" said Aurora, running a finger along her scar.

"Possibly," Hugo answered. "Or the victims may have torn the air themselves in some last act before death."

Aurora noticed Finn's feet. "Are you wearing those claws to your Completion Ceremony?"

So cosy were they, Finn had completely forgotten he was wearing the giant slippers. His face reddening, he opened his mouth to answer only to be distracted by a giggle from Emmie.

This was followed by a loud snort from the sleeping member of the Twelve. "Three!" he announced.

"Does Stumm the Eleventh wish to contribute?" asked Estravon.

Stumm the Eleventh belched in his sleep slowly, as part of his natural exhalation at that moment. Hugo's impatience practically radiated from him as he took the chance to glance again at the scanner. Returning to his seat, Finn looked too, and could see that Broonie was moving deeper into Darkmouth.

"Or they may be the marks from whatever Glad uses to snatch his victims, or vaporise them, or whatever he's doing," Hugo continued, his focus back on the room.

"Two!" blabbed Stumm the Eleventh, sitting up sharply from his apparent slumber. His eyes were wide open, pushing up his pile of eyebrows. Every member of the Twelve and their assistants looked at him. Apparently satisfied with his contribution, Stumm the Eleventh nodded off again while the fur of his robes rose and fell to his snores.

"He's telling us it's a countdown," said Steve, from where he leaned against a curved shelf at the back of the room. "That's what Stumm is saying. Three. Two. And presumably—"

"One!" shouted Stumm, not even opening his eyes.

"There you go," said Steve.

Aurora looked at Finn. "And Mr Glad said, *'Tick, tock'*?"

"Yes."

"Then it would certainly appear to be a countdown," she said. "He's planning something. Building up to something. And he wants us to know it."

There was a brief outbreak of whispering and discussions between the members of the Twelve and their assistants. Finn saw his own father silently berate himself.

He was so distracted by Broonie's escape he'd missed this vital deduction.

While this was going on, Finn noticed that the impassive assistant to the sleeping Stumm, light bouncing off his utterly bald head, carried a square briefcase. It was red and weathered, the gold paint of its locks largely peeled away. Spotting Finn eyeing it, the assistant gripped the briefcase just a smidgen tighter.

"I wonder what's in that case?" Finn whispered to Emmie.

"I don't know," she said, leaning forward on her beanbag for a better look. "Their lunch?"

"They handcuff their lunch to an assistant?" He had noticed a chain running from the man's sleeve to a cuff at the case's handle.

Cedric cleared his throat. "If it's a countdown, then what is it counting down to?"

"More victims?" wondered Estravon.

"Or something bigger," said Steve.

"What of the Hogboon who arrived here from the Infested Side?" asked Aurora. "Were we able to extract information from him?"

Finn hoped they didn't see his eyes widen at the mention of Broonie.

"He is contained," said Hugo calmly, even as the scanner at his feet showed Broonie loose about Darkmouth. "Besides, I think he answered all he could. There was a fair amount of prodding."

"True, there was prodding," said Cedric. His blond assistant leaned in and whispered something. "And quite a lot of poking," concluded Cedric.

Finn could see that the blue dot was on the move. Not towards the wormery at the allotments, but further into town. It looked like Broonie was heading for the main street. Hugo was doing well to hide his anxiety, but they both knew that this was about to get very messy indeed.

"About Mr Glad," said Aurora. "Tell us again how he died. It was, I believe, in this very room."

Finn and Emmie exchanged a glance. They'd both been there at that terrible moment.

"I pushed him," Finn answered. "Into a gateway. And he became sort of stuck in it."

"He wriggled," said Emmie. "Tried to get out."

"But it was like he was being bitten, and the jaws were tightening," said Finn. "Eventually, it became too much and when the gateway closed he just kind of vaporised in a spray of light."

"Golden light," said Emmie. "Right over there." She

pointed to the spot where it had happened, now betraying no evidence of the strange events that had taken place there not even a year before.

"If he was caught between gateways, could it be that...?" Aurora asked quietly, addressing the rest of the Twelve.

"Could it be what?" Emmie whispered to Finn, who shrugged his shoulders.

"Such a phenomenon was never proven," Cedric spluttered. "Rumoured but never proven."

"Yes," replied Aurora, "but there is one important place where it was once rumoured to have occurred."

"What are they talking about?" asked Finn.

"The Trapped," said his father bluntly, as if it was something he had hoped to avoid saying. "They're talking about the Trapped."

"Ahem, if I may," said Estravon, taking a few steps towards Finn and Emmie. "The Trapped are a myth even among myths, talked of but never seen. They are those souls caught in gateways, between worlds, and said to live in that space thereafter."

"But they do not come back," said Aurora with certainty.

"There have been stories," said Cedric. "At least one Legend Hunter who believed they could."

"That is for another time," Hugo said, sounding like

he wanted to cut off this discussion before it got any further. "For now, what is the plan? I presume that as Darkmouth's Legend Hunter I will be expected to deal with this situation?"

"Yes," said Cedric, glancing at the other members of the Twelve.

"Good," said Hugo, making to stand up.

"And... no," said Aurora, leaving Hugo to hover, neither sitting nor standing. "This is a big day for our kind. The biggest in many years. Our greatest triumph in decades. A new Legend Hunter. After which you will join us as a member of the Twelve. Then, perhaps, we can start making plans for Emmie here too."

Finn blushed. He sensed Emmie sitting a little taller at the compliment.

"We must not hesitate," said Cedric.

"If necessary," continued Aurora, looking to the bald assistant attached to the case, "we must take extraordinary measures. You will deal with it for now, Hugo. But if things are not resolved quickly we will intervene."

Hugo glanced at the case too, sighed. "Fair enough."

Finn looked down at the scanner. It showed Broonie wandering straight into the centre of Darkmouth. There would be chaos out there. And disgust. Panic. Excitement.

Trouble. His dad was obviously thinking the same thing.

Further along the row of the Twelve, another member stood, a very tall man in a black robe with light blue leather edges, and a medallion bearing the number 2. The skin sagged on his face and on the finger he raised.

"Lazlo the Second," announced Estravon, realising he needed to introduce him as was the way of things.

The rest of the room hushed. Lazlo inhaled, working himself up to what was obviously going to be a very important intervention.

"In my blighted village we have a saying," he said. "Hairy feet are no substitute for comfortable shoes."

Lazlo sat again, with the aid of his assistant who draped his black robe over the back of a floral kitchen chair.

No one seemed to know quite how to respond.

"I'm going to have to find a way to break up this meeting," Hugo mumbled to Finn as the thrum of elders and assistants rose again.

Finn had a moment of inspiration, words so powerful that for a long time after he would be shocked by their impact. "Who needs to use the toilet?"

There was quite a rush for the door.

13

They hurried the ten members of the Twelve and their assistants from the house without wanting to give the impression they were pushing them out.

They jumped in the car without wanting to give the impression they were hurrying anywhere in particular.

They tracked Broonie through Darkmouth without wanting to look like they were tracking anything at all.

Blip went the scanner.

"I can't believe he escaped," went Hugo.

"Sorry," said Finn.

"Just as the Council of Twelve turns up."

"I know."

"While Half-Hunters are being vaporised by Mr Glad."

"That bit's hardly my fault," said Finn. He wasn't so sure, though.

The scanner told them the Hogboon was scampering

around the centre of the town, apparently in some kind of panic judging by the pattern. In and out of alleyways, trying to find ways into backyards, hugging the edges of every wall. But one thing was clear. He was heading towards Broken Road, and the calm of the unsuspecting people of Darkmouth was about to be shattered.

"There's to be no screwing up this time," said Hugo, with such a grip on the steering wheel that his knuckles were white.

"You're the one who left me alone with a choking Hogboon," replied Finn. "Anyway, you're just taking all this out on me because the Council of Twelve has shown up and you're trying to pretend we're in control of things."

"Hold that Desiccator," said Hugo sternly. "We're about to turn sharply."

He swung the car round a corner while Finn held the Desiccator on his lap, praying it wouldn't accidentally discharge and shrink the car door. Or the entire car.

It wouldn't be the first time Finn had accidentally shrunk something. Almost a year ago, when Mr Glad first turned on them, Finn had desiccated half a fishing boat in the harbour. Still, compared to some unfortunate Legend Hunters of the past, he wasn't doing too badly. Most famous was André the Clumsy, who had inadvertently desiccated his mother-in-law during their very first meeting – which wouldn't have been so bad if she hadn't been on a bicycle at the time. It is said to have taken him four weeks to properly separate the woman from the bike, and even then a bell rang every time she hiccuped.

"What's in the briefcase, Dad?" Finn asked.

"Briefcase?"

"The one that assistant had chained to his wrist."

"I can't tell you."

"I know you'd tell me if you needed to," responded Finn.

"It's the worst thing I can imagine," said Hugo. "So we're going to make sure they don't need to open it. Now tell me where Broonie is on that scanner."

"He's gone into Scraper's Lane," said Finn, watching their target move on the map. "Hold on, he's back out on Broken Road now."

At that moment, his father pressed on the accelerator in order to dash through the lights just as they went from orange to red, a short scream of the tyres giving an indication of his urgency. Hugo almost clipped the front edge of a small oncoming car, and gave the driver a wave of forced jolliness that was supposed to make up for the fact he had almost crushed him pancake-flat.

They arrived at the top end of Broken Road.

"There!" shouted Finn, pointing towards a spot further down the road, where the scanner said Broonie should be. The place was obscured by parked cars and the usual mix of Darkmouth locals and Half-Hunter tourists. None seemed as yet to have noticed the rogue Legend.

"Let's draw up slowly beside him," said Hugo, keeping his speed steady. "Get good and close for a shot."

They moved on, the blue dot on the scanner getting very near.

Blip. Blip. Blipblipblip.

Still Broonie was obscured. Finn saw a low figure flit between a gap in some parked cars, hugging the ground. "There!"

In just a few more metres, Hugo would get a clean shot through a space between cars. He took the Desiccator from Finn's lap, kept his other hand on the wheel. Nerveless. Steady. He pulled in to the kerb, waited for Broonie to emerge. "Ready," he said. "Three. Two. One…"

"Hey, Hugo!" Nils, the Norwegian Half-Hunter stuck his head right in the window. "And it's the boy Finn. What a hero! Oh wow, yes."

"Listen," said Hugo, trying to look over his shoulder, "we're in the middle of something here so—"

"Great car," said Nils, oblivious to the urgency. "Does it have an ejector seat?"

Finn watched the scanner as the dot approached the street side of their car.

Blipblipblip.

"No ejector seats either," replied Hugo. "Look, we'll have plenty of time to—"

"But it has Desiccators in the bumper, right?" asked Nils, undeterred. He pushed his arm into the car. "I love gadgets. Have I shown you my souvenir cufflinks? I wanted something really explosive for my trip and—"

"Dad," said Finn as the dot passed right by them, hidden by parked cars and Nils's big head. Hugo pushed open the door, practically shoving Nils out of the way. Finn got out of his side of the car, the scanner held low under his hooded jacket. *Blipblipblip. Blip. Blip.*

"He's gone down the alleyway to our one o'clock," said Hugo.

"What's at one o'clock?" asked Nils, standing in his way. "Can I come?"

"Nils," said Hugo. "Do you want to know a Darkmouth secret?"

Nils nodded with the enthusiasm of a toddler.

"That postbox over there is a spring-loaded Legend trap. You should go and have a look. But *only* look. One touch and you might lose a foot."

"Oh wow." Nils bounded away.

Hugo grabbed the Desiccator, tucked it tight under his armpit. "I'll take this alleyway, you take that one just behind us. They meet at a dead end. There's nowhere for him to go."

Finn jogged back to the alley known as the Gutted Narrows, eye on the scanner, watching the Hogboon move along the curve between them, just ahead out of sight. Each time he thought he might glimpse Broonie, the creature scuttled on a little further, before stopping at the very corner where the two laneways met.

Finn rejoined his father there, at a fruit and veg shop at the elbow of the two paths. On one side of the door was a tall rack of potatoes and onions. On the other, boxes of apples and melons. And, in the middle, the door inside which they knew would be a cowering Hogboon.

"It's quiet," whispered Finn.

"Not for much longer," replied his father.

They burst in, Desiccators high, ready to fire, Hugo shouting, "Right, you little scut, it's bedtime!"

The shopkeeper shrieked and dropped a lettuce.

Kenzo's rabbit hopped over to where the vegetable lay and nibbled on its leaves. Finn bent down. On the animal's neck was a locket with a combination lock on it.

Finn remembered loosening it when it was on Broonie's neck, but now wasn't *entirely* sure he'd locked it properly afterwards.

"Any idea how Broonie got out of that lock?" Hugo asked.

"No clue," said Finn.

He wanted to hide now. From responsibility. From everything. He felt like his face might burn up with guilt.

"You've always been a terrible liar, Finn."

N ear the harbour, at a spot where the wind whipped off the sea, carrying with it a low moan like bored ghosts, stood a church. About the building was the usual array of decorations. Stained glass. Plaques. Crosses. And, high up on the clock tower, gargoyles.

Those statues were weathered and grimy after years at this exposed point, smacked by salt water, slapped by flecks of slimy seaweed, and were only there because many, many years ago they had been bought cheap from a cathedral that had ordered far too many stone creatures for its own needs.

There were three gargoyles perched on the sides of the bell tower, gazing across the sea, appearing somewhat silly with their blank eyes and eroded beaks. There should have been four, but one had been dropped during the building of the church, crashing to the ground and

leaving an empty stone pedestal just beneath where the clock's hands slowly trundled round its face.

The pedestal was not empty now.

Instead, it held something that did not particularly resemble a gargoyle, but was close enough that it could hide there for a while without being noticed.

And Broonie had, at least, once met an actual gargoyle.

He crouched in the shallow alcove, pressing as hard as possible against the rear wall to prevent the wind blowing him out and down to his death. While Hogboons were known for always being able to land on their feet, he knew that if he was to fall from this height his feet would become fatally acquainted with his brains.

A young girl passed on the street below. Bouncing a ball, she paused to look up. Broonie froze, stared out as blankly as he could while salty air tickled his eyeballs, until the sound of the bouncing ball heading away told him it was safe to move again.

Across the maze of the town, he could see the distant but distinct figures of Finn and Hugo. Their confusion and bewilderment were clear even from this remove. They would have to hunt for him now. Sooner or later, they would find him. And what they would do with him then was yet another weight on a mind already laden down with dread.

"We need a plan, Broonie," he mumbled to himself. "Use that big brain of yours to think of something. You've done it before. You've escaped deep pits of bones, flown from certain death. There was that time you ran out of shoes and fashioned new ones out of discarded nostril hair. You are resourceful. Clever. Handsome. So, come up with a plan. Think. *Think*."

The bells rang out in the tower, crashing at his ears. He almost leaped clean from the alcove with fright. As each *bong* counted the hour, Broonie slumped back, the breeze pulling at his toes, resignation dragging at his mind, hunger nagging at his belly already.

He had absolutely no idea what to do next.

15

Finn didn't get back in his dad's car. He wanted to walk home – or, more accurately, mope home, drag himself through the streets, regardless of the attention he'd get. The alternative was to sit in the car with his dad, but if he was to guess how that might feel it would be a bit like being inside a car in a crusher at the scrapyard. While that crusher was being crushed by a bigger crusher.

But there was no escape from things now. He turned a corner and could see the stage where the Completion Ceremony was to take place. Regardless of everything going on, the boiler-suited Half-Hunters were still preparing for the big day, apparently oblivious to the growing crisis in the town.

Finn watched them go about their work, carrying scaffolding and rigging and various bits and pieces of equipment, pulling them in over the stage, dragging

them underneath the heavy drapes that skirted below it from platform to ground. It was a level of decoration that seemed ridiculous to Finn. But then the whole thing seemed ridiculous to him at this point.

He just wanted it over with. Wanted his town back. He could feel things unravelling, and knew his father was feeling that way too. He didn't want that to happen. Not now. Not after everything they'd been through.

He scratched at his neck where his locket itched. Frustrated, he released it and examined it. It was decorated with an elaborate swirl, almost like the coil of a snake. This was, though, the least exotic thing about it. The dust *inside*, the remnants of a crystal from the Cave at the End of the World, was a route to the Infested Side – maybe even a part of it. And a means of travelling in time.

It was, all things considered, a strange piece of jewellery.

Yet he'd earned it. Having for so long wanted to avoid becoming a Legend Hunter, he now found he didn't want to lose out on it.

He was temporarily blinded by the flash of a very big camera, held so close to the side of his face it might as well have been up his nose.

"Excellent!" announced the stocky Half-Hunter

behind the camera, not able to believe his luck at nabbing this prize picture.

"Not now," said Finn, rubbing his eye. He fished for the bag on his back, put the locket into it and, as his vision returned, he looked up and immediately decided he preferred being temporarily blind.

The traffic was being blocked by a large van trying to manoeuvre a trailer down the street towards the stage. On the side of the van was a somewhat disconcerting image of a snake with a tarantula perched on its head.

Finn recognised a familiar sensation. Whatever was in that van, it wasn't good. And it certainly wasn't good for *him*. And, as that thought was bouncing about his mind, Estravon appeared at his shoulder, clipboard in hand.

"That's Animal Al, the Half-Hunter who handles the wildlife for us," he said. "Whatever happens about the whole Mr Glad business, there is still much to sort out between the monkeys and the scorpions."

"Hold on," said Finn, alarmed. "I'd heard there were six hundred scorpions for the Completion Ceremony, but I didn't believe it."

"Of course not," laughed Estravon, striding off towards the stage, clipboard aloft. "That would be completely ridiculous. Six hundred scorpions. Ha ha. No, no, not at all. It's only three hundred."

While Finn's mind was whirring away with this worrying information, his eyes stayed fixed on the commotion further up the street, where a few people were complaining about Animal Al's clumsy attempts to turn a narrow corner, and the florist came running out of the shop as the truck edged on to the path and clipped a display. But the van was already revving up and moving away again.

Finn turned to head back home, his chest squeezing in on him at the scale of all of this.

Because he was anxious to become a Legend Hunter, to not let down the family tradition, even if he wasn't so anxious to be attacked by actual Legends.

Because Emmie would get her turn to be a Legend Hunter once he took his.

Because he feared whatever Mr Glad had turned into.

Because of the scorpions.

Because of *everything*.

And he would have remained completely wrapped up in those confused feelings if he hadn't been startled by a screech of brakes behind him, immediately accompanied by the wrenching of metal and a lot of screams.

Turning, he saw the van driver swerve suddenly to

avoid a collision. He lurched dangerously towards the street and its pedestrians, then tried hard to pull away again, to get back on the road. The vehicle righted itself, but the trailer clipped a postbox, flipped on to two wheels and detached from the van.

Pedestrians and Half-Hunters dived away from the out-of-control vehicle.

A woman jumped behind a car.

A man jumped behind the woman who had jumped behind the car.

The trailer narrowly avoided them and ended up against a wall, resting two wheels against it for a second, before it dropped on to its side on the street.

Its doors flopped open. Hundreds of scorpions found themselves with a freedom they had not expected and scuttled off in every direction.

The people and Half-Hunters of Darkmouth ran for it in every other direction.

Except for one person. Finn stayed right where he was, even as the fleeing crowds began to stream around him. Because he wasn't looking at the van or scorpions. He was looking right at what had caused the vehicle to swerve so disastrously in the first place.

Mr Glad.

16

There were scorpions scrambling and fleeing and clinging on to whatever they could, be it trees or cars or hair.

There were shoppers flailing and swatting as if – well, as if they'd suddenly found themselves in the middle of a river of fleeing scorpions.

And there were about half a dozen Half-Hunters arriving on the scene, so stunned at this sudden eruption of chaos that they simply stood still and gawped, although one of them raised an arm to point dumbly at the supernatural figure that had materialised in the middle of the road.

Mr Glad stood within the melee. Or what *looked* like Mr Glad did. It was as if he was constantly melting and re-forming, his hair an oil slick crawling on his back. He was stretching out a hand, testing it, turning it in the air.

At the opposite end of the road there was a squeal of

tyres. Finn turned to see Hugo's car bouncing off a kerb, alert to the unfolding trouble.

Emboldened by the arrival of his father, and without really thinking, Finn ran. Towards Mr Glad. He ducked under the arm of the frozen Half-Hunter in front of him. Towards danger. It felt necessary. It felt right. And it felt like his dad would get there before him to sort out the problem anyway.

"Everyone out of the way!" he shouted while crunching on something, but deciding not to see how much squashed scorpion was stuck to the sole of his boot.

Animal Al himself had leaped from the van and yelled at the panicking crowd, "They're only Emperor Scorpions! They don't sting!"

Darkmouth's postman went screaming past with a scorpion on his ear.

"Not too painfully anyway," said Animal Al. "And it would be far worse— "

A large window on the side of the trailer flopped open.

"—if the golden monkeys escaped," he groaned.

Monkeys poured from the van in a golden cloud of screeching, leaping, furry fury.

Finn was almost at Mr Glad now. He became aware of his own breath, his muscles, every movement. Aware that he would reach him before his father did and that he didn't know what he'd do when he got there first.

He spun past a shopper barrelling along wildly to his left. He pushed off the bonnet of a car that skidded to a halt to his right. He ignored the monkey that bounded so close to his face that he could smell the stink of its breath.

On the road, Hugo's car was close. The roar of the approaching engine seemed to catch Mr Glad's attention, and he turned to look over his shoulder, his face passing through his head to the other side.

Finn stopped to avoid a shopping trolley shooting in front of him, just about missed its shopper following close behind, then resumed his chase. As he reached Mr Glad, he realised he had nothing with which to attack or to defend himself. Still running, he pulled his backpack from his shoulder and swung it at Mr Glad.

It met him on one side and, after a brief moment of resistance, exited the other.

But it stopped Mr Glad. Sent a ripple through his form. Seemed to leave him struggling and distorted for a moment.

Mr Glad turned to Finn, slowly and menacingly, then noticed Hugo's approach. He flowed towards a car abandoned on the road in front of him, touched the rear wing of its petrol tank, drew a line down it. With a loud crack, the vehicle burst away from him, spinning in a ball of flame and smoke that landed on the front edge of the bonnet as Hugo slammed on the brakes.

Finn stopped. Hugo scrambled to the passenger door, throwing himself out of it just before the thrown car exploded. The blast caught Hugo in the back and Finn in the chest, lifting them both and throwing them to the ground.

The monkeys went crazy.

Finn didn't notice. He just felt like he'd been kicked in the chest by every one of the hooves on a Sleipnir.

Sleipnir

His bag spilling out beside him. His father sprawled face down on the road, unmoving.

"Dad!"

Pain shot through his chest as Mr Glad loomed over him, reaching for him with a spectral finger.

F inn felt stretched across the skin of the universe. He could see its connections, the vibration of its strings, sense every molecule as if they were grains of sand pouring through the neurons of his brain. Could feel them flowing between the worlds, the never-ending drift between realities.

The pain burned, ate at him like acid, and built into a rage grown in the darkest corners of his mind.

His eyes saw two worlds at once. His own and the Infested Side, that burning world beyond his own, and, standing at the centre of it, a fierce Fomorian with a helmet lined with broken teeth.

And, between both worlds, he could hear voices. Screaming, distressed, calling out for vengeance, help and release. They were in his head. Outside his head. Everywhere. Were these the Trapped? Finn was being pulled into their world. Their cries were in him, part of him.

His cry was part of theirs.

His hold on himself was floating away, and the strangest sensation of all was that he felt an intensifying desire to let go. He couldn't fight any more. It was easier to be taken. It was like slipping into a dream, wanting to give in to sleep, fighting off reality. He could hear Mr Glad's voice, summoning him, controlling him...

Suddenly, unexpectedly, there was pain again, as if he was being hauled back to his own world. Then it was over.

Mr Glad recoiled, rippling like a stone thrown in a puddle. Finn didn't understand why and had no time to think about it.

Instead, he found himself struggling to regain his senses. Suddenly he was Finn again. A person. With a body. With a mind pieced back together, like a jigsaw with a couple of pieces missing. Just for a moment, he'd been ready to let go of everything, slipping under the control of someone else. Of some*thing* else...

Shaking his head, he tried to get a grip, realising that as the pain in his chest dissipated it was being replaced by an ache in the fingers of his right hand where he was, he saw, gripping hard on to his backpack, as if clinging desperately to his own world by pure instinct.

Mr Glad eyed him, the fires in his irises flaring, and then turned his hand out. And Finn could immediately see why. He had set his eyes on new prey. And Finn could see who it was. Clara was standing before him, dental scrubs on, probably having appeared just to see what the commotion was and finding someone she had never, ever expected to see again.

Mr Glad moved towards her, folding into her path rather than walking.

"Mam!" shouted Finn.

Mr Glad stretched for her and, just as he was about to touch her, she was forcefully pushed out of the way. Steve stood in her place.

Mr Glad touched him at the neck, drew his fingers down to the chest, opening a shock of light that convulsed Steve, held him in place.

Finn pushed himself up, his body aching.

Mr Glad's blood-bruised eyes watched him struggle to his feet, even as he kept hold of the convulsed Steve, light boring through him. Finally, Mr Glad spoke, scorched words that seemed to have been dragged from the depths.

"*Tick, tock.*"

Sparkling light burst from Steve's chest; his back

arched grotesquely. It could have been a thing of beauty if it wasn't killing a man.

"Time's up," said Mr Glad. "An army is ready."

Mr Glad evaporated on the breeze, a foul leer the last thing to go.

Steve clung to the world for a moment longer, silently reaching for help. The gateway expanded suddenly, shockingly, then imploded just as quickly. Steve was gone with it. All that was left was a symbol floating slowly upwards like a belch of smoke.

Hugo staggered towards Finn, through crazed pedestrians, crazier monkeys, shocked Half-Hunters and a man in a jungle outfit rounding up scorpions on an Irish street.

And beyond the scratch in the air that marked the spot where her father had been only seconds before, stood Emmie, her face white with the shock of what she had just witnessed.

Steve, her dad, was gone.

18

Broonie saw it happen.

He was in a bin at the time, chowing down on whatever rubbish and wrappers he could find, having slid down the side of the church, stone tearing at him until he landed with a crunch on the ground.

His stomach had, eventually, won the battle for attention. He didn't want to get caught, but he didn't want to go hungry either.

He had slunk through the town, found a quiet road on which to scavenge from bins, when a human family shuffled into view. A man, woman and boy-man thing. Broonie couldn't be sure. He looked sort of in between.

The man was carrying a camera. The woman was wearing a strange outfit, with flapping scales on its top half and something like snakeskin for trousers. The boy

wore a look of annoyance with the world that reminded Broonie of what generally greeted him when he looked in the mirror.

"I'll take a photo," he heard the man say, crossing to the other side of the road while the mother and boy stayed where they were.

"It's a hole in a wall," said the boy, his boredom as clear as the air. "Like every other hole in a wall. How many holes in walls do we have to stop and look at?"

Broonie moved around to hide behind the far side of the bin, while cramming a banana skin into his mouth.

He heard the woman scream and presumed it was because she had seen him. Peeking over the bin, he realised her scream was instead aimed at something around the corner from them, out of view. It was accompanied by the sound of a vehicle screeching, then crunching. This was followed by a rumble through the ground, the shock wave from whatever was happening.

The three humans were rooted to the spot, watching. Broonie moved around for a better look, and saw it.

A figure seemed to have formed from black smoke, like a corpse leaked into the world. Around him was carnage. Humans. Monkeys. Scorpions. Mangled vehicles. A van lying on its side.

"Now *this* is cool," said the teenage boy.

And among the wreckage was the boy Finn, bent double, hand out, reaching to help someone, but unable to do it. For the phantom had his hand on – no, *in* – Steve.

Broonie watched as a gateway was sliced open right at Steve's centre. It sent a shudder through the Hogboon, reminding him of the fate that awaited him in this world. Of Desiccation and becoming frozen in time, waiting to be brought back to life in a manner that felt like being pulled nose first through a keyhole.

Then he saw what no one else seemed to notice. A second tiny gateway was hovering in the air. Right where a car had been unceremoniously propelled into Hugo's vehicle. A tear in the world opened by Mr Glad, it was small but was probably just about the right size for, say, a limber Hogboon to fit through.

Broonie's mouth dropped wide enough for the old butter wrapper he was chewing on to drop from it. This was a way home.

He weighed up the options.

What did he have to look forward to here? In this

world of humans, he was faced with Desiccation, interrogation, the torture of Hugo's terrible music, the total lack of anything really putrid to eat.

But, if he went back home, what awaited him there? So many punishments, of such a great variety. He remembered the story of a Hogboon who had tried to escape Gantrua's mines: they said he was made to balance a spear on the tip of his tongue, pointed end down, while he simultaneously juggled three knives. All while standing in a trough of biteroaches. And he did that for forty-three days straight. After which, he was sent to the mines again.

Broonie stood, ran a hand across his mouth as he considered.

The boy-man from the little family he'd been following screamed at the sight of him.

"Look, a goblin! This is *brilliant*!" said the teenager.

Broonie knew he had no choice. It was bad here. It was bad there. But at least he had his own hovel over on the other side and he might get one more night in it before whatever new and novel torture life had cooked up for him came along.

Broonie ran for the open gateway and jumped through it an instant before it slammed shut.

A moment later, his mind feeling like it had been whisked, scrambled, poached and fried, he lay on the Infested Side. He gulped in the delightful stench of home, let its stink flood his grateful lungs.

He was on a hillside. High up, with a wide view of the world in front of him. There was no human here. No ghost. No one but himself, for now at least. He needed to think quickly, to find shelter, to get out of here and hide for as long as possible. No more humans. No more resistance. No more anything. Just a quiet life from now on for Broonie.

As he stood and dusted himself off, something caught his eye. There, fixed on this side of the world was a scar, vivid and large. The flip side of what had been drawn in the air on the other side of the invisible fabric between worlds.

It burned in the sky of the Infested Side, a freshly carved beacon.

"Look who it is," a terribly familiar Fomorian voice said.

Broonie turned, and very much wished he hadn't.

"Would you like to hit him, Cryf?" asked Trom.

"After you," said Cryf.

Not surprisingly, this was the last thing Broonie heard before being knocked unconscious.

LIECHTENSTEIN:
SEVEN WEEKS EARLIER

*I*n the basement of the Council of Twelve HQ was a dark, windowless cavern known as the Department of Destructive Studies. It had been put down here because its previous room fifteen storeys above had been blown up when, predictably, one study proved just too destructive.

Now two people in white lab coats were moving between beakers of different-coloured powders and flasks of varying liquids. They were taking one or other and adding them carefully to the contents of a silver bucket. From within was a dull, reddish sparkle, its hue changing depending on what was mixed with it.

"It needs more mush," said one of the scientists, his moustache long enough to reach his earlobes.

Watching from the very edge of the room, Lucien sipped on his coffee. In his hands was a top-secret document titled THE TRUE FINDINGS AT DARKMOUTH. It was so secret, in fact, that it was supposed to self-destruct two seconds after it had been read from start to finish.

But Lucien had fooled the document by beginning at the last page and working backwards from there.

The other scientist in the room, a tall woman with hair that shot like electricity bolts in all directions, withdrew a palmful of sparkling clay and carefully attempted to rub it against thin air, like a particularly bad mime artist.

Nothing was happening.

"We need to add more mush," said the moustached scientist again.

Lucien returned his attention to the top-secret report, specifically a page listing all the things found in the mess after the battle at Darkmouth. These were:

- 5,387 tonnes of rubble, stones and bricks
- 211 desiccated Legends
- 1 twisted lifebuoy
- 1 leg from a pair of trousers
- 3 bits of old fishing nets that may in fact have been one old fishing net torn in three
- 1 old fishing net that may in fact have been 3 old fishing nets tied together
- Dust
- Lots and lots of dust

But it was what they had found inside the dust that mattered. More dust. Scarlet. Fine. Mysterious. It was the dust of the crystals found in the Cave at the End of the World, and which Finn had used to open a gateway to the Infested Side. Under a microscope, it appeared almost alive, wriggling and dancing with light. It was this dust that they were now testing, seeing if it could be used to make more gateways into the Infested Side.

But still nothing was happening.

"I'll add even more mush," said the tall scientist.

Lucien watched. Every failure of theirs was another moment in which he and everyone around him was condemned to stare at pages, not portals.

He pushed at his glasses. They slid back down the bridge of his nose.

A colleague entered the room beside him, eating a small bun. Axel, a fellow Half-Hunter who worked in the Office of Snacks. "Have they opened a gateway yet?" Axel asked.

"No," confirmed Lucien.

"I hope they make a breakthrough soon," said Axel. "We need it. I was not born into a long line of Legend Hunters purely for the purpose of ordering three hundred mini-muffins and a box of cheese crackers each Wednesday.

Speaking of which, your mini-muffins have arrived. Raspberry icing, just as you like them."

Lucien remained silent, thoughtful, his growing frustration at missing out on the Darkmouth excitement pushing dark thoughts into his mind.

"Maybe that stuff only works in Darkmouth," said Axel, wiping crumbs from his mouth.

"Which would mean only Hugo the Great and his son, Finn, get to try it out there," said Lucien.

In front of them, another attempt to open a gateway failed.

"Too much mush," the scientists agreed.

"Well, that family does seem to enjoy trips to the Infested Side," said Axel as he took the top-secret document and, before Lucien could warn him, flicked quickly through the self-destructing document from first page to last.

"No—" Lucien cried.

Three seconds later, and accompanied by a good deal of yelping, they both learned just how horrible burnt fingernails smell.

19

cross Darkmouth, shops flipped their 'Closed' signs early. Locked their doors. Pulled their shutters. The townspeople retreated indoors, once again in the shadow of disaster. But the Half-Hunters filled the streets in anticipation of a great and glorious showdown to come.

Amid the excitement, Finn had been examined by his mother, who grabbed him by the face, by the shoulders, by the head, checking him over. And over. And hugging him. And only stopping once he told her that, while he seemed to have broken no bones, every hug hurt him in molecules he didn't know he had.

She tried to soothe Emmie too, who was sitting on the kerb. Numb. Disbelieving. Quiet. That disturbed Finn most. Emmie was never quiet.

When Clara went to Hugo, a medical assistant had come over to Finn. She had arrived with the Council in

the aftermath of the incident. All ten present members, in full regalia, a shock of colour and pageantry in a scene of devastation. They conversed with their various assistants, while Estravon made notes on his clipboard.

The medical assistant gave Finn the once-over.

"Where were you hurt?" she asked, and Finn could only look back dumbly, because there was no answer to that. He hadn't been hurt exactly; he'd almost been imprisoned between two worlds. He turned the locket in his hands, tried to recall the details. It was already a fading memory, like a dream he was trying to remember. But he knew it had been real. He'd heard voices. Had a vision of…

He couldn't hold on to it. It was frustrating him. He felt his anger rise. It had been him, until Mr Glad was distracted. It should have been him. Not Steve.

Behind him, a house alarm went off. Was his stress triggering that? The problem was he couldn't be sure. Finn forced himself to calm down, to count his breaths. The last thing anyone needed was for him to explode.

The medical assistant continued to examine him, declaring that she could find nothing wrong with him and went to check on Hugo and Clara.

Finn waited where he was, watched. He'd never seen

his father as he was now: his face ashen and drawn. They'd been in trouble before, they'd been challenged before, but this looked like something Finn had not truly seen. This looked like defeat.

To his other side, the Twelve were still in consultation with their assistants. Finn could see that their focus was on one in particular: the bald assistant with the battered red briefcase still handcuffed to his arm.

"Something's happening," Finn said to Emmie.

She didn't seem to even hear him.

"I think it's a weapon," he added as he edged a little closer to the huddle, trying to make out what they were saying. But they stopped talking and, instead, started to move away, two by two, from the scene.

"What's a weapon?" said Emmie flatly.

"That briefcase," said Finn.

Emmie stared at him, blank-faced.

As the Twelve filtered away, Finn looked to where his parents sat. He didn't want to cause trouble where there was none, especially not after everything that had happened. But something was going on, and he needed to know what it was.

"I know you don't want to move right now, Emmie," he said. "But we really have to. Please. Look, I don't know where your dad is, but I don't think he's gone altogether. I think he's out there somewhere, in some way I can't explain, but what happened to him nearly happened to me, so you have to believe me when I say I just know it. So, we need to know what the Twelve are planning. It could help find your father." Finn didn't know if this was true. But he felt it was. That would have to do.

Still half stunned, Emmie nodded, slowly got up from the kerb and together they followed the Twelve and their assistants. Finn led the way, crouching low while having to practically drag Emmie through the streets after the elders, pushing her into corners when he thought they might be spotted, pulling her along when it was time to move again. Her body was there, but her mind was stuck somewhere else entirely.

They trailed the group through the streets until they reached their destination, the hotel.

They waited until they had all gone inside, then followed, seeing the last of the lurid robes disappearing into the hotel's function room. They crept to the door, which was open just enough for them to slide in through. On hands and knees, they hid behind a row of stacked chairs, rusty from years without use.

They peeked through gaps in the chairs, seeing the

Twelve settle around the dark wooden dance floor, their assistants helping them, pulling up seats. All the while, Estravon waited, with clipboard in one hand and a thin screen in the other.

Aurora the Third was the first to speak. "Things are happening here in Darkmouth."

Estravon held up the screen. Finn could see some kind of bright graphics on it, and a string of numbers.

"Almost as soon as we arrived," he said, "I began tracking background energy levels to try and see what is really going on here. Three years' studying Crystal Dynamics, you see. I know a lot about it, as it happens. Though, to be honest, I don't know what's happening here exactly. But what I have found is that every time there is an attack, these energy readings spike. Coronium readings crucially. The very substance that opens gateways from the Infested Side into here. The same substance that I myself discovered growing in the cave in Darkmouth."

A murmur broke out between all the Twelve, and Estravon waited patiently for them to quieten again. Finn had to restrain himself from protesting Estravon's claim. Finn and Emmie had found that cave and the crystals all those months ago. In fact, Estravon had tried to stop them.

"Where is the Coronium coming from?" asked Aurora.

"That I don't know yet. But it seems that Mr Glad, if it is him, almost swims through this energy, that he requires the right conditions to be able to appear here and strike."

The hum of talk broke out again.

Finn kept his head down, pressed his eye to the gap in the chairs. Emmie couldn't help but listen too.

"There is one other thing," said Estravon, raising his voice to cut through the chatter. "The Coronium energy readings have dropped after each attack, but not as low as they had been before."

"Meaning what?" asked Cedric.

"That next time he will come back sooner. Much sooner." Estravon held up the screen, with a graph rising, falling, a little like a heart rate. But it was moving steadily upwards towards a red line. Beside it was an electronic timer, counting down. "Eight hours twenty-seven minutes," he said. The minute ticked down. "Eight hours twenty-six minutes actually."

Again, the room broke into discussion.

"And, after that, I calculate he'll be able to come back again after only six hours," said Estravon. "Around about midnight tonight. He said 'tick, tock' to Finn. The clock is indeed ticking."

Cedric stood and calmed them with a coughing fit, while he held a hand aloft. He sat again as he asked the important question.

"Until *what*?"

Aurora turned to him. "We have had a III, a II and now a I. At least one countdown is over. I think we can safely assume that whatever happens next will be bad."

"A bigger attack?" wondered Cedric. "To disrupt the ceremony perhaps? The man has a grudge against Hugo and his family. He must especially want to kill young Finn."

More murmuring.

Finn swallowed.

But he thought back to when Mr Glad had tried to trap him between worlds, tried to hold on to the dream that was slipping from him with every moment.

It hadn't felt like death. It had felt like something bigger. Like Mr Glad was gathering his victims. Preparing. Finn didn't know what for, but it had left him sure that when Mr Glad returned he would not be alone.

"I recommend we all set our alarms for eight hours and… twenty-five minutes," said Estravon. "That is when he'll be back."

Many of the people in the room fiddled with their

watches and phones, setting timers. Finn set the alarm on his own digital watch too.

"This is getting out of control," one of the Twelve said, twitching in his leopard-skin robe.

"We cannot wait any longer," said another, draped in bottle green with leather cuffs.

Lazlo the Second stood, one long finger poking through his droopy black sleeve. "There is a saying in my Blighted Village. If the sun does not rise tomorrow, you should not wait for the mushrooms to grow legs."

That silenced everyone for a few seconds.

"You do have to wonder," said Aurora, scratching the scar that ran across her face. "If it's not rogue gateways, then it's crystals in caves. And if it's not that it's traitors and Minotaurs. Darkmouth is supposed to be under Hugo's control, but I don't see it under any kind of control."

Finn and Emmie silently shared a worried glance.

"Weapon," snorted Stumm the Eleventh without opening his eyes.

Aurora turned to him. "Is it too soon, though? We don't know what we're facing, let alone how to face it."

Finn realised for the first time that he couldn't see the assistant who carried the battered red briefcase everywhere.

"We cannot," said Cedric, coughing while looking for a hanky.

"It would be unprecedented," admitted Aurora.

"It would result in certain death," said Cedric, taking a handkerchief proffered by an assistant and spluttering into it.

At the word 'death', Finn and Emmie looked at each other again, still as puzzled but far more concerned now.

"When we open that briefcase, it must be in the most desperate of circumstances possible," continued Aurora. "This is the weapon of absolute last resort."

She let those words settle. Through the chairs, Finn watched, wondering what would happen next. Curious to know what this weapon was. Worried he might find out.

Aurora looked around. "But these *are* desperate circumstances."

The eleven members of the Twelve looked at each other solemnly. Behind them, assistants whispered to each other, exchanged glances. Watching from the other side of the chairs, Finn could see the worry in those looks.

"Does anyone object?" asked Cedric.

Stumm mumbled something that made his eyebrows dance.

"You're right," said Aurora, "Hugo won't be happy."

"Hugo had his chance," said Cedric and cleared his throat.

The room fell silent.

"It seems clear," said Aurora, her words heavy with regret. "We have no choice. We must detonate the weapon. Now."

20

Something very strange was now going on at the hotel. There was a hum of anticipation among those in the room, where the ten current members of the Twelve sat in a circle around the dark-wood, long-quiet dance floor in the hotel's function room, their various robes hanging over the back of chairs, or draped on the carpet.

Cedric the Ninth and Aurora the Third were a little further forward than the others. Near them, even Stumm the Eleventh was making a valiant effort to stay awake.

His bald-headed assistant was the only one missing – and his briefcase too. Behind every other member of the Twelve, the assistants stood, their suits not seeming so bland any more in a room of deep brown walls and mustard-yellow carpet. Each was poised, attentive. Meanwhile, Estravon moved between them, engaging

in quick, whispered conversations while ticking things off a checklist.

"I should have told my dad," Finn muttered from where they hid behind the rows of stacked chairs.

Emmie didn't answer. She was still blank, muted. Her father was gone. Finn hadn't seen her like this before.

"I have to let him know," Finn said to her, pulling out his phone and hurriedly typing a message.

WEAPON! HOTEL! HURRAY!

He realised his jaunty spelling mistake too late.

At the dance floor, Cedric the Ninth scraped back a chair, stood. His blond assistant made to help, but Cedric waved him away. "I'm fine. I'm fine."

All present fell quiet. Even Estravon let his clipboard drop by his side. There was a sense of something solemn about to take place.

Cedric cleared his throat, phlegm catching in his first words. "Mass forces are darkening," he said. His assistant leaned in to whisper in his ear. "Yes, yes, I mean, dark forces are massing. Great events are taking shape. We must again rise as warriors."

He broke into a violent coughing fit, requiring him

to sit for a few moments to get his breath back and take a sip of water.

Aurora took over from Cedric, a ripple running through her robes, shaking the scales at her collar, as she lifted her chin and stroked her scar. "It is time to take our most desperate step."

"Can you see the weapon?" Finn asked Emmie, his face pressed against the back of a chair, watching through its slats.

Emmie simply shook her head, as if hardly hearing the question at all.

Finn sent his father another message.

HOTEL! NOW!

"Bring in the briefcase," Cedric said, in a loud voice.

A door at the rear of the large room opened and Stumm's assistant emerged, briefcase in hand, chain still attached to his wrist. Daylight pierced a hole in the curtains, bouncing off his shiny head.

The assistant walked forward, not too fast, not too slow, until he reached the dead centre of the dance floor and lifted the briefcase above his head to display it.

Finn looked anxiously back at the door, hoping his

father would burst in at any moment.

Cedric's blond assistant then stepped forward. Using a small key, he released the cuffs from the bald assistant's wrists. He in turn placed the briefcase carefully on the floor, front side up.

"Thank you," Aurora said to the bald assistant. "You have borne that burden for many years. You have slept with this briefcase on your wrist. You have eaten with it by your side. Exercised with it. Bathed. You have carried it in every activity of your life, for every moment of every day for many years. You are now free."

Rubbing his raw wrist, the bald-headed assistant merely nodded and took his place behind Stumm's chair.

Finn sent another message to Hugo.

DAD! HURRY!

Cedric the Ninth leaned forward in his chair, assessed the space. "We must avoid the sunlight, for fear of blindness. Pull the curtains tight. Turn off the lights."

What is *this thing?* thought Finn, truly nervous now.

Two assistants stepped back to close gaps in the curtains, where the eyes of several curious Half-Hunters were pressed against the window. The last slice of daylight, along with their view of the room, was shut out.

Another assistant left her place and started towards the heaped chairs behind which Finn and Emmie were hiding. It seemed to jolt Emmie, and along with Finn she curled up tight in an attempt to remain unseen. The assistant came close enough that Finn could have pulled the leg of her suit, but she was interested only in the light switches on the wall, her head turned over her shoulder away from them as she watched the bulbs overhead.

She stood on her toes, reached up and pressed a switch.

Disco lights burst into the room. The glitter ball over the dance floor began to twirl. The whole room was briefly a riot of bright flashing colours and sparkles, while the assistant searched desperately for the right switch to kill the lights.

"Sorry," she said, just as she managed to turn them off, followed by every bulb in the room, so only the muted sunlight of the world outside brightened the shabby walls.

Cedric the Ninth stood shakily, and with the assistance of Aurora the Eleventh walked slowly forward. Reaching the briefcase, each gave the other a look and, duly synchronised, creaked their way into a kneeling position, waving away the twitching anticipation of their assistants.

Together, they placed a thumb on each of the briefcase clasps and, following a last glance to acknowledge the apparent magnitude of what they were about to do, flipped open the locks.

Thunk.

They opened the briefcase and stood up once again.

From inside the case emanated a dull golden glow, filtered through a thin film of blue smoke.

Peeking between the piled-up chairs, Finn couldn't see what was inside, couldn't yet make out what it was that was so awesome about its contents. But he could sense everyone in the room exhaling, as if they had only that moment remembered to breathe.

"Sceptre," said Aurora, like a doctor asking for a scalpel. She held out her hand and waited as her own assistant produced a long rod. Finn couldn't be sure from where, or whether he had been holding it all along. But at the end of it was a bulbous container, a sphere coated in glimmering jade.

Finn had seen similar things lying around the library. They were not decorated like this, and not handled with such ceremony. This was a Reanimator, used to bring back desiccated creatures – and he began to guess that what might be inside the briefcase was stranger than any weapon he had imagined.

Aurora held the sceptre high so that its point almost pierced the disco ball above her head. Then she spoke, her voice harsh and challenging.

"I must ask the three questions," she announced.

"Yes," said every voice in the room. The Twelve, their assistants, Estravon too.

"Are we ready to bring into this world one who long ago left it?" asked Aurora.

"Yes!"

"Are we prepared to condemn to death one who is long dead?"

"Yes!"

"Does anyone in this room object to the action we are about to take?"

"Yes!" shouted Hugo.

He stood at the door to the function room, a dark figure against the blur of daylight behind him. He was heaving for breath, blood smeared on his forehead and a deep bruise rising on his neck from the earlier encounter with Mr Glad. "Darkmouth is my Blighted Village. This is my battle," he told them. "You cannot do this."

"It is not your decision to make," said Aurora, sceptre gripped tight.

Clara arrived in the room behind Hugo, clearly unsure what was going on, but realising it wasn't going to be good. At that, Finn stood, revealing himself. Every eye in the room flicked to him, then back to his father. Emmie stood too.

"This can't happen," insisted Hugo.

"We gave you a chance," said Aurora. "But things have gone too far for you. Too far for any of us. Mr Glad will be back, there is no doubt about that, and so there is only one answer to this problem now."

"You can't do this," Hugo said again, but Finn heard the hollowness in his voice. He had never seen his father look so powerless in his own Blighted Village. "*Please* don't do this," he begged.

"We have no choice," said Aurora.

She lowered the tip of her sceptre, touched the sphere and activated the weapon.

21

The light was phosphorous-bright, a spitting thunderstorm in the room that Finn had to shelter his eyes from.

It burned out quickly, but the sound did not. It was the cry of someone being dragged from the deepest of sleeps. The noise filled the room. Filled their ears. Haunted them. And just at the point when no one in the room felt they could take it any more…

…it stopped.

As it faded – the light, the noise, the shock – Finn's eyes took a few moments to adjust, for the flares and after-images to clear and for him to be able to see properly in the dimmed light. Gradually, a figure became apparent. Tall. Broad. As if carved from stone. Standing ready.

Hugo wasn't looking, though. He had his head down. Shaking it slowly.

This was the weapon. And it was a person.

"Is that…?" Finn heard his mother say.

Finn peered at the figure, silhouetted against the rectangular smudge of light from the curtained window. He began to recognise the features, to figure out who this was—

Someone flipped a switch. The disco lights came on again. The glitter ball began to rotate, throwing diamond shards of brightness around the room.

"What on earth is going on in here?" asked Mrs Cross, incredulous.

No one answered. No one was interested in her.

"Somebody turn those stupid lights off," spluttered Aurora.

The figure in the middle of the room winced at the sudden intrusion of roving, blinding rainbows. An assistant smacked at the wall and the disco lights wound to a halt, then two spotlights converged to light up a face long gone from this world, a man so terrifying his name had only been spoken in whispers.

Gerald the Disappointed.

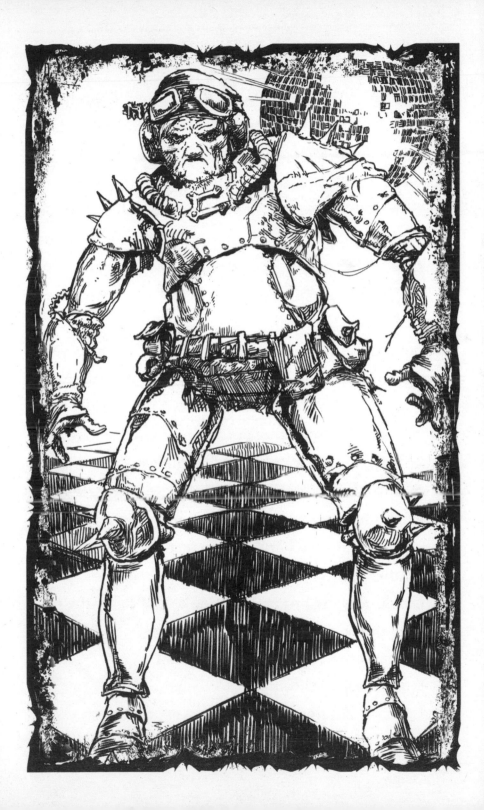

"How…?" started Finn, but couldn't quite get his question out.

Gerald the Disappointed. His great-grandfather. A figure so forceful and fearsome and, well, so thoroughly *disappointed* that his portrait sent a shudder through you even if you just passed it in the Long Hall.

"Why…?" Finn tried again.

"I don't believe you brought him back," Clara said. "Actually, on second thoughts…"

Hugo had simply begun rubbing his stubble with his knuckles – this time hard enough that he was in danger of wearing a path right down to the skin.

Gerald appeared to be adjusting to the light, the air, his very presence in the world.

"The boy didn't know?" asked Aurora.

Hugo shook his head.

Estravon clearly saw this as an opportunity to show

off his knowledge to the gathered crowd of elders and assistants. "Years ago, when the gateways began to close," he said, "and the Legend Hunters were not needed like before, it became clear that we were facing a crisis unlike any other."

"We became weak," said Aurora, "ill-prepared, inexperienced. So many Half-Hunters had to get *jobs*."

"It was obvious that, should there ever be an invasion, we would be woefully underprepared for anything other than counting the dead," said Estravon. "So, an operation was put in place, a secret weapon devised, something that could be used in case of emergency. It was called Operation Hardball."

Hugo stepped in, perhaps in an effort to show he still had some control. "They desiccated the Legend Hunters of various Blighted Villages, Finn," he said. "Including here in Darkmouth."

Only now beginning to understand what was going on, Finn's eyes moved from his father, to Gerald, and back again.

"I never really told you what happened to your great-grandfather," Hugo continued. "You just presumed he died years ago. I didn't give you any reason to think otherwise. But that's not what happened at all. Instead—"

"They *desiccated* him," concluded Clara.

Face ruddy and cracked, Gerald blinked, trying to get his vision back. Finally, he growled. "This had better be worth it."

The medical assistant stepped forward, carrying a small torch and a doctor's bag. She tentatively approached Gerald, who wore old-fashioned armour, spikes at the shoulders, spikes at the knees, a spike on the toe of each boot. The assistant shone the torch first in his ears, then moved to wave the beam at his eyes, but he shot her a look that stopped her dead. She turned to Cedric for some guidance, then, apparently deciding the examination could wait, stepped back again.

"What idiot has allowed Darkmouth to become so threatened as to need me?" asked Gerald, intolerance dripping from every word.

"Well…" said Cedric.

Hugo stood forward, chin up. "I will answer that."

Gerald peered at him, as if trying to place him, or to recall a face from the distant past. Finally, it dawned on him who this was. "So, it is you, my grandson Hugo. All grown up," he said, without a trace of sentiment. "I would say it was good to be home, but if you have brought me back the place must be a mess."

"I've protected Darkmouth long enough without you," said Hugo, refusing to be cowed by him.

"Ah yes, that's why you reanimated me," sneered Gerald. "To tell me it's all just fine and not to worry about a pretty little thing."

"It was not my idea to bring you back," said Hugo.

"It was ours," said Estravon, gulping. "Under the emergency protocols established through section 7G of the..."

"It's strange," said Gerald, glaring at Estravon, "but I hear someone talking as if they're a Legend Hunter, yet they're wearing a suit that looks like it was designed by hyperactive children."

Estravon retreated, chastened.

"*I didn't tell you to stop talking*," Gerald barked at him.

Estravon stepped forward again.

"Things have changed since you've been gone," he said in a nervous voice. "Darkmouth is now the last Blighted Village left. We brought you back because we are facing something different from the usual Legends. We seem to be dealing with one of the Trapped. And he, in turn, is making people disappear. He also seems to be counting down to something. Something bad, we assume."

Gerald didn't respond. Instead, he turned his attention

to Finn. Immediately, Finn wanted him to switch his attention somewhere *else*, because it was deeply uncomfortable. "You remind me of someone," Gerald said. "Someone I never want to see again."

"That is Finn," said Hugo. "My son. Your great-grandson, the latest in our long line of Legend Hunters—"

"That would be why he looks like Niall Blacktongue," said Gerald, unimpressed. "How old are you, boy? You look barely able to dress yourself, let alone fight."

Finn felt heat rise in his cheeks, but his courage fought through, pushing aside his instinctive need to shrivel up in front of this man. "I've been to the Infested Side," said Finn, just about forcing the words out. "And I survived. Dad too. He was there for over two weeks."

"What?" said Gerald.

"Finn has already done more than you or I have in our entire lives," said Hugo, eyes narrow. This was no happy reunion of long-lost relatives.

"What age are you?" demanded Gerald of Finn. "Eight, maybe nine years old?"

"I'll be thirteen tomorrow," Finn replied, hurt.

"No, you're younger than that," insisted Gerald.

"He's going to be made Complete tonight," said Hugo.

"We've to see what happens first," Estravon pointed out.

"That is not your decision to make," Hugo informed him sharply.

"You fought on the Infested Side?" Gerald asked Finn.

"Yes. Well, I didn't fight exactly, but we were both there." Finn jabbed a thumb at Emmie. She pushed her hair back, sadness still hanging from every gesture.

"Yes," said Gerald, "I can imagine the girl doing it. She's older. Stronger."

"We're the same age!" said Finn.

"But you, boy, I'm not so sure." Gerald looked around for someone to complain to. "*I need some water.* Has no one noticed I've been a dried husk for decades?"

The blond assistant went to get some water and, as he left, Gerald finally focused on Clara. "Are you Hugo's wife?" he asked, suspicious.

"I am Clara, yes," she answered, and Finn could see that she was using the very polite, very cold voice she employed when trying to stop herself from shouting at rude patients. She held out her hand to shake his. He didn't respond.

Every member of the Twelve and their assistants were watching this unfold, like it was a play on a stage.

Estravon was half wincing at the impending clash. Finn just wanted a Legend or something to invade to break the tension.

"What is your Legend Hunter lineage?" demanded Gerald. "How far back does your family go? What Blighted Village? Who have you defeated?"

"Well—" she started.

"When did you become Complete?"

"Actually—"

"What scars do you have?"

"I am not a Legend Hunter," she finally blurted out.

Gerald snapped his head back at this. "You're not Complete yet? At your age?"

"*Excuse* me?" said Clara, insulted.

"What's the delay?" asked Gerald, taken aback. "Why don't you just get on with it?"

Clara was clearly deeply offended by this and now in no mood for putting up with such insults, but Hugo interjected on her behalf as she opened her mouth to tell Gerald what to do with his questions.

"Clara is a dentist," he said.

"I don't understand," said Gerald.

"She fixes teeth."

"I understand what a *dentist* is," he growled. "I just

don't understand why you're married to her." He turned to Clara. "That is not meant to offend you, Hugo's wife."

Finn had seen some shocking things in the past year. Gerald's attitude was right up there with the worst of them.

Clara opened her mouth again to make it clear just how offended she was, but again Gerald spoke first. "Hold on a moment, that means that the boy here is a…" he looked at Finn in withering disgust, "…a *half-civilian* too."

A jolt of anger shot through Finn. The energy crackled in him. He felt like he might explode. Wondered briefly if he would. The lights flickered, but so fleetingly only Finn noticed it.

Calm, calm, calm, he told himself.

Clara took a step right up to Gerald. "You want to know what my Legend Hunter lineage is?" she said, indignant. "You are looking at it. I am the mother of that remarkable young man. How far back does my family go? We've survived famines and wars and ice ages and everything else that all families needed to get through to make it this far. Oh, and I've been to the Infested Side too. Twice as it happens. I was at a little thing called the Battle at the Beginning of the World, but you're so freshly thawed out you won't even know what that is."

Finn felt his humour lift, his anger drop. A good thing too. There was a crackle in the air around him that he didn't like at all. He wasn't sure, but thought he could hear the distant sound of a car alarm from outside.

Gerald prepared to speak again.

"What else?" Clara said. "Oh yeah, my scars. I have them, trust me. They may not be on my skin, but they are fresh and raw and came from meeting things far scarier than you. And finally, for a man who's been dried out for so long, you have a very heavy bead of sweat running down your brow."

They eyeballed each other. Finn noticed that a bead of sweat was indeed trickling down Gerald's ridged forehead, running round a mole, through the crevices of his brow, towards eyebrows that stuck out like waves.

"Has anyone *else* here been to the Infested Side?" he asked eventually.

Cautiously, Estravon put his hand up.

Finn elbowed Emmie.

She blinked at him. Then she raised her hand too.

"So, I sleep for a few years and when I come back the Infested Side is a holiday destination," Gerald sighed. "I think I preferred being desiccated."

23

Gerald turned slowly, taking in every one of these people who so clearly disappointed him. "So, you are expecting half-civilians to do the job of proper Legend Hunters. You've run out of Legend Hunters anyway. The Infested Side is apparently somewhere children and men in shiny trousers can just wander in and out. Now one of the Trapped is here. Am I missing any other disasters?"

"Nothing we haven't been able to cope with," said Hugo angrily.

Again, Gerald ignored him, faced the Council instead. "And you have brought me back because many years ago I warned the Council they existed."

"You did," said Aurora.

"But I was told it was superstition and nonsense."

"You were," admitted Cedric.

"Well, you are lucky I refused to listen to anyone else,"

said Gerald. "So, what's he doing, your Trapped visitor?"

"He's appeared three times over the past two days," said Estravon. "Each time he has evaporated a Half-Hunter. Disappeared with them into thin air. Or maybe killed them."

Finn saw Emmie stir in silent protest. He thought he should speak up, but didn't get a chance.

"He is trapping them," said Gerald as if it was the most obvious thing in the world.

"Explain," said Cedric.

"He is not killing them, he is trapping them," said Gerald in a louder voice, as if talking to an idiot. "Bringing them with him into the space between worlds."

"You're here two minutes and you think you have it all figured out," said Hugo, and Finn could see this was a challenge to Gerald, as if Hugo's territory had been encroached on, his expertise suddenly bettered.

"I had it figured out *decades* ago," he snarled. "It's only now anyone's bothered to listen to me."

"What do you know?" asked Aurora.

"That there were many old stories about the Trapped," continued Gerald, "and some tell of how they can be far more than just wisps floating in limbo. Fuelled by torment, they can become strong, powerful. They can return to take others with them."

"It's more than that," blurted Finn, talking almost before he could stop himself.

Gerald gave him a laser-beam stare that suggested the interruption had better be worthwhile. Finn felt like every eye in the room was giving him that same look now.

"Go on, Finn," Hugo said, seeing he was hesitant.

"He's controlling them too. I think."

"You think?" asked Gerald, sceptical.

"Give him a chance," said Clara.

"Mr Glad almost trapped me. That's what it felt like anyway. I'm trying to get that feeling back. It's all a bit fuzzy. I could hear other voices there. See… things. I can't remember it all properly. But, when he was doing it, he was in my head. I *know* that. It was like he was able to control me. I was fighting him, but it became easier to give in to it, to let it happen. I almost did."

Finn stopped, realising that everyone was looking at him, mouths agape.

They continued to watch him expectantly.

"Um, yeah, that's it," he said.

Gerald was nodding, though. "He's building an army," he said. "An army of the Trapped."

"But why? What does he *want*?" said Cedric.

161

"We have little time left to figure that out," said Aurora.

"He's coming back quicker each time," Estravon informed Gerald. "And he has left marks in the air. A countdown. Three marks, then two, then one."

"That news is about as welcome as the tie you're wearing," said Gerald. "Who wears a tie to a battle?"

"Incredible," sighed Clara.

"No," said Hugo, resigned. "This is what I grew up with."

"How long until the next visit?" Gerald asked Estravon, without looking at his grandson.

"Just over eight hours now," Estravon answered. "And we expect he'll be able to return a short few hours after that again, about midnight."

"Well, his next visit must be his last," said Gerald.

"We really didn't need your help," Hugo said to Gerald, and Finn thought his father was acting pretty much like he usually did when he was being pushed into something he didn't want to do.

"You will if this Mr Glad is coming back," said Gerald. "Especially if he can bring other Trapped."

"If Mr Glad's coming back," said Emmie, as if waking from her trance, "will he bring my dad back?"

"Is your father Trapped?" asked Gerald. Emmie nodded. "Then yes, he'll be back."

Hope crossed Emmie's face.

"Although he will not be your father in any meaningful sense. If this young boy is right, when you meet him, he will likely try and trap you," Gerald said.

Finn's mouth hung open.

"Or kill you," added Gerald, nonchalant.

"Unbelievable," said Clara.

"Really all too believable, I'm afraid," said Hugo.

Gerald had already started to walk from the dance floor towards the exit. He paused, turned to all those watching him somewhat stunned. His family. Emmie. The Twelve and their assistants. Estravon. "Well, come on then," he said, exasperated. "You brought me back so I could sort this mess out and I want to do it before I die for real this time."

24

Broonie awoke in a great hall he recognised, with a seismic headache that was also all too familiar. Tied upright to a pillar, he tried to force open eyes still swollen shut from the blow that had knocked him out in the first place. He could hear the grumbled conversation of Trom and Cryf, but also a chant somewhere else in the room. Incantations and pleadings in a language he recognised as containing all the bitterness and bile of Troll.

Broonie knew this hall as the place where fires had once blazed, in which crystals were forged in anticipation of taking over the Promised World. Now it felt cold.

Then Trom and Cryf's conversation, and the constant stream of Troll language, were drowned out by the sound of screeching metal. Broonie raised his head to see the sparks from Gantrua's sword as the great Fomorian leader arrived in the hall, emerging from the corridors, dragging

the weapon along the ground, his eyes alive with an anger that seemed to exceed even his usual levels of rage.

Broonie saw that the weighty cauldrons that had once blazed with fires that were never put out now hung lopsided from rusting chains. No wonder it was cold.

And there was something new, an addition to Gantrua's armour: great broken wings, folded at his back, but jutting above his fierce, domed head. Then Broonie saw the dried blood where the wings met the armour. It looked as if Gantrua had ripped them from a serpent, one of the enormous flying creatures that had been fighting Gantrua's army at the Battle at the Cave at the End of the World, and tied them on somehow.

A thin, curving tooth dominated the grille of Gantrua's helmet, reaching from jaw to forehead, no doubt another souvenir of the battle against the serpents. It was the biggest tooth on a row of many different types and shapes. Their owners were most probably too dead to miss them.

"*Yygggghh*," murmured Broonie, a string of bloody saliva hanging from a gap where one of his own teeth used to be. The tooth itself was now some metres away, on the floor, being gnawed by a scabmaggot.

"Just kill me," he said. "Release me from the torment that is my life."

Gantrua stopped in front of where he was tied up. "Do you think you matter enough to kill?" he asked. "I have had far more important victims than you."

He triggered a mechanism at the left edge of his armour, and the great broken leather wings on his back opened in the most alarming fashion, wide and intimidating, once attached to a living being and now hacked away and strapped to the back of someone who was not built to fly.

"You see the red daubed on these wings?" asked Gantrua. "That is not paint. It is the blood of the traitors who tried to take advantage of this time in which crystals are rare and the Promised World is being cut off from us. But that rebellion has been crushed. The serpents lie dead. I enjoy taking a souvenir after I have won a great victory. And, in a few hours, the humans will be next. I will finally conquer those who abandoned us here like stinkrats, and who selfishly hold on to the world of light and growth that they stole from us once, so long ago." He leaned in to Broonie, then bent and picked up his tooth. "*And, when I am done, I will cover this armour with their skin.*"

Gantrua moved further along the hall towards the plinth and its hard throne, carved from the glassy hardness of a petrified tree. As he pressed into the throne, there was a terrible sound of cracking bones as the leather wings pushed up at his back.

The Troll incantations were quickening now, growing louder. As Broonie's vision cleared some more, he could see their source to the right of the plinth.

It was indeed a Troll – lumpen, bulbous-headed, stooped over a massive upturned skull filled with claws and what Broonie thought could be entrails, although he had never seen them so far outside of where they were supposed to be coiled. The Troll was rubbing dust in his hands as he chanted,

letting it crumble into the skull. Broonie guessed he was casting some sort of spell, using the magic of hatred to bring more darkness into the Infested Side.

"We destroyed the Cave at the End of the World, where the humans came through," said Gantrua. "We tore that place apart, dug every last handful of dirt from it in search of Coronium, to find a way through to the Promised World. But all we found was dust, the decaying remains of crystals. Useless."

He examined Broonie's tooth, turning it over in his giant hand.

The Troll's spell grew ever more insistent.

"They tried to open gateways with it, to find a way for that soft dust to become a knife that would cut through the walls that trap us here. They failed. They paid the price." He crushed Broonie's tooth between his fingers, licked its remnants from his fingers. "Now I trust only my own Fomorian kind. They will not betray me. They are loyal. They will fight."

The Troll was calling out louder and louder, quicker and quicker, in language harsh and demanding. More dust was clapped into the skull. Cryf and Trom stood back, as if wary of what was about to come.

"Although, my Hogboon turncoat, the dust did bring

us something quite wonderful. It revealed one ally, a figure who came screaming into our world, and who we now control. We found that the dust can release those trapped between worlds, that in its purest form it can bring them back. But if you dilute the dust, control it, use it expertly, then you can have the best of both worlds. We can fill the air with dust and…"

The Troll released dust into the foul castle air. As it fell, its dull shimmer strangely beautiful in this ugliest of places, Broonie could have sworn he saw a face. A human face.

Gantrua stood once again, waited while a figure formed from the dust. Broonie recognised it as the same human he had seen tear a gateway in the Half-Hunter in Darkmouth. He knew this was the one who had so occupied the thoughts of Finn and Hugo and all those bags of skin in the human world.

The one they called Mr Glad.

Mr Glad did not pour into the Infested Side in the way he did in his own world.

He struggled and thrashed with the pain of being in two worlds and none at the same time. It was as if he was being plucked into reality, atom by atom.

The Troll continued his work, chanting, dusting the

air, but Broonie could see that even he looked terribly nervous about all this.

Gantrua, though, remained unmoved, upright, in charge.

"We saw your message in the sky. The last victim is trapped," he said, when Mr Glad finally stopped twisting and warping, settled into a semblance of a person. "Can we begin the attack on the humans?"

Mr Glad's mouth opened so wide it actually swallowed the rest of his head, turning it inside out until it reappeared in the right place and his face followed. When he spoke, it was in tones of deepest anguish. "Promise me."

"I have promised you already," Gantrua said, his voice edged with annoyance.

"Then promise me again."

"If your army helps take Darkmouth," said Gantrua in a bored tone, as if he'd said this many times, "then we will give you back your body. We will take the dust that has brought you here and purify it, thicken it, fill the sky with it so that it will not bring you back in some half-form any more, but re-form you completely. No more of this life between lives. You give me Darkmouth, I promise I will give you life again."

Mr Glad seemed to breathe out, his body shedding half

its molecules while he steadied himself.

"They trapped me," he said. "Hugo and the boy trapped me. Promise me too that you will make them suffer."

"Oh, I will make them suffer a thousand times over. Believe me."

Mr Glad began to thrash and fade, but reappeared as the Troll worked feverishly, crushing dust and throwing it into the air.

"Soon you will return to Darkmouth. You will help us destroy them. And then I shall return you to your body," Gantrua told him, then motioned to Trom. "Start the timer."

The Fomorian guard turned a large hourglass, and what to Broonie looked very much like blood started to drip slowly through.

"When the last of the blood falls," Gantrua said to Mr Glad, "you shall have all the vengeance in the world."

Mr Glad thrust his shoulders back, chest forward, summoned his last scraps of energy.

"Vengeance in two worlds," he said, before scattering across the ceiling and disappearing. Nothing was left but the exhaustion of the Troll, and the horror on the watching Broonie's face.

"Hold him," Gantrua instructed, and Trom and Cryf

grabbed the Hogboon from either side, as if preparing to tear him apart.

Gantrua stood before him and pulled the sharp serpent's tooth from his grille, held it to the Hogboon's thin skin.

"Do what you want," muttered Broonie, helpless, yet finding a defiance that pleased him in these, his last moments. He knew this was the end for him, and some fleeting, final scenes from his life flashed through his mind.

He thought of his mother and the way she would entertain him by licking her own earhole.

He thought of the home he'd grown up in, allowed his memory to flood his nostrils with the comforting smells of ripe feet, freshly boiled scaldgrubs, the polluted earth they would sleep so close to every day.

Broonie dropped his head again. Awaited his fate. And lifted it back up only when it became clear to him, with some surprise, that Gantrua was using the serpent's tooth to saw through his restraints and free his arms.

"Just because you are worth more alive *now* does not mean you will not eventually die in a most terrible way," Gantrua said. "I have a plan for you that requires you to be breathing. Then, when my plan is carried out, you will pay for living among the humans. You can be sure of that. When I am done, only then will you truly know what it is like to wish yourself dead."

The last string of rope snapped.

"But first," Gantrua told him, "we will go for a walk."

LIECHTENSTEIN:
FIVE WEEKS EARLIER

TWO WORLDS — ONE VICTOR

*L*ucien of the Office of Lost Arts needed a trusted source for his investigation. Someone who he knew would give an honest, reliable and loyal account of what had happened on the Infested Side. Someone who played by the rules, even when the rule book had been torn up, then burned and its ashes shredded just to be sure.

"Good morning, Estravon," he said, pouring tea for them both. "I have asked you here under rule 33x of— "

"—subsection 87/b of the Guide to Subliminal Investigations," interjected Estravon as if answering a quiz question. "It's one of my favourite subsections."

"Have a mini-muffin," Lucien said, sliding a plate across the desk to Estravon.

Estravon had been on the Infested Side and had the extensive notes to prove it. He furnished Lucien with these notes and sketches and a large bill for the dry cleaning needed on the suit he had worn when he was there.

"Did anything there strike you as strange?" Lucien asked him.

Estravon almost choked on his mini-muffin at that question.

"I'll take that as a yes," he said while Estravon wiped raspberry icing from his chin. "I'll rephrase the question. What happened when you met Niall Blacktongue?"

"Well, I didn't meet him myself," explained Estravon. "I heard about him. I might even have glimpsed him in a forest at one point."

"Might have? And what about the boy? What did you see of his explosion and defeat of the Legends?"

"Not much. Nothing actually. He looked crispy around the edges when he returned, though. And the Legends I met on the Infested Side seemed to back up his story."

"Legends confirmed his story?"

"Yes," replied Estravon. "In some detail. They did help Finn and Hugo escape after all."

"So, I'm just going to throw an idea out there," said Lucien, smiling. "Do you think there's anything, I don't know, suspicious about all of that?"

Estravon was quiet. He felt a bead of sweat run down his temple, crawl along his ear, tickle his neck before settling into the collar of his shirt. It was a new shirt. Expensive. Tailored.

Bought just for this meeting. The damp spread of sweat was seeping into his armpits.

Lucien didn't wait for an answer, but simply topped up his tea. "So, tell me, Estravon. How have things been for you since you left Darkmouth?"

"Honestly?" asked Estravon.

"Honestly."

"Dull. Boring. Nothing like the adventure and excitement and wildness of what I went through in Darkmouth and the Infested Side." He stopped himself, realising he was rising out of his chair while gripping the edge of the table. The tea sloshed in its cup. "I thought I'd at least get a medal or two out of it. I know another Assessor who got one just for fixing a broken microwave."

"Life is boring," agreed Lucien.

"Unexciting."

"You had such an incredible experience, something we've all dreamed of. And now you're back to this."

"This," agreed Estravon, looking out of the office window at the ranks of assistants sitting at row upon row of computers, typing monotonously.

"That's our lot now. Office work when we should be – could be – warriors." Lucien straightened up, clasping his hands on the desk between them and leaning forward.

"Estravon, I could get you a medal. I could get you a medal tomorrow. A dozen medals if you wanted. Each hanging from a gold ribbon."

"That would be quite—"

"But what would you say if I told you I could get you something even better than that? Something I know you'll treasure far more than any mere trinket."

Lucien took a breath. Estravon held his.

"Estravon, I have a mission for you. In Darkmouth."

"You got rid of the great skull from the front door," Gerald snarled as he approached the doorstep.

"It didn't seem appropriate," said Hugo, catching Clara's eye.

"Appropriate?" said Gerald. "What's appropriate got to do with it? Maybe it should have been painted some nice shade of lilac to match the colour scheme, uh? Maybe you could have surrounded it with flowers to make it look less fierce."

"This might have been your home once," Clara told him, "but it's ours now."

They began to step inside, but Gerald stopped and turned to the trailing gaggle of elders and their assistants. "Family only," he told them. "Darkmouth is still this family's Blighted Village to protect after all. Although the girl can come with us too. She's been to the Infested

Side. I like the seriousness of her. She looks useful."

"She just lost her father," Hugo pointed out.

"Good," Gerald responded. "A bit of anger could be needed."

Emmie didn't react; she had retreated into numbness again. Clara placed a hand round her shoulders, comforting her as best she could.

"I'll come too," said Estravon, making to follow them.

"No," said Gerald, a hand out. "I don't like your trousers."

Finn hesitated as Gerald walked straight for the door to the Long Hall, eventually following only after giving the crestfallen Estravon a sympathetic look. They had, after all, been on the Infested Side together.

Inside, Hugo pressed the panels of the door in a sequence and, when he pulled it open, Gerald inhaled deeply of the interior's musty smell, before pushing on through to the corridor burrowed through a whole street of houses.

As they bustled towards the library, Gerald scanned the portraits, ran his fingers along the frames and door handles, while the spikes of his armour scraped the walls. "Shay Gutbuster," he said, stopping at a painting.

"Here we go," sighed Hugo.

Shay Gutbuster

"My great-great-grandfather," Gerald explained to Finn, looking up at a portrait of a very rotund Legend Hunter. "Shay Gutbuster lived in very difficult, hungry times in Ireland. Had to make do with what he had. So, he hid in the belly of a washed-up whale to avoid detection from a rampaging Legend. Once he was done, he fed the whole of Darkmouth with the same whale. That's the kind of spirit that ensured this family and this town survived for so long. Are you one of those who'll swim in whale guts for Darkmouth?"

Finn didn't even have time to answer such a ridiculous question. Gerald was already striding on again.

"Next time you get to time-travel," Clara said to Finn, "maybe you'll go back and advise me to marry into a family in which all the dead people are actually dead."

Before the steps at the end of the Long Hall, they reached the final portraits. First was the woman who would have been Finn's great-grandmother, Elsie the Patient. She had a serenity about her that could not have been easy to maintain when living with Gerald.

Further down was that of Niall Blacktongue. Father and son were side by side on the wall. Gerald cast a disdainful eye on Niall, who was staring at a selection of items it transpired contained clues about how to get to the Infested Side.

"That traitor should be turned to face the wall," he said.

"You don't know the whole story," Hugo told Gerald.

"He abandoned this town," he snarled.

"He abandoned *me*, his son."

"Leaving me to raise you," said Gerald.

"Don't I know it," muttered Hugo.

Finn looked on, bristling from listening to the constant arguing.

Gerald turned away from Hugo and took the briefest of looks at his own portrait, where he appeared as deeply upset with the world as was humanly possible. "And that looks nothing like me at all. A chimp would have done better." He stormed on.

"Actually," Finn said to Emmie, "he looks positively cheery in that picture compared to real life."

Gerald burst into the library, practically taking the

door off its hinges, and looked around him while tutting for no obvious reason, or perhaps for a thousand reasons. It was hard to tell.

He assessed the sweeping walls, stuffed with jars of Legends caught long before his time and long since. He saw the detritus of inventions, half started, half abandoned, scattered about the floor. He tried to mask his surprise at the computer on the desk at the centre of the room, technology too modern for him to immediately comprehend, yet surrounded by the ancient armour standing proud throughout the room.

He pointed at a spot near the curving edge of the library where a dark stain was smudged on the floor. "Is this where it happened? Is this where you pushed the Fixer into a gateway?" They'd filled him in on the events with Mr Glad on the way back to the house.

Finn nodded.

"So, this is how you trapped him." He glowered at Finn.

"Yes, but only because—"

"You did the right thing," said Gerald, surprising Finn. "It just had the wrong results. What do you know about the Trapped?"

"Um. They're a rumour. A story. Or at least that's what people thought until just recently."

"And what do the rumours say?"

"It's not a test, Finn," said Hugo.

"It's OK, I learned a bit about them before," said Finn, stepping to a section of the library that actually held books and pulling from it a colourful, frayed copy of *101 Astonishing Myths of the Legend Hunters*. "When I was younger, I read about them in here."

"You don't need books," tutted Gerald. "I *am* books."

"The page is here somewhere," Finn said as he searched for the right chapter, but instead fell on an old wives' tale about how some old wives had tails.

Finn found the page. The story told of an anonymous Legend Hunter who had seen a phantom in the sky, the reappearance of a warrior long ago thought to have been lost through a gateway. "Shall I read it out?" he asked.

"No," said Gerald.

"It says that the Legend Hunter became obsessed with finding out the truth of the Trapped and even began to study how the Trapped might be rescued again."

"I don't need to hear it—" insisted Gerald.

"But he was called a bit of a fool for his beliefs, it says here," continued Finn. "Everyone mocked him."

"—because the Legend Hunter in that book was me," growled Gerald.

Finn slowly closed the book, its spine cracking a little bit as he did.

"Like the book says, I saw one once," Gerald said, a little subdued for the first time since arriving. "It was in battle, here in Darkmouth, and at the opening of a gateway I saw, well, I saw *something*. A face, in the sky. Not properly human, but I recognised it. It was that man, our ancestor, Shay Gutbuster. He was said to have given his life for Darkmouth, said to have chased a Manticore straight into a gateway, never to be seen again."

Manticore

He walked to a suit of armour, his lava-red face distorted in its reflection. "The vision was gone soon enough, but the agony of his expression burned into me. I couldn't forget it. I was young enough that I almost let them convince me I was talking rubbish. But I'm not soft. I know what I saw. And I sought out every story ever whispered about the Trapped, every sighting, every Legend Hunter dismissed as crazy because of what he said he'd seen."

He turned again. "And I found that sometimes they come back and take others. And when they do." He clapped his hands shut, like imitating the snap of a crocodile. Finn wondered if everyone saw him jump. "That's when you have your chance to get them back."

Emmie perked up again. "You can rescue my dad? Please say you can."

"Yes," said Gerald. "In a way."

"How?" asked Hugo.

Gerald lunged forward, snapped the sparkling locket from Finn's neck before he could react.

"What's in this?" he demanded, holding it up.

"Dust," said Finn.

"Crystal dust," said Hugo. "From here, in Darkmouth. We found them growing in a cave."

"Did you have that on you when Mr Glad touched you? When you avoided being trapped?" asked Gerald.

"No," said Finn. Then he paused. "Actually, I did. I mean, I wasn't wearing it. But it was in my bag. I took it off and put it in there because it was itchy around my neck. When Mr Glad attacked me, I must have grabbed my bag without realising, clung on hard. I was holding it tight when it all ended. And this was in it. No, I remember now. Mr Glad let go of me when I did that."

"And your father, girl. I'm willing to bet he didn't have any dust on him?"

Emmie shook her head mournfully, while removing Steve's locket from her pocket. "He didn't wear it this morning. Said it made him too itchy. He put it down. I took it. I didn't want it to get lost."

"I didn't have mine on either," said Clara. "I don't wear it at work. For hygiene reasons and all that."

"That is something many stories about the Trapped have in common," said Gerald. "Coronium. Either as crystals or as dust. The ancient stories were always the same. Those rare shards of crystals would be sought out and used as charms, as protection against the Trapped."

"Why?" asked Hugo.

"I died before I could find out," said Gerald. "Maybe

it's poisonous to them. Destroys them perhaps. But *if* Mr Glad let go of Finn because he caught hold of his bag, with the dust in it, then that would suggest the protection works."

He considered all this. "What matters now is that the Coronium energy levels are building all the time and Mr Glad and the Trapped are most likely coming back in a few hours. And you had better have enough dust to go around or a lot of Half-Hunters are going to die fighting them."

"But you said there was some way to get my dad back," Emmie reminded him.

"Yes," said Gerald. "Hugo, there used to be a Desiccannon in this house. Big long thing on wheels. You put bombs in it and fire them at Legends. Is it still here or did you replace it with maybe a comfy sofa?"

"We have it," said Hugo, biting his tongue. "It's on the stage for Finn's Completion Ceremony. For decoration really. It hasn't been used in years."

"That doesn't matter," said Gerald decisively. "We need serious Desiccation firepower, and we need it quickly."

"There's a problem, though," said Hugo. "To make the bombs, we have to fill them with Desiccator fluid, but we used up a huge amount of it in attacks over the past year and it hasn't been restocked fully. The stuff doesn't exactly flow from a tap."

Gerald's face lit up into something that Finn thought might be, or at least was very close to, a smile. "That's where you're wrong."

"Of course I'm wrong," muttered Hugo. "I'll always be wrong."

Gerald stepped back to the suit of armour standing proud at the edge of the library. "Have you shown the boy what's under here yet?"

"Not yet," said Hugo. "I've been saving that for after his Completion. It's Highest Level Information."

"Highest Level Information?" said Gerald. "Rubbish. I was sharing Highest Level Information with you before you were even born." He yanked the tip of the lance held in the gloved hand of the standing armour. It moved aside steadily, revealing a wide hole in the floor. A deep hole. It was dark down there. Finn couldn't see the bottom.

Finn looked into it. "Is that a hole?"

Gerald dropped to the edge, dangled his feet over it for a moment. "Of course it's a hole," he said. "You know for a moment there I thought you might be a smart wee fella, but that's a daft question."

"You can't say that," Clara said.

"I'm dead!" bellowed Gerald. "I can say whatever I want."

With that, he dropped down into the hole.

The Fomorian kicked Broonie forward, shoving him along the sharp ground, a path roughly tramped down by centuries of wheels and feet, heavy bellies and dragged tails. The Hogboon shuffled as best he could without falling over, the manacles tight at his thin wrists, rubbing at his even thinner legs.

The path skirted the edge of a cliff that formed one great wall of a chasm so deep its bottom had never been seen. Instead, the sheer wall of the mountain disappeared into blackness. Many creatures had fallen in there in the past. Many more had been pushed. They could still be falling for all Broonie knew. For this was the Chasm of Bewilderness. No one knew what was down there, only that finding out would be the very last thing you would ever do.

Trom kicked Broonie again.

"I won't walk any quicker if I have to use my face

as feet!" complained Broonie, just about keeping himself from falling nose first into the dirt.

"It's all right," said Trom, "I won't be kicking you again."

"No," said Cryf. "It's my turn now."

Ahead of them, Gantrua considered kicking them *all* into the chasm, but restrained himself, concentrating instead on the steady sway of the Sleipnir beneath him, its snorting and bucking needing occasional restraint, using the sharp bones in his feet to plant firm digs into its ribs. Gantrua glanced behind him, at the phalanx of Fomorians in his wake, a couple of dozen of them, compliant but sullen, carrying various weapons. Clubs. Crossbows. Swords. And, at the rear, a giant trundling along a catapult.

The Fomorians' only mission for eons had been to bring further brutishness to this already brutal world. Soon he would offer them a chance to take it to another realm altogether. The Promised World would be theirs.

But first there was business to do.

"Stop!" he commanded.

They stopped, the halting of the line confirmed by the grinding screech of the catapult at its rear, already sprung back and held ready for action. Beside it, the line

of rocks clacked as they settled.

The cavalcade had reached what appea to be some form of long bridge, but one th it had grown organically from the detritus, mists.

"You can just tell me what's on the oth Broonie, peering across at where the bridge into the general gloom. "We don't need to g look ourselves."

"There would be no enjoyment in that," sa "Kick him on."

Because neither Trom nor Cryf could be of them he was talking to, they both kicke together, sending him flailing forward, his feet to keep the rest of him up, the shackles bash legs.

Gantrua motioned his Sleipnir forward and legs moved almost as one as it began to cross th The line of Fomorians followed, the catapult b to slowly build up momentum again at the back.

As he took his first small, faltering steps or bridge, Broonie couldn't help but gulp. The freezi whipped at him, buffeted him, tried to force him edge. It took many terrifying minutes to reach th

side, and even in his desperation Broonie felt a large measure of relief that he hadn't died. Yet.

They had reached a long ridge that swept along at the base of a sheer wall of rugged, deep brown stone. They were so tight against it that even looking up, it was impossible to get a sense of how far up it jutted, only that there was wall, and there was cloud, and they met at a sharp angle somewhere high above.

They waited for the Fomorian soldiers to haul the catapult carefully across the narrow bridge, the stone of the structure crumbling under its wheels as it occasionally teetered dramatically close to disaster.

Broonie heard a deep rumbling. It took him a few moments to realise it wasn't coming from the catapult, but from deep within the stone facing them.

He listened carefully, felt a thud that shook the loose tooth in his head.

Sweat ran down his brow, through his wild eyebrows, tickling the edge of his eyes. He pulled at his manacles to try and swipe it away, but couldn't.

The catapult finally joined them on the ridge, pulled by four clearly relieved Fomorians who were roped to it. They were all squeezed on to the ledge now, with little room to move except for the space carved out by the jolting of Gantrua's Sleipnir.

"You think we brought the catapult to attack something?" Gantrua called down to Broonie. "No. It is to defend ourselves against what lies within."

Gantrua stroked the neck of the Sleipnir, calming its clear agitation. "It took us many, many years to cross to the far side of the Chasm of Bewilderness. And when we arrived we realised why this chasm was here in the first place. It was dug with bare claws millennia ago, to keep the rest of the world safe."

"Safe from what?" asked Broonie.

"Something beautiful," said Gantrua, a wry smile apparent even within the ranks of teeth at his grille.

Trom and Cryf hurriedly moved to opposite sides of the wall, and began to push at slabs almost indistinguishable from the filthy rock surrounding it. With a sound not unlike a mountain being torn in two, the great stone wall began to part. It was no wall, Broonie realised, but a pair of mammoth doors, creaking as they opened, so tall their tops seemed to drag at the clouds above.

As they slowly parted, the doors forced aside rubble that danced away down the edge of the mountain and into the chasm below, until eventually they were opened fully. It revealed something that greatly surprised Broonie.

More doors.

These were equally as formidable as the stone ones that had just opened, but were made instead of iron beams bracing tight ranks of the widest tree trunks Broonie had ever seen.

Gantrua nodded a signal, and the Fomorian ranks stepped forward to pull at thick ropes hanging from the handles. The soldiers heaved and hauled and grunted and strained as these doors commenced their slow grind open, revealing a space beyond, a great square of dim daylight and more cliff ledge. And, beyond *that*, something that made Broonie's heart sink.

"Oh look, more doors," he remarked, long ago having lost his fear of showing such cheek to Gantrua. "Is it doors all the way down? Any chance of a window or two?"

He earned a clap on the back of the head for that comment, and was perversely pleased to get it because he felt it a reward of sorts for his continued bravado in the face of mounting disaster.

Gantrua stepped towards the door. "Don't worry, Hogboon, in a few moments you will be wishing that doors were all you would ever see for the rest of your life." While still looking at Broonie, he landed three mighty thumps on this latest door.

The crunching response from the other side was so sudden, so deep, that every Fomorian except Gantrua recoiled. Broonie's fright was evident in the rattle of his manacles and inwardly he felt every organ of his body almost leap back of its own accord. His heart beat heavier. His lungs heaved harder. His blood pumped faster. His brain made a greater effort to shut itself down and leap from his ears and run away to safety.

"What," he asked through a dry mouth. "Is. *That?*"

A figure appeared beside him, emerging from the throng. Broonie had not seen him before, had no recollection of his presence during this arduous journey. He was not Fomorian. He did not have their face. Nor their head. He did not have a head at all.

Instead, he had a brass plate across his chest, a gouge across it, and burrowed within it were two eyes. Broonie knew this fellow was a Blemmyes, a member of a tribe few had seen, but who had a reputation for doing the dangerous jobs no one else liked to do.

The rest of his leathery skin featured an impressive array of scars and scratches, some old, some new enough to still glisten with congealed blood.

The Blemmyes pulled a slat across the chest plate, roughly where his ribs might normally have ended.

It revealed a mouth. "He'll have to do, suppose," he said. "Bit chewy. Smells of…" he sniffed at Broonie, "…stupid."

"And who are you, judging me with a nose where your belly button should be?" asked the insulted Hogboon.

"Wrangler."

"Funny name," said Broonie.

"No. Wrangler. My job." He slapped his chest plate. "Wrangler."

Blemmyes

"Wrangler of *what?*" said Broonie, only now fully appreciating that this odd fellow was also missing a chunk from his right forearm.

The Blemmyes pointed to the door. "That."

Thunk.

The sound vibrated through the floor and walls, sending tiny rocks dropping from the ceiling far above. It was followed by what appeared to be a growl. Or a snort.

Or a grort. Several of them. Broonie began to wonder if there wasn't more than one creature in there.

Those manning the catapult began to get busy about it, pulling boulders from the rear and lifting the largest awkwardly into its cup.

Gantrua waved the rest of the Fomorians away, and they retreated, pulling the wood and stone doors closed behind them so those left in the high, narrow corridor in the rock were only Broonie, Gantrua, the Wrangler and an emergency catapult primed for launch.

"She quite nice when you get to know her," said the Wrangler.

"Who?" asked Broonie.

Ahead of them the doors were already opening, revealing a huge cavern carved into the mountain, lit by the meek daylight trickling in through a small hole in the roof far above. In the darkness beyond there was the sound of deep, growling breaths. Several of them.

From a terrifying height, a head snapped into the light, a fang-lined snout on a long crimson head. Broonie jumped back.

"Careful," said the Wrangler. "It bites."

Another two heads appeared from the darkness,

snapped at the Hogboon.

"They all do," said the Wrangler. He slammed shut the slot over his mouth.

Into the light lurched a creature so big Broonie couldn't take it all in. A Legend he'd heard of but never seen. One he'd never wanted to ever come near. He stared at it, his jaw hanging open in shock.

With all fourteen eyes of its seven heads, the Hydra stared right back.

One by one, they dropped into the hole after Gerald. Hugo, then Clara, and finally Emmie and Finn.

A metal ladder brought them down a narrow tube and, before they had reached the bottom, the suit of armour above slid over again leaving them clinging on in complete darkness until, slowly, soft yellow light began to rise.

"Tunnels," said Finn, making out the shape of the corridor curving away from them.

"Very old tunnels," said Hugo. "Two hundred years old in fact. There was an incident before that when lots of Legends invaded Darkmouth, and the entire population tried to hide in one farmer's cowshed, but there wasn't room for everyone, even after they kicked both the cow and the farmer out. So they built these. The idea was that the population of Darkmouth could hide in here until a battle was over and the all-clear was given."

"Why didn't you tell me about them?" Finn asked.

"It could be dangerous down here after so much time. I didn't want you running around, treating it like a playground."

Gerald's frame almost filled the tunnel in front of them. "While we would all love to stand around chatting, this town has very little time until it is invaded by beings from between worlds. We need to move."

He walked off.

Clara shook her head. "You know, Finn, now I've met this man, at least a few things about your dad are beginning to make sense."

"I heard that," said Hugo.

They followed Gerald deep into the tunnels. Above them, they could hear the footsteps, voices, vehicles of Darkmouth. But at this depth it was warm, the sound muted by curved brick walls with stone seats cut into them and the occasional sign on faded wooden boards pointing towards exits or telling people not to smoke.

Finn pushed at a loose door, and inspected the chamber inside. Emmie followed and they examined the cupboard filled with shelves of tinned food and old sheets and coats. Finn picked up a can that bore the words *Industrial Tomato Sauce* in big black letters on a plain white label.

"My stomach churns just thinking about how this tastes after whatever amount of time all this has been down here," said Finn.

"Three weeks actually," said Hugo, putting his head round the door. "The local supermarket was getting rid of these tins and the owner thought, rather than waste them, they could come in handy if, you know, the world was ending or whatever."

Emmie held up a can of *Auntie Maisy's Just-Like-Celery Soup*. "I think I'd rather take my chances with the Legends up there."

Back in the corridor, they passed beneath more hatches. "Each one leads into a part of Darkmouth," explained Hugo. "A phone box covers one. A bin another. You know the big plastic ice-cream cone outside the ice-cream kiosk? It's right above us. Pull the chocolate flake on it and it'll slide directly across."

Next to most of these hatches, Finn noticed, were signs with unusually worded warnings.

PLEASE STAY IN – OR YOU'LL LOSE A LIMB.

DON'T END UP A PATIENT! JUST BE PATIENT.

OPEN DOORS MEAN BLOODY FLOORS.

"Delightful," said Clara. "But they do make me wonder: if the tunnels are meant to be a place to hide when Legends invade, then what's the plan if the Legends get in here with you?"

"They won't," said Gerald, affronted. "We'll keep them out. That's our job. Legend Hunters built the tunnels, but they were never meant for *us*. Civilians hide. We fight. That's the natural order of the world. Which is why I have brought you here. To show you something that could come in very useful. And here we are…"

Gerald had led them to a narrow corridor off the main tunnel, at the end of which was a metal door with a sign saying

ELECTRICITY. HIGHLY DANGEROUS. KEEP OUT.

Ignoring the warning, he pushed down hard on the rusted handle, yanked open the door and led them into a dark room lit only by the low blue glow of the liquid contained in a giant steel-rimmed vat at the centre.

Hugo looked as surprised as anyone, his mouth hanging open. "Desiccator fluid? Why didn't you mention this before?" he asked.

"Because I've been dead," Gerald answered with immeasurable gruffness. "And if it was ever necessary to bring me back—"

"It wasn't," said Hugo, but Finn didn't think he sounded as convinced now as he did before.

"—then I needed a fail-safe, something that would help us in what would clearly be a very serious crisis."

"But what use is all this against Mr Glad?" asked Clara, her face lit by the low glimmer of blue. "If he's a ghost or whatever, how can you desiccate something that's not really there?"

"Because in order to do anything here, in the real world," explained Gerald, "the Trapped must *become* real themselves. And if they're real they can be desiccated. We have a Desiccannon. We have Desiccator fluid." He placed his hand on a large tap sticking from the vat, slapped it with satisfaction. "And, once the Trapped appear, we will have them."

"And my dad," said Emmie, hope-fuelled excitement filling her now.

"Yes, well…" said Gerald, half-hearted.

Finn noticed a few things. He noticed how his father looked at the floor at that moment, as if something wasn't quite right. He noticed how mightily pleased Gerald was with himself, the lines of his face stretched flat with puffed-up pride. And he noticed that the vat of fluid went through the ceiling, as if going up into the street above. But it couldn't be. Finn would have noticed a tank of Desiccator fluid in the middle of town.

"Where's the rest of the vat?" he asked.

"Follow me and I'll show you," said Gerald, walking back into the main tunnel, where he stood at a choice of two corridors. "We'll go up this one over there." He led them to a ladder leading to another hatch.

"You sure you want to go up that way?" Hugo said. "She won't be happy."

"Who won't be happy?" asked Clara.

But Gerald didn't hear – he'd already gone up the ladder, followed by Clara, Emmie and Hugo. Finn was last. Eventually clambering back above ground, he found himself facing a shabby shopfront dummy in the window of the local fashion store. The dummy, with a straw-like wig askew on its bald head and a long lime dress hanging loosely from its frame, looked somewhat nonplussed to have been shoved aside.

Finn turned around to find the shop's owner staring at them all.

"I am not happy with this," said the owner.

As he tried to shuffle aside, Finn almost lost his balance, but righted himself by grabbing the dummy's arm. It came off in his hand. Clara roughly pulled the dummy back into position.

"I am not happy at all," added the shop owner.

"Sorry," said Clara.

"Me too," said Finn, making a brief and vain attempt to push the dummy's arm back into its socket, but giving up and instead handing it to the very unimpressed owner as the five of them climbed from the window display and left through the shop door. "Very sorry."

The owner slammed the door so hard behind them the little bell fell off its hinge and tinkled to the ground. In the window display, the mannequin's head toppled off.

On the street, Gerald pointed at the grey obelisk tapering skywards. "You think that was built just to make the town look pretty?" he asked and walked over to it, stepping through the flowers around its base.

"The fluid's inside the obelisk?" said Finn.

"Actually, it's filled with raspberry jelly," said Gerald. "*Yes*, it's full of fluid."

Finn stared at the monument. He'd passed it day after day, treated it as little more than a colourful roundabout. And inside it, all this time, a great vat of Desiccator fluid.

"To desiccate all four of the Trapped, we will need to flood the sky with fluid. The bombs will do that, and still leave us a bit to spare," Hugo said.

Gerald grunted. *Maybe*.

"So that's the plan?" asked Clara. "You're going to bomb the sky. And what if that doesn't work?"

"It will," insisted Gerald.

"We do need a Plan B," admitted Hugo. "Do you remember that time when we were attacked by those wolf-like Grendels and you thought a dog whistle would distract them, but it only drove them mad?"

Grendel

211

"I don't remember you having a better plan."

"I was *six years old*."

"*Pfft*," said Gerald. "You always had an excuse. Why couldn't you be more like these young ones? They've been to the Infested Side and survived."

"So have I," said Hugo. "Twice."

"But not when you were eight years old like Finn."

"I'm thirteen tomorrow!"

"So tell me, Hugo," Gerald said, ploughing on, "do you have a better plan?"

"*I* do," said Clara.

"With all due respect, Clara—" started Gerald.

"Don't," said Clara, holding up her hand. "Because the words 'with all due respect' are inevitably followed by words showing no respect whatsoever. Your problem, or rather one of your growing number of problems, is that you look at me and think I'm just a civilian. Regardless of how much time I've lived with a Legend Hunter. Longer, as it happens, than any of you have. But you're ignoring the one special skill I have, which is that I'm *not* a Legend Hunter. I don't think like a Legend Hunter. I don't act like a Legend Hunter. And I am not always looking for a fight like a Legend Hunter. And I can see the plan you're not seeing."

Finn felt the warmth of pride flood him. His mother had faced bigger monsters than this. He stepped beside her, almost without realising it, because it made him feel stronger under Gerald's glare.

"What's your plan?" Hugo asked.

"Mr Glad is coming in…" She looked at Finn.

He checked his watch. "…less than ninety minutes."

"And he has the power to trap anyone he touches. But *you* have these tunnels, built to evacuate the townspeople," she said. "So use them."

28

Broonie had reached a point in his life where he would use the wildest edges of his imagination to think of the absolute worst, most insane, most unlikely things that could possibly happen to him. And then, when he'd thought of them, he tried to imagine something worse.

Even in his most fevered, most beaten-up, most desperate moments, he had never imagined himself in a large cavern on the far side of the Chasm of Bewilderness. Strapped to the bucking back of a Hydra.

He had been forced to climb up on to this great beast and strap himself into the harness on its back, his feet locked into the stirrups, his hands manacled to reins that were so small they clearly did nothing to control the Hydra, but simply offered Broonie something to hold on to so he didn't fall to his death.

"Hydras have some very particular traits," Gantrua

had explained as the Wrangler used a very large pronged stick to keep the beast in relative stability in the corner while Broonie climbed up to it. "When they are born, they attach themselves to the very first creature they see, and they will always protect its kind from there on in. It just so happens that the very first creature this Hydra saw was a Hogboon. A snivelling, knock-kneed Hogboon just like you."

"So," Broonie had asked, looking for a foothold in the Hydra's welted skin, "why not use him instead?"

"Because the mother Hydra was there too, and she ate the Hogboon immediately."

The Wrangler had laughed at this, a wheezing guffaw through his teeth that made it sound like he might be about to keel over and die. He then shuffled off into a deep crevice, mumbling about needing to fetch something.

A couple of Hydra heads clashed around Broonie. They seemed to bicker almost constantly. Most of them anyway. Two were particularly aggressive, repeatedly shunting aside or snapping at others. One had a scar right down its eye and seemed particularly irritated by the very presence of the heads around it, hissing and growling at any other head that came near it.

Another had a white stripe down its crown, like a

smear of paint starting at the base of its neck and ending at the centre of its forehead. This head liked to stare at Broonie with worrying intent, breaking off only to headbutt whichever one drifted closest to it, the sound of colliding skulls enough to send a ripple of fear to the very centre of his core.

The heads fought over not just space, but control of the body they shared. At one point, Broonie realised that a particularly violent episode of juddering and bucking had been caused by a struggle between two heads for which one of them could scratch an itch first. They clashed fiercely, so much so that the other heads veered out of the way, pushing themselves at awkward angles to avoid the scrap as the two necks swung at each other, the heads crashed together, the fangs tried to stab from within their muzzles.

And yet two of the heads – one with a long fang sticking out of the side of its mouth; the other with a tuft of blue hair on its crown – were dozy, unbothered, maybe even beaten. They hung, listless, from the body of the creature. Broonie wondered what had happened to them.

As Broonie found his place, Gantrua continued to talk. Broonie tried to listen. He tried to hear past the *thumpety-thump* of his own heart, the scraping of the Hydra's feet, the cracking of neck on neck as they jostled for position all around him.

"Another thing about a Hydra," said the Fomorian, "is that once a battle is done, it feeds on its pilot and then they get another Hogboon. It's a sort of reward. You understand that the pilot is you, don't you? And *you* are about to take this fearsome creature into battle. You deserve a front seat for the invasion." Gantrua walked away with the headless Blemmyes Wrangler in tow, into the murk beyond as the door began to close around them. "You have, my Hogboon corpse," he called over his shoulder, "so much to look forward to yet."

Now Broonie was alone in the cavern, with just a raging Hydra for company. The head with the white stripe kept staring at him.

"You think you have it bad?" Broonie asked it. "Of all the indignities I've suffered in recent months, this is getting close to being one of the worst. And that's saying something. I've been frozen and thawed, clobbered, starved, insulted, mocked, chained, kicked, kicked again, prodded, poked, beaten, kicked some more, and now I am here, staring you and death in the face. And you know what the worst thing about it is?"

The stripy Hydra's head kept staring at him. It licked its lips.

"The worst thing is wondering just what's next." He yanked at his bonds. "I'm wondering what's to come, wondering what's out there still waiting to get Broonie, and wondering what *is* that scratching noise in the shadows down there?"

It was getting louder and louder. A scratching deep within the darkness. It was starting to cause the Hydra to snort and snap.

Broonie tried to see what was making the sound, craned over the beast's back as it rose and fell, giving him intermittent glimpses of the floor below. The scratching came again, followed by some sort of hissing noise, as if air was being released from something. Or the sound that might be made by a...

"...Snake!" exclaimed Broonie, seeing a green, arrow-shaped head emerge from the dark, a flick of its tongue, its eyes catching a glint of the weak light high above them. Broonie began to pull at his restraints, panic creeping into him. He hated snakes. Despised them. Because snakes in this world were not mere snakes, they were always something else. The snakes on a head. The snakes in a giant's mouth. If there was one thing he had learned in his years in this benighted world, it was that there was a never-ending array of ways in which a snake could be attached to another creature.

And he hated every last one of them.

"Stamp on it!" he told the Hydra. It ignored him, its heads busy instead fighting or dozing or scratching themselves against the rock wall. Except for the stripy head. It just kept staring at him.

"Stop panicking," said a calm voice in the darkness. Thin. Nasal. And edged with fatigue as if life had dragged it through the dirt on too many occasions. "You will give everything away."

Cornelius emerged from the darkest shadows. A large ageing dog, apparently so low on energy it could just about muster the effort to push through the shadows. It walked fully into the light, and now Broonie could see the bright green of the snake attached to it as a tail. "The last time we met, we helped you escape to the Promised World. We saved you," said the snake-tail, Hiss.

"You did a glorious job too, as you can see," said Broonie, from up on the Hydra. But he relaxed slightly. Rescue was at hand. A couple of heads swung past him, smashing like felled tree trunks. "How did you get in then?" Broonie asked when the Hydra settled.

Hiss looked up, its body curving upwards towards the shaft of light high above them.

"Ah," realised Broonie, "the Quetzalcóatl. Those rebellious serpents. Causing trouble again. So, you're going to get me out that way. We're flying up, right?"

"I am afraid not," said Hiss.

Broonie sighed. "Of course not. Why should it ever be so straightforward?"

"You will be staying on the Hydra."

"Wonderful," said Broonie.

"We have conversed with the creature, used the power of suggestion, spoken as one multi-headed soul to another, and we have given it a few instructions," said Hiss. "We were not entirely successful, in truth."

"Fantastic," said Broonie.

"We think it will be enough to delay it, however, from killing us and everybody else for at least a while longer."

"Of course," said Broonie, resigned to whatever new twist of fate would befall him.

The Hydra had calmed momentarily, its heads at peace briefly.

"We have managed to subdue two of the heads," said Hiss, flicking his tongue towards the noticeably dozy parts of the Hydra. "When the time comes, you will need to say

Orthrus

one word. This single word will act as a trigger, waking the hypnotised heads, putting them at war with the rest. But you can use this word once and once only. Its power will be exhausted once you, and you alone, utter it. Say this word only at the right moment."

The doors to the cavern were opening again, a shuddering grinding of steel on stone, cracks of light breaking the seal into the cavern.

"What's the word?" called Broonie.

Cornelius coiled and jumped, leaping on to the body

of the Hydra, dodging swiftly through its snapping heads, climbing up its back until Hiss was so close Broonie felt the disgusting tickle of the snake's flickering tongue.

The snake said a word. Then repeated it. And, before Broonie could ask what that even meant, the Orthrus was leaping again, clasping on to the wall, and then into mid-air where it hung for a moment in what looked to Broonie like a death plunge before, from a crevice high up, a pair of wings unfolded, widened, swooped, and a serpent that had been waiting hidden in the dark caught the Orthrus just at the point at which a Hydra's head was going to make a meal of it.

And then it was gone, up to the ceiling and the circle of grey light from the world above, disappearing into the shadow, away from the oncoming Fomorian soldiers, led by the Wrangler.

As the Hydra was led out, with Broonie trapped on top of it, the word spoken by the Orthrus echoed inside his mind, distracted him from the pain of the chains stretching his limbs, tearing his skin. The final instructions of the Orthrus were clear.

"Say this word only at the right moment."

He would. He would hold it in his head and use it as a weapon only when the time arrived.

Now seemed as good a time as any.

At which point, the Wrangler reappeared and began bounding up the side of the Hydra with an agility belying his bulk. "Gantrua tolerate whingeing," he said, "but me, no. Hydra, no."

With that, he put a muzzle round Broonie's mouth and, no matter how much the Hogboon screamed the word, it could not be heard.

"*Sssssggsssss!*" he moaned. "*Sssssggsssss!*"

And, on the ledge outside, Gantrua held the hourglass aloft, triumphant. The last drops of blood were falling. The battle was about to begin.

29

Finn's watch told him there were only ten minutes left until time ran out and Mr Glad returned.

Slowly, like the fading of a rainbow, each of the scars left by Mr Glad had faded from Darkmouth's air. What had not disappeared was the feverish excitement of the Half-Hunters staying in town. They were invigorated, almost delighted at this turn of events. If Estravon was right, Mr Glad would be able to return imminently. They had arrived as tourists, but would leave as warriors.

And for those who had never seen action, only hearing of it from their parents or grandparents, all this death and uncertainty was making for a quite wonderful holiday.

They scurried to wherever they had found a bed, or parked their camper van, or pitched their tent, and grabbed the very things they weren't supposed to have brought in the first place.

Weapons.

They took them from their bags, their jackets, their ceremonial pouches. Pulled them from their boots, from their socks. One Half-Hunter, in full view of the hotel's owner, Mrs Cross, produced a long baton from somewhere under his armpit, and, when she glared at him with a mixture of contempt and bemusement, simply shrugged, broke into a grin and ran back out of the door to join the flow towards the rendezvous at Finn's house.

There waited the members of the Twelve and their assistants, plus Hugo, Gerald, Finn and Emmie. Estravon was with them, clipboard in hand, still looking somewhat wounded that he'd been kept out on the basis that Gerald didn't like his choice of trousers.

The Half-Hunters crowded up the street.

Finn stood alongside Estravon, their backs to the wall outside, which was tall and imposing and beyond which lay nothing but wasteland and rubble piled up from years of digging their house through the street.

"How are you feeling?" Hugo asked Gerald above the noise.

"Feeling?" replied Gerald, utterly disgusted at the very word. "I don't have time for feelings."

Hugo turned to Finn. "I'm sorry if I was ever like this with you," he said. "Please tell me I haven't been."

Finn's brain wasn't able to come up with a lie quick enough for his mouth, and he ended up just kind of burbling a bit in response. Emmie turned to him. "Do you want me to say it?" she asked.

"No need," Hugo sighed.

But Finn knew why his father had asked Gerald how he was feeling, because he could see his great-grandfather wince every now and again in some kind of pain, had noticed him grip his side once or twice to quieten some spasm or other. He seemed to be struggling with an injury, although Finn couldn't be sure where he'd picked it up.

Before Finn could dwell on that any more, Hugo stepped forward to silence the giddy throng. "The time draws close. The readings show the sky thickening with energy somehow, from somewhere. It seems to be forming most in the Black Hills there." He pointed to the lumpen rim of hills surrounding the inland edge of the town. "The clock ticks down, and we will be ready."

He held up Estravon's screen showing the countdown.

Five minutes left.

The crowd was practically riotous with the excitement.

"You came here for a celebration, for a Completion, for a birthday party. Not to fight a battle."

227

A battle was all they wanted. Hugo had to calm them down.

"We will have the Completion Ceremony," he said. "We will have the party. But first, a battle must be fought."

The Half-Hunters were practically dancing with anticipation.

"My father might be one of the ones they're attacking," Emmie said to Finn. "They can't celebrate anything if he's dead."

Finn didn't like seeing this slavering for a fight either. He had been in battles, and knew that they shocked the bravado out of you very quickly. He knew they thought this would be easy. And Finn knew they were wrong.

"We have a Desiccannon which will freeze Mr Glad or any other Trapped when they appear," said Hugo. At the rear of the crowd, the weapon was mounted on the battered remnants of Hugo's car. "And each of you has been handed a packet of crystal dust for your own personal protection."

Every Half-Hunter present rummaged through their pockets and produced the packets as proof.

Gerald stepped forward. "*Do not* lose these," he barked. "If you do, then you will be lost and we will not come and find you."

"We need to see what other weapons we have," said Estravon, clipboard in hand. "In case the cannon doesn't work for any reason. Step forward, please."

A woman approached. On her head she had a helmet that was too big for her, but looked ferocious. Spikes of various sizes stabbed out from it. It gave her the appearance of a mutant hedgehog.

"What's your name?" asked Aurora the Third.

"I am Kate of the once-Blighted Village of Sinister, Surrey!" she bawled loud enough for Cedric the Ninth to rock back a little even if this Half-Hunter hardly reached his shoulders.

"And what do you do now?" Aurora asked.

"I fix washing machines."

"*Snort*," snorted Gerald.

"What weapon do you have?" asked Cedric the Ninth.

She stayed rigid, silent.

"It's the hat, isn't it?" Hugo suggested.

Kate nodded and a spike shot out of the helmet, fizzing with a loud *wheeee* between their heads, causing everyone to duck, and embedding itself in the wall behind them.

Estravon made a note.

"Take that thing off your head before it downs an aeroplane," growled Gerald. She did, but not carefully enough to prevent another spike whirring off uncontrollably and causing mayhem among the assembled ranks behind her.

She was sent back into line.

The next Half-Hunter approached, his fighting suit a rusty orange. On further inspection, it might simply have been rusty.

"How times have changed," complained Gerald to Hugo. "This lot are more a danger to themselves than any Legends. You have to put up with this?"

Hugo gave a very small nod.

"You have patience, I will give you that."

The Half-Hunter presenting his weapon was busy trying to find the switch on the very small egg-shaped device he was carrying and, when he did, it burst in his hand with a loud bang. He dropped it, shaking the pain from his hand, and whined as its goo ate into the concrete, desiccating a patch. "That was a family heirloom. I knew I shouldn't have brought it."

That broke Gerald's tolerance. "Right, this is ridiculous!" he cried out. "I fought at the Battle of the Little Big Horns, where we brought down Legends using only the horns of particularly small bulls—"

Hugo stepped up, cutting Gerald off, drew in a deep

breath, his chest filling his fighting suit. Finn could see the bruise on his neck from where he had been hurt during the earlier attack by Mr Glad. He was ready to deliver words that would carry them into battle, that would fill them with pride and determination and knock away their fear.

Over the Black Hills edging Darkmouth was a silent roll of lightning behind the late afternoon cloud.

On every wrist, in every pocket, of every Half-Hunter, alarms began to go off. Beeps. Chimes. Jingles. Music.

Finn's watch did the same. He pressed a button to silence the alarm. But he couldn't quieten the suffocating tension taking hold of him.

"It is time," said Hugo.

LIECHTENSTEIN:
TWO WEEKS EARLIER

TWO WORLDS — ONE VICTOR

*I*n the corridor of the seventh storey of the Liechtenstein HQ stood a little girl with pigtails in her hair and a very large vaporising weapon in her hands.

"How did you get hold of that?" an assistant asked her, while a crowd looked on tensely.

"That room," she said and waved it around, causing everyone to gasp and duck for fear of having their head vaporised.

"You need to put that back in the museum, OK?"

She nodded sweetly. "OK," she agreed and put the weapon down on the floor, much to everyone's relief. "But can I keep this?" She pulled a grenade from her pocket, causing the corridor to scatter.

It was Bring Your Kids To Work Day, and those assistants who had children had brought them to the office as they did every year. And the children were running wild, as they did every year.

Lucien's were there too. Elektra and Tiberius were seven

233

and five years old and had been given bold warrior names in anticipation of how one day they would grow up to become bold warriors. Right now, they were seeing who could spin fastest on their dad's office swivel chairs.

Elektra won. "I feel sick," she said, dizzy.

"I want to win!" screamed Tiberius.

"Seriously, Daddy, I'm going to be sick."

Lucien brought the wastepaper bin to Elektra and sat it on her lap.

"Howdy," said Axel, arriving in the office. "Who wants some sherbet dip?"

Elektra, magically better now, grabbed a packet first, tore it open and shoved in her fingers to root out the unnaturally pink sugar within.

"Put that skull down!" Lucien heard someone in the corridor outside shout. A kid went running by the door with a Legend skull on his head.

"What do you want to be when you grow up?" Axel asked Tiberius.

"Famous," he answered.

Lucien shook his head.

"Famous for what?" Axel asked him.

"Just famous," said Tiberius as if Axel's was the stupidest question ever asked.

"When I grow up, I'm going to work in an office like this," Elektra said, sugar caking the rims of her nostrils. "It looks dead easy."

Lucien tightened his jaw. He then saw that Axel had come in to deliver something other than sherbet.

"Why don't you two go and play with the vending machines in the corridor," he urged the children. "If you put your hand up the slot, it sometimes gives you free sweets."

"I feel like I'm going to puke again," said Elektra.

"Excellent," said Lucien, ushering her out after her brother.

"Such great kids," said Axel.

"Do you want them?" Lucien asked him. "They were supposed to be the latest in a long line of Legend Hunters, stretching back generations on my side and their mother's. Then again, we were supposed to be the same. Instead, I'm here stapling reports and my wife makes cheese."

"She makes the one that tastes like feet wrapped in a plastic bag."

"It's won awards for its tastiness."

"I'm not surprised."

"It's going to happen again," said Lucien.

"What is?"

"Darkmouth," said Lucien. "I can sense it. With Hugo

and the boy Finn at the heart of it, I'm sure. They're always at the heart of it, have you noticed? It's always Darkmouth. Never anywhere else. Never our kids. Always them."

He watched Elektra and Tiberius take turns to put an arm up the vending machine. "Why are they so blessed over there? Why does the trouble come to them? Surely you've asked yourself that question too."

"We all have," admitted Axel. "The Twelve are going there, though. For the boy's Completion Ceremony."

"While we've been ordered to stay behind. As we've always done. Just sitting here, waiting for trouble to arrive. We've waited so many years. It hasn't come, but still we wait. And wait."

"What else can we do?" asked Axel.

"Well, I've been examining the trail of events at Darkmouth, and I have an idea. A plan. But you must keep it to yourself for now. Promise?"

"Promise," said Axel. "Although you should do one thing first."

"What?"

Axel pointed at the girl in the corridor. "Free Elektra's hand from that vending machine."

On the other side of the curtain separating the world of the humans from the Legends, the Half-Hunters waited on the slopes of Darkmouth's Black Hills, where the energy readings were highest, where whatever was going to happen… was going to happen.

A clamour for a fight rippled through the ranks, their previously unused armour shuddering and creaking. A handful of the assembled Half-Hunters had Desiccators. Others had a variety of odd weapons. They crouched behind advertising hoardings grabbed from the local football pitch to use as emergency protection. Everything shuddered, because everyone was nervous.

Lightning rippled through the sky. Again, no thunder followed. Finn wished it would. Without the sound, it felt like the tension would never break.

"The energy levels are off the scale," said Hugo, his

eyes on the small screen in his hand.

Gerald coughed, and it sounded like a chainsaw failing to start.

Finn was going to ask him if he was OK, but thought better of it. He, Hugo, Gerald and Emmie were waiting behind a hoarding for the local sports shop, *Batty for Balls*.

Gerald was taking in the sight of the Half-Hunters around them. Some were in fighting suits, some in colourful formal jackets they'd brought for the Completion Ceremony, while others wore boiler suits, having been fetched from where they'd been working on the stage.

"The one on the left is wearing tracksuit trousers." Finn looked again and realised it was true. "What a world I've woken up in. Why didn't he just wear his pyjamas if he wanted to be comfortable? At least you've dressed properly, Hugo. And the boy here. The red-streaked helmet. The Minotaur illustration. The epaulettes." He eyed Finn up and down. "Nice touch that."

Finn looked around him. Behind the crouched Half-Hunters were the Council of Twelve, their robes incongruous splashes of colour against the green of the grass and the brown of the mud. Aurora and Cedric stood again to the fore, refusing the offer of a seat. Stumm was seated, but even he was awake, his eyes hardly blinking in fact.

They'd all arrived, with the assistants ranged behind them, in cars and vans that had churned up the ground, and which formed a convoy ready to leave hastily should things get too risky.

Finn could see that the assistants looked far more nervous than their superiors. He reminded himself that the Twelve, now so old to him, had once been spry Legend Hunters in a world where Blighted Villages still posed a grave threat. They had fought. They had won. They had the medallions to prove it.

Between them all were two Half-Hunters manning the Desiccannon where it had been rolled on to the grass. Estravon stood with them, ready to take the order from Hugo, and to give it to the two Half-Hunters hovering over the muzzle, a bomb in their hands, ready to drop it in. One was visibly shaking, even from this distance.

A minor flare of light in the sky regained Finn's attention.

Gerald flinched, but it was not what was up there that was causing the problem. Finn could tell it was something inside him.

"Is Gerald OK?" he asked his dad in a low tone.

"Of course I'm OK," Gerald said, his hearing obviously better than Finn had realised. "I'm here, aren't I?"

"We should tell Finn," said Hugo, clearly not happy that this discussion was happening now.

"Tell me what?" asked Finn.

The light flickered in the clouds again, purple skittering across the sky. Still no thunder. Still no relief. The needle on the graph pushing so hard now it was in danger of breaking through.

"You can only bring the Preserved back once," Hugo told Finn.

"The Preserved. It makes us sound like some sort of jam," snorted Gerald. He looked at Finn. "I *hate* jam."

"Why?" asked Finn. "I mean, not why do you hate jam. Why can you only come back once? We've reanimated Legends loads of times."

"Because I can't be bothered saving you every time there's a minor crisis," sniffed Gerald.

"That's his attempt at a joke," said Hugo. "In reality, human and Legend biology differs," he explained, eyes still on the sky, Desiccator resting against the chipped metal of the hoarding. "You can bring a Legend back many times. But the moment you reanimate a human, their cells begin decaying. Gerald is dying."

"I have a few hours left at most," said Gerald.

"You did this *knowing* it meant certain death?" Finn asked him.

"A life without battle is death already," said Gerald.

Emmie sat forward from where she had been waiting, watching intently for her father. "Hold on," she said, a fact dawning on her. "You mean, if you desiccate my dad with that cannon, he'll only survive a few hours once he's reanimated?"

"Up there!" a voice shouted. A Half-Hunter in a feathered fighting suit was pointing skywards, where cloud was flooding slowly across the sky, pinching off the bloody sunset.

Finn touched his chest, where his locket of dust was kept. He saw several Half-Hunters do something similar, patting pockets, grabbing wrists, reassuring themselves that the protective dust was where they'd put it.

He looked behind him again, where the Council was arranged, on their trucks, assistants at the wheels, not ready to give instructions, but certainly poised to flee.

"They're going to kill him," said Emmie. She stood, desperation showing clear on a face lit by the dying glow of the day. "You're going to kill him, not save him!"

Hugo pulled her by the arm to get her down again.

Finn looked at her, saw her horror, felt it too. Felt that he had let her down, betrayed her without even realising it.

There was a flash in the sky above. A crackle of light, then a flickering smudge in the cloud. Yellow, pink. No sound. Just silent light, coalescing in the sky, fixing into one bright star. It separated, three lights pulling away from the central one.

Then they drifted slowly towards the ground.

31

On the Infested Side, an army of Fomorians waited on a road of black glass, cut across a darkscape of dead plants, broken bones, crushed life. Their weapons were arrows and blades hacked from the glassy trees of the Petrified Forest. As one, they pounded their shields, a menacing rhythm that shuddered through the shards at their feet, that drummed out their anticipation of the fight ahead.

And in time with it were the words of a Troll as it mixed dust, the last crystals of a world that was once replete with them. Then the Troll smeared sparkling paste on the air, throwing its hands back as it mumbled its constant incantation.

"Hear those words?" Gantrua shouted up to Broonie.

Broonie could not answer, because of the muzzle. Being strapped to the back of a bucking Hydra didn't help either.

"Those words are still useless," said Gantrua, the long sweep of the serpent fang swaying at his jaw. "But I know what they mean. We tear open a path between the worlds."

The cloud above them was almost within reach. It felt to Broonie like he was in a wide coffin, built for an entire army. The Legends were packed in here, swaying in anticipation of the invasion ahead.

Within the cloud, around it, the flashes of lightning. Building. Becoming more frequent. But no thunder. And the light was unnatural – even in a place where light meant only that it wasn't entirely dark. It was as if a torch had been lit behind a curtain. It leaped and flickered.

Still, the Troll called out. Wailed. Rubbed the dust and crystal, attempting to smear it on the invisible dark.

"This world was beautiful once," Gantrua said to the stricken Broonie. "It had vivid colour. It had fresh life. Its rivers did not peel the flesh from those who swam in them. You probably think I just want to take the human world because of greed, because of some basic evil that burns within me?"

Broonie couldn't answer.

"You have spent too long with those puny bags of flesh and bone," Gantrua told him. "They have poisoned your mind like they poisoned this world. I want that world because it is ours. I am not stealing it. I am taking it back."

The lightning flickered, crawled across the sky above them.

"Ssssgggggsssss," was all Broonie could manage by way of a reply.

The sky groaned, as if awaking from the deepest slumber.

"Before this night is out," said Gantrua, "I will walk their streets."

On the Black Hills on the Darkmouth side of the world, the Half-Hunters watched the three lights drift towards the ground and instinctively took a step back, a ripple of armour carrying all the way to the anxious souls manning the cannon, and the elders of the Council of Twelve, each of whom leaned forward in anticipation.

"Wait for my order," Hugo called to Estravon at the Desiccannon.

"Don't get this wrong, Hugo," said Gerald. "Not now."

"When?" Estravon responded.

"Not yet," said Hugo, a closed fist in the air.

Finn counted the lights. *One, two, three...*

"Dad," he said, standing up for a better view.

Gerald coughed again, hacking loudly. "Get your head down, boy," he said, his voice caught on phlegm. "Unless you want to go home without it."

"Don't fire yet," commanded Hugo, his voice just about audible over the rattle and clatter of the surrounding Half-Hunters.

"Dad," said Finn, trying to get his attention, "there's something wrong."

"Don't screw up this timing," Gerald was telling Hugo. "Let me take over if you're going to do that."

"I've got it," said Hugo, hand still raised, eyes narrowed. He was counting the lights drifting into place.

"There are only three lights," said Finn.

As if being tipped from a jar, liquid light poured from each hovering glow, building a body from the ground up. Streaming beings of flesh and nothingness, bodies forming from pure agony. A collective howl came from them. And one by one they took shape. A sort of shape anyway. Writhing masses, their flesh fighting for coherence.

Douglas first.

Then Kenzo.

And, finally, they saw Steve. A version of him. Torn apart. Being torn apart, reassembled, over and over.

"Dad!" called Emmie, and Hugo had to grab her by the arms and hold her back as she attempted to climb the barrier and run towards her father.

Finn stood with her. He knew this thing was only part

Steve, only part human. He was a body between worlds. A mind torn asunder and put back in a rough order, a slave to Mr Glad. Like the other two, Steve was distorted, smeared across a patch of air. But there was something else. He was trying to cling to the sky. Douglas and Kenzo were doing the same.

"Where's Mr Glad?" asked Finn. But then he realised that the three Trapped weren't trying to grab *hold* of the sky, they were pulling at it as they dropped. Tearing it, leaving trails of light. Above them a star remained, unmoving.

"What are they doing?" Finn asked.

Hugo didn't answer, but the electricity in the air matched the crackle of noisy tension emanating from the massed ranks of Half-Hunters on the hill. Finn glanced back at the Desiccannon, where its two operators were ready, waiting for Estravon to give them the order to fire.

But Estravon was waiting for Hugo to give the order first. And he wasn't.

"You're losing control," Gerald insisted as the din from the Half-Hunters grew louder. "Give the order now."

"Not yet!" he shouted.

"Don't do it, please," pleaded Emmie.

The three trails of light where the Trapped had torn at the air were lengthening, widening.

"Wait," said Finn, understanding finally. "They're *gateways*. They're opening gateways."

Then a fourth light dropped, glowing brighter, flattening out and spreading like a spill across the air.

Clearer than the others. More human. Dropping to the ground, long coat and hair unmoving in the breeze. For all that he looked human, the grin growing on his face like a scar was utterly monstrous.

It formed Mr Glad.

He floated downwards, but he did not land fully.

His voice carried like a rumble of thunder across the hill. "*Tick. Tock.* Time's up."

Mr Glad raised a hand and pulled downwards as if yanking a curtain free.

"They're opening the sky!" shouted Finn.

"Fire, Hugo!" demanded Gerald.

"No!" shouted Emmie. "You'll kill my dad!"

"Fire!" ordered Hugo.

"Fire!" yelled Estravon.

The Desiccannon fired.

33

For a moment, the grey sky was splashed with a wondrous blue, as if the world was being dashed with paint.

The liquid bomb arced from the cannon at the rear, over the heads of the Half-Hunters, whose eyes followed its trajectory towards the Trapped. Finn stood, ignoring his father's orders to get down again, and could feel the suck as it tore through the air.

The bomb exploded in the sky over where the Trapped had stood, spraying a bright blue drizzle that slowly fell in a curtain. But it became very apparent, very quickly, that something had happened. Or, rather, not happened.

"The Trapped are gone," said Finn.

"Where are they?" asked Emmie, standing upright.

"You missed!" Gerald called back to the Half-Hunters manning the cannons.

"We didn't miss," said Hugo.

"Where's *Dad?*" screamed Emmie.

Gerald stood tall, furious. "How could you miss?"

"*We didn't miss,*" repeated Hugo, finally earning Gerald's attention. "The Trapped were already gone. They disappeared before the liquid even reached them."

"Oh, thank goodness," said Emmie.

"I don't think it's anything to be thankful for," said Gerald ominously.

The curtain of liquid was drifting on the hill at the foot of the gateways. Where it landed, it ate into the grass, soil, whatever poor crawling creatures had the misfortune to be near the surface. The sound of the land being scrunched up like tinfoil should have been utterly alarming, and would have been if anyone had been paying attention to it, but there was something much, much more worrying to distract them.

"They've left something behind," said Finn, stating the obvious.

Through the gloom, four streaks of light remained, high off the ground. Dashes down the sky. Each was golden, fizzing.

Emmie stood beside him, staring at the holes in the sky, hoping to see her father.

Hugo was rubbing his chin with his knuckles. "Why

make four small gateways. In the same place?"

Finn watched the gap between two of the golden marks, could see it was narrowing.

"Because they're not making four small gateways," said Gerald.

The Half-Hunters sensed it too, began to rustle with nerves, to tap at shields, to fidget with weapons.

Hugo nodded slowly. "It's one very big gateway," he said.

The gateways began to join, to seep into each other. End to end. A gouge the height of two houses carved in the night sky, its glow brightening, the golden edges becoming a foreboding light show.

The Half-Hunters flinched, a synchronised scrunch coming from their fighting suits as they moved back. At their rear, the growl of truck engines drilled through the night sky, assistants ready to evacuate the Twelve.

"This was never about any army of the Trapped," Gerald said. "This was about something else, something bigger."

"He's still working with the Legends," said Hugo, a new understanding dawning on him.

"Dad's gone, isn't he?" Emmie was saying, disbelieving.

"So sorry, Emmie," Finn said.

The gateway was spreading, widening, its centre brightening in intensity, a hole being bored between worlds.

Finn, who had seen more than enough gateways in his life, in the past year alone, knew exactly what this meant. "Mr Glad must have known we could protect ourselves with the dust," he said. "He was never going to fight us directly. He was trapping the others so together they could open a huge gateway. To the Infested Side."

Hugo paled. "It's an invasion," he said.

From the other side, still invisible to them, they could hear the thumping rhythm of sticks on shields.

The Half-Hunters took another step back, the mulch of their boots on wet grass competing with the jolting engines of the trucks hosting the Council of Twelve.

"Do not back down," Hugo said.

"Do not retreat," Gerald ordered.

A single screaming Fomorian burst from the vast gateway, his chunky legs propelling him down the hill towards them as he waved his stick. Hugo fired and his shot was true, striking the Fomorian square on the chest and desiccating him instantly.

He was followed by a couple more screaming Fomorians. And then three more.

"This would never have happened in my day!" said Gerald.

"Fire!" shouted Hugo.

Those few with Desiccators let loose. Some missed wildly. Others hit targets so that lumbering Fomorians disappeared with a stifled *whoooop* drowned out by the maelstrom of the battle.

"You and Emmie get back," Hugo ordered Finn.

"I don't want—" Finn started to protest.

"You two have to be safe now," said Hugo, desiccating another Fomorian as it appeared through the gateway. "Go."

Finn hesitated. Emmie was still simmering with anger.

Gerald fired his Desiccator. "Listen to your father, boy. You're the future of this family. A brighter one than I had reckoned, to be honest. So, if you don't go now, I'll use the spike on these boots to send you on your way."

He and Hugo stood and fired again, in unison.

Finn realised he had no choice: he pulled Emmie's arm to encourage her to leave with him. She didn't budge, but he pulled again and finally she moved. Together they crouched and ran towards the rear, the noise and light of battle briefly behind them. Ahead of them now, Finn could see the Half-Hunters hurrying to fill the

Desiccannon with the second bomb, while Estravon shouted at them to, "Load it, load it, don't drop it!"

They dropped it.

Every one of the Council of Twelve and their assistants held their breath as the bomb rolled away and finally settled, unexploded, on a clump of weeds.

Finn and Emmie reached the rear as the Half-Hunters scuttled over to pick up the bomb and once again attempt to load it. At the top of the hill, Fomorians were pushing through the open gateway, but continued to get picked off by Desiccators.

Finn and Emmie held their Desiccators out over the back of a hoarding (*Eye Spy Opticians*) to be prepared. To their right they could see that the Half-Hunters at the Desiccannon were growing increasingly panicky, their inexperience beginning to overcome them.

Aurora was watching them too, fidgeting with impatience, seemingly finding it impossible to stand by as disaster approached. "Right!" she shouted from where she stood among the Twelve. "Leave this to the experts."

She rolled up the sleeves of her robe and marched forward. Without hesitation, Cedric followed. So did the others. One by one, the Council of Twelve advanced, each of these people Finn had until recently only known through the stories of their past glories, the adventures they had once lived. He watched as they dragged robes across the mucky ground, found their once-tired legs reinvigorated.

Only Stumm struggled to rise from the chair he sat on. Cedric turned to put a hand on his shoulder, a wordless recognition that he didn't need to move.

Their assistants tried to help the Council of Twelve as they went, lifting the hems of their robes, leaning in to whisper to them, asking them not to do anything rash. Cedric turned and calmly said to his assistant, "Let us be young again. Just this once."

The assistants stood back, and these ancient members of the Twelve began to lift the slippery bomb from the ground and together placed it smoothly in the Desiccannon chamber. Every one of them left their great age behind, and found the strength and focus they'd had in the glory days when every day brought a battle.

At the gateway, the Fomorians still came.

"We're winning!" a Half-Hunter shouted. Finn recognised him as Nils, the always chirpy, weak-bladdered, gadget-loving Norwegian he'd met at the house and on the street. He was chirpy even now. "We're pushing them back!"

It was true. Gradually, the Desiccators were beginning to eat away at the Legends' numbers, to block the entrance, to have an effect. Some of the Half-Hunters began to cheer.

Finn watched. He'd seen enough before to know that things were not always as they seemed. He focused on the gateway rather than the invaders. Its centre was darkening, a shadow within the lake of light, growing, approaching. "Emmie, why do they need a really large gateway?"

"For all those Fomorians," she answered.

"But they're not nearly tall enough to need a gateway that size." He thought about it, while the Desiccators fizzed and the elders finished loading the bomb. "Maybe it's a large gateway, because something—"

"—very large is coming through," said Emmie.

The dark spot grew.

"Not a step backwards!" they heard Gerald cry.

Everyone took a step backwards.

The shadow enveloped the light. And, just as suddenly, a Hydra was in the world, impossibly huge, building-huge, cliff-huge. It towered above them, its many necks rising up into the sky. Heads. Teeth. Roaring from every mouth.

Finn stared up in horror, barely able to comprehend the size of the thing.

"As the ancient saying goes," said Lazlo the Second, stepping back from the Desiccannon, "we're in big trouble."

34

The Hydra reared up, before dropping back on to its feet with force enough to jolt every Half-Hunter, send a shock wave through the crowd, shuddering through the Twelve at the Desiccannon, sending the trucks and cars into a roar where they revved engines in an unbearable need to escape.

One Half-Hunter turned from his place on the hill and ran, crashing through the shocked throng, fleeing as he shouted, "I'm a tennis coach, not a warrior!"

"Don't fire your Desiccators at the Hydra!" Hugo called to all around him.

A Half-Hunter fired a Desiccator anyway and a spreading blob of blue arced through the twilight and caught one of the heads, snapping it down immediately, like a snail retreating into its shell.

"It'll only make it worse," growled Gerald.

From the Hydra's wounded neck, a bud appeared.

And another. Each one growing, bubbling into life, until something resembling eyes appeared on each one, then something else most definitely approximating teeth. After a last, violent spasm of growth, there were two heads at the end of one neck.

35

Finn had been at the centre of the beach battle.
He had been cornered
by a Minotaur.
He had fallen from a
tower of bones tall
enough to pierce clouds.
He had *exploded* in
another world. But this
was frightening on a level
so deep it shook parts of him
he didn't know existed.

Gerald and Hugo had
no choice but to move back,
abandoning their protective
hoarding for another a
couple of metres in front
of Finn and Emmie.

Minotaur

The Hydra stomped steadily from the entrance to the gateway, while Fomorians poured in behind, using the enormous Legend as a shield.

"We need to get under that beast," said Gerald, gritting his teeth at whatever pain his disintegrating body was causing him. "The only way to shrink a Hydra that big is to ram Desiccator fluid right in its guts."

Around the Hydra's legs, behind its belly, out of the flaming jaws of the gateway, they could make out more Fomorians pouring in. A legion of them. From behind the Hydra there came the sound of arrows being shot into the air. Except they weren't arrows, but long, deadly shards of the fossilised trees on the Infested Side, and they sliced the earth around Finn and Emmie with terrible effect.

Finn dived out of the way, heart pounding, as one buried itself in the ground where he had been standing. He picked himself up out of the mud. The Half-Hunters fired their Desiccators, but now understood it wasn't even worth targeting the colossal creature, instead trying to lob fire over the Hydra that stood between the humans and the incoming Fomorians. They launched stones, waved wooden swords, flung clumps of dirt, whatever was to hand.

A couple more turned and fled for safety.

Hugo waved back at the Desiccannon. "Get that thing up here!"

Gerald stood upright, shooting his Desiccator from the hip. The blue fire arced towards the edges of the Hydra, scorching past a gaggle of Fomorians peeking out from its rear.

Finn was sure that in this moment of great madness, Gerald was loving every minute.

Three blades landed in the grass in front of Finn and Emmie, cutting deep into the earth and forcing them to drop down for safety. When Finn popped his head up again, he saw the colossal Hydra, its teeth bigger than a person, most of its heads snapping and biting and swinging at the oncoming humans. But Finn noticed that a couple of heads weren't engaged. It was almost as if they were dozing, or comatose. *Odd*, he thought.

Then he saw something far more surprising on the Hydra's back. A small figure, strapped and helpless as the battle raged no more than the width of a Hogboon's earlobe away.

"That's Broonie!" he told Emmie. "On the Hydra."

"Can't be." She peered into the flares and colours of the battle. "It is!"

"Why?" said Finn. "How?"

With that, figures came running towards them, and they tensed until they realised they were only more Half-Hunters, dodging the falling dagger-like shards dropping all around them.

"Heave!" The Twelve were trying to move the Desiccannon forward to where they could aim it at the belly of the beast.

"Heave!" Its wheels were stuck in the mud of the hill.

"We need to help," said Finn, dashing to the Desiccannon to push. Emmie joined him. Before they knew it, other Half-Hunters were there too. Nils was just ahead of Finn, Estravon behind him. "I am never wearing new trousers to a battle ever again," he grumbled.

"Use the robes!" Aurora yelled, and the Twelve started to pull the garments from their necks to place beneath the Desiccannon's wheels to form a silk pathway in front of it.

"Heave!" shouted Aurora. They heaved. Heaved again. Finn wedged his shoulder in, pushed as hard as he could, felt the ground slip under his feet, but replanted them and went again.

The Hydra was a great silhouette against the light of the gateway, heads like tentacles seeking out victims.

A Half-Hunter just managed to vault a barrier as a Hydra's neck smashed through it so easily the metal wrapped round its chin. It shook it clear, and the hoarding sliced over the heads of those at the cannon.

"Heave!"

The Hydra found its grip on a Half-Hunter, a tooth piercing his jacket and lifting him high. He managed to shake himself from it before hitting the ground with a thump, rolling and then running away as the Hydra swallowed his coat.

"Heave!"

The Desiccannon moved. A few centimetres. Then a few more. The wheels found their grip on the robes and it jerked forward suddenly. Finn fell, face down, taking Estravon and Emmie with him. He looked up to see the Desiccannon gaining traction and speed, rolling steadily across the grass.

Behind it was the unlikely force of ten aged Legend Hunters, and Nils cheering at the back.

"Light the fuse! Light the fuse!" Aurora was shouting. Cedric just managed to smack the flint, and it sparked, sparked again. Lit.

The Desiccannon trundled straight for the Hydra's belly. Its fuse burning down, bomb ready to fire.

Something glinted in the sky. It was an arrow, a shard slicing through the air from the gateway, and heading straight for the Desiccannon. Finn identified its source. It was a newly arrived Fomorian, larger than the rest, his helmet rimmed with what looked like teeth, dominated by one serpent's tooth, and he had wings stretching wide across his back. In his hands rested a hefty bow.

Finn knew who this was, recognised him from the stories, from the things Broonie had told him. And he remembered him now from his vision when Mr Glad had almost trapped him.

"Gantrua," he muttered to Emmie where she lay. He pulled her to her feet, jumped, shouted above the melee. "Gantrua!"

Gantrua's arrow dropped fast and true, hitting the muzzle of the Desiccannon at the precise moment its fuse triggered the release of the bomb. The two met in a piercing flash, an explosion within the weapon, running through it in a devastating cascade.

Aurora's face froze for the merest moment.

Then she spoke.

"Oh no."

The bomb burst over everyone attached to the Desiccannon – Aurora, Cedric, Lazlo, every other member of the Council of Twelve there, and Nils whose eyes were wide open with terror.

There was a pulse, then a stifled *whoooop*, and it desiccated them all at once, together.

Shock grabbed hold of Finn, shut down his vision so that all he could see was the ball left behind. A brightly coloured horror. All those people. Fused into one.

Everything seemed to slow down. Sound seemed to dull.

"They're gone," said Finn.

"No, we can reanimate them," said Emmie. "Even just for a day, we can bring them back."

"They've been desiccated together. When two beings get fused like that, it's hard to separate them. But all of those, in one go? Impossible."

"Oh…" said Emmie, but there was nothing left to say. All they could do was stare at the large multicoloured ball that had been the Twelve.

Dead. Or as good as. The oldest, wisest, most experienced Legend Hunters in the world. All gone.

Then Finn realised something had landed at his foot. He picked up a cufflink. Nils's cufflink. The last thing left of him.

The heads of the Hydra rose up and roared with a terrifying fury that shook the hill.

Suddenly Gerald and Hugo were there, climbing over the final barriers, directing a retreat of Half-Hunters.

"We've got to run," said Finn, recognising an instinct that had served him well so many times before.

"This family does not go backwards," insisted Gerald, and looked up at the chaos descending upon them. "But the boy is right."

"We have no choice," said Hugo, facing the hordes pouring through the gateway into Darkmouth. "We have to evacuate. We have to use the tunnels. We have to let the Legends take Darkmouth."

antrua stepped into a world he had always yearned to see. The first thing he did was to close his eyes.

He drew breath through his nostrils. Filled his senses with the scent of this place. The crispness of its air. The life that filled every crumb of soil. The manure of whatever creatures had passed through was the most glorious he had ever encountered. He savoured it.

"My Lord of Unbound Death," said Trom, "what do you command us to do?"

"Ask him again," said Cryf. "In case he can't hear…"

Gantrua roared in Cryf's face. His eyeball bulged so hard a blood vessel popped and filled a corner of his left eye with fresh blood. He kept roaring, a sound not just of fury but of victory, of relief, of a long lifetime aching for this exact moment that had now been fulfilled. It quietened the entire hill, every Legend and every insect.

When he finally shut down his roar, it carried on across Darkmouth, a wave pounding against the town below.

The Hydra bucked. Broonie held on through instinct, even as the chains ensured he could not possibly fall anyway.

"Sssssmmmmmmffff," he said. "Sssssmmmmmmmmmmffffffff!"

Gantrua, chest heaving with violent breaths, reached down and scooped up a palmful of dirt and grass and one very confused worm.

Behind them the gateway closed.

"This is our world now," said Gantrua, then turned to the army, raised his sword and commanded, "let us take it!"

Crushing the earth in his hands, he led the Legends into Darkmouth.

LIECHTENSTEIN:
TWELVE HOURS EARLIER

TWO WORLDS — ONE VICTOR

"Tell Lucien about it," Axel of the Office of Snacks said as he bit into a cheesy cracker. "Go on."

The Half-Hunter remained behind his desk, a hand on the computer keyboard, and narrowed his eyes. In front of him was a small name plaque that confirmed that he was Karl, Department of Rumours, Legend Sightings and Bathroom Maintenance.

"They say there's a face appearing in the sky in Darkmouth."

"A face?" prompted Lucien.

"Or maybe legs. We're not sure. But what is happening is that Half-Hunters are being killed there. Zapped. Just turned to dust."

Axel ate the last of his cheesy cracker, swept up the crumbs from the table and tipped them into his mouth.

"The point is," said Karl, "it's all kicking off there again."

"You were in Darkmouth, weren't you?" Lucien asked him. "At the battle by that cave."

"It was incredible," said Karl, animated. "It cost me a week's holiday to make the journey to Darkmouth when Hugo disappeared, and I got a bit lost on the way, but it was worth it to see that battle on the beach. But now I'm back to..." he turned his computer screen to face Lucien, revealing numbers, charts, "...ordering toilet paper."

"Well," said Lucien, studying the Half-Hunter, "we don't want civilisation being flushed away, do we?"

"Hmmm," said Karl, and pulled the screen back towards him and hesitated before continuing. "We've all heard about the experiments in the basement, that you're attempting to make that Darkmouth dust work, to see if gateways can be opened from here."

"It is important scientific knowledge," said Lucien, cautious not to give too much away.

"Of course it is," said Karl. "Of course."

A head popped round the door, an older assistant in the same grey trouser suit that all the women in the building wore. "You got that toilet-paper order in yet, Karl?" she asked.

"Just doing it now, ma'am," Karl replied.

"The fifth-floor bathroom is almost on its last roll. Don't

let us down again." She left.

Axel stuck his head out of the door to see if she was gone before closing it for privacy. "What Karl is saying is what many of us are saying. We've been waiting a long time to see what would happen with the Legends, to see if they'd return, to see if we'd ever live up to the legacy of our ancestors."

"But while the Council of Twelve talks about glory," said Karl, "all I talk about is toilet paper."

Lucien bent forward, placed his hands on the edge of Karl's desk, pushed his face towards his. "Are you saying you'd prefer war over peace?"

Karl pulled back a bit, his uncertainty reflected in the thick lenses of Lucien's glasses.

"Are you suggesting, in fact, that you yearn for a reason to fight?" Lucien pressed. "That we should put some sort of secret programme in place that allows us to get in on all the action denied us for so long? Is that really what you want? Really?"

Karl was sweating.

Axel was munching.

Lucien began to smile.

37

"I need the toilet," said a woman deep in a darkness lit only by the low glow of mobile-phone screens.

"Hey, who's prodding me?" asked a man. "Is that a sword? It better not be a sword."

It was packed in here. An entire town crammed into the tight space, the evacuation having been quick and panicked. Some had been reluctant until it had been pointed out to them that if they needed persuasion, they simply had to look up at the Black Hills above the town. That glimpse of hell got them going.

"I'm hungry," said another Darkmouth evacuee. "I was halfway through making my dinner."

"Don't mention dinner," said someone beside him. "Now *I'm* hungry."

"I was making a Brussels-sprout soufflé."

"You know what, I'm not so hungry any more."

276

They had since been joined by the retreating Half-Hunters and the assistants who had been left without anyone to assist. Only the bald assistant, once the proud carrier of Gerald the Disappointed's desiccated husk, had his superior with him. Stumm was awake now. More awake than he must have been in years. His eyes were wide open, vivid in the unnatural light of tiny screens. He was clearly reliving the sight of his colleagues being desiccated into one great mess of people and steel.

The sight of so many bedraggled Half-Hunters squeezing in alongside the people of Darkmouth was not a welcome one.

"So we're in here, and you're in here," a woman said to a Half-Hunter in now shredded furs. "Is that your great plan? I'd like a better one than that."

In the middle of all this, Clara gritted her teeth. Took a deep breath. Regretted taking a deep breath because of the accumulated smell of a few thousand people all crammed into one space together. It was her own fault. This had been her idea after all. She'd had the notion of evacuating the town, but hadn't reckoned on being the one landed with being in charge of it. Yet the logic had been annoyingly sound. She was a civilian married into a Legend Hunter family. It made her the ideal candidate to negotiate between the two.

Besides, she knew these people, had grown up with them, had stared into many of their mouths and knew the deepest secrets of their deepest cavities. The people of Darkmouth trusted her. Sort of.

"Where's the sergeant?" asked the hungry person.

"He could be here for all we know," said his neighbour. "He spends so much time hiding away that I don't even know what he looks like. Or if he's even a he at all."

Clara tried to remain calm. And upbeat. While wondering if they were about to be invaded by rampaging Legends at any moment. Wondering if Finn and Hugo were OK out there. Wondering why she had to marry the only guy within a thousand miles with relatives who not only refused to stay dead, but also liked to complain about the miracle of resurrection.

"What's the plan, Clara?" asked a man above her. He'd found a space on a statue plinth.

"Hugo, Finn and the others are putting their fallback plan into operation, don't worry."

"I don't mean to sound, you know, downbeat, but what if the fallback plan doesn't work?" the man asked while swinging his legs off the plinth's edge. "Is there a fallback to the fallback?"

278

Clara didn't know how to answer him, because the truth might have caused panic. There was no fallback to the fallback. There was only defeat.

There was murmuring and movement in the throng as Finn appeared through the crowd. Emmie was with him, and behind them came Gerald and Hugo. All of them out of breath.

Finn's mum checked on him, tilting his chin to assess him for signs of damage. He let her. He felt his pulse tapping quickly at his neck. They'd had to run pretty fast to make it to a tunnel entrance before any of the Legends arrived in town.

He noticed that the Savage twins were right there, squashed in with everybody, eyeing him, one taking a picture – *snap* – while the other grinned.

"What are those dangly things on your shoulders?" mocked Conn Savage, spotting his epaulettes.

"I think they're cup holders," said Manus Savage.

"You know Legends track victims' bad odour," said Finn. He sniffed the air in their direction. "So you two will definitely be the first to get eaten."

"They're all here?" Hugo asked, no greeting preceding the question.

"Yes," said Clara, now giving Emmie a squeeze.

"We're all here," said the hungry man. "But *so are you.* While out there—"

Out there was the sound of thumping feet, getting closer.

Gerald pointed a finger at the man. "Out there are things you don't want to invite in here, and they don't know about the tunnels. So, unless you want to find yourself suddenly stranded on a street full of Fomorians even angrier than me, you might want to keep your voice down."

The hungry man kept his voice down.

Gerald tried hard not to show it, but even in the near-darkness Finn could see him fight against spasms of pain now wracking a body that didn't have much longer to live. "Did they always moan this much?" Gerald asked Hugo, by way of a distraction. "I don't know how you put up with that all these years."

Hugo began to push his way through the crowd again, and Gerald followed. Together they turned to Finn and Emmie.

"Come on, you two," said Hugo.

"Come on where?" said Emmie.

"Up there," said Gerald. "We're going to end this."

38

"**G**rass," said Gantrua.

The army had walked down the hill, into Darkmouth and on to Broken Road, without a fight.

Or rather not so much walked as snarled and snapped and pushed and drooled. At least one Fomorian had marked its territory in a most unpleasant way, leaving a stench behind that would probably take several generations to scrub out. Should Darkmouth have any humans left alive to do so, that is.

"I remember grass," continued Gantrua, nose in the air, eyes closed. He sniffed and the wings on his back almost opened with the sensations. "I remember grass. A blade of it grew in the forest near my ancestral lands. Here it is so plentiful it grows through the cracks in the stone."

"Their trees seem sick," said Trom. "They have these green things growing on them." He picked off

a leaf to chew on it.

"What's that taste like?" asked Cryf.

"Better than the nicest toenail you've ever bitten," said Trom. "But not as chewy."

Broonie watched and heard all of this, from above the Hydra, with his elevated position affording him a view down the town, through the roofs of buildings. Whenever it wasn't being obstructed by snarling heads and gnashing teeth anyway. Still, two of the Hydra's heads remained disinterested, snoozy. The others were fully enraged by their circumstances, and by each other.

Broonie tried to pull his arms free from the straps binding them, and flicked his head about to loosen the muzzle pressed tight over his mouth. Nothing budged. All that changed was that he became more exhausted, and the green of his skin flushed with the yellow of his blood.

Gantrua moved on, the curving serpent's tooth on his grille catching the orange of the street lights as he took in this world he had long striven to enter.

"The humans live in straight lines," he said. "They live behind glass and squares and metal." He gently punched a small car as he passed, and it burst into a riot of flashing lights and a high-pitched beeping sound. This briefly shocked the Hydra, causing it to clip a corner of the street's bookshop with one head, punching a chunk out of the wall and freeing books to flutter and fall to the ground.

Another head clattered an electricity pole, which bent over, snapping wires and whipping electricity about the street's edge. A Fomorian soldier picked up a wire to see what the strange fizzing substance tasted like and was blasted across the road in a shower of sparks.

"Ssssssgguusssss," said Broonie desperately.

Gantrua did not flinch. "This world is soft. I can feel it in every step. The black of this road is soft. The bricks are soft. The air is soft. The smells are of sweetness and luxury."

He picked up a bunch of roses from a display at the hastily abandoned florist's. Water dripped from its roots, ran along his arm. "They have such life here that they can afford to cut it down, display it, leave it lying around." He dropped the flowers to the ground. Trom grabbed them, shoved them into his mouth and then made a face that suggested he wished he hadn't.

"Not good?" asked Cryf.

"Like licking a Manticore's tail."

"Sssssssssggggggggggsssssss," said Broonie.

The street was now wild with Fomorians pulling at car mirrors, chewing on hanging baskets, pressing their flat noses against shopfronts.

Something attracted Gantrua's attention. He tapped a shop window, sending a crack through the pane until the glass shattered and fell about him. He reached in, yanked a mannequin from where it stood, held it out so he could examine it.

"Fake humans?" he asked. "What kind of trickery is this? And what are these thin threads on their bodies? How much softer can this world get?" He pulled the dress from the mannequin, handed it to Trom, who held the flowery green frock up against his hulking body and for a

moment seemed genuinely taken with it. Seeing the look on Gantrua's face, he threw it aside.

"Not my colour," he said.

"Ssssgggsssss!" Broonie kept shouting, muzzle clamping tighter every time he breathed in.

Gantrua stepped back into the street, calm amid the celebration and madness. He sniffed the air. Sniffed again. "Why did the humans run?" he asked. "They spend a hundred lifetimes squashing us into our own world, and then scurry like dung-ants when we finally break free."

From above, Broonie saw something roll from under a car, a white, egg-like object that wobbled across the road until it nudged at Trom's biggest big toe. Trom picked it up.

"No!" shouted Gantrua, but it was too late.

The egg popped, a purple residue spraying across Trom's face. He pulled a finger through it, tasted it. "Spicy," he said.

Then he burst into purple flames, a swirling plasma that first tightened his skin so that his eyeballs stuck out alarmingly. *Schlloop.* He was shrunk into a small lumpen square hardly bigger than Gantrua's left foot.

39

"Trom!" shouted Cryf, loud enough to send a tremor through the entire street, the rest of the Legends sensing immediately that something had changed. That the celebration was over. That they were still at war, even if the battlefield was a playground to them.

Cryf cradled the uneven box that was the desiccated Trom, reassuring his old friend that everything would be OK. Behind him, a figure darted across the dark road, sprinting from one laneway to another.

"There!" said Gantrua. Three Fomorian soldiers peeled away to follow the movement, chunky legs propelling them towards the entrance to the lane. They came to a swift halt when they found a human standing stock-still, one hand on its hip, the other outstretched, holding a handbag, eyes dead, face lifeless.

"Another fake human," Cryf said, arriving on the scene.

"A trap?" Gantrua asked.

"I don't know," said an upset Cryf as he cradled Trom in his hand, while pushing through the panting Fomorians. "But it's wearing a very strange hat."

The mannequin suddenly tilted, as if pulled over, and smacked to the ground. The many spikes of the hat fired off in every direction, embedding their tips in the ground, the cobbles, and three Fomorian backsides. It sent them instantly into jabbering craziness.

"*Trap!*" shouted Cryf.

Tied to the Hydra, Broonie ducked just quick enough to avoid a flying dart, which embedded itself in the neck with two heads on it. A thin blue vein rose where the dart had stabbed, creeping upwards until, as if making its choice, it diverted into the head on the right side of the neck. The mind attached to that part of the Hydra instantly went burbly, its eyes swivelling in different directions, its teeth drowning in spittle and it began to snap at its neighbour, at the other heads, at itself.

"*Sssssssgggggsssss!*" said Broonie again, trying to get the word out that would save them all. Or make the Hydra fall over and kill them. Or do whatever, but at least just end this torment once and for all.

At the top of the street, another human ran across.

Then two more. The sparking electricity of the fallen street lamp glinted off their armour. Then they were gone.

From somewhere to the right of them, there was a sound of sliding metal, of something dropping in an echoed *clang*.

Gantrua turned his head, the bones creaking in the wings on his back.

He walked to the phone box where the noise had come from, looked at it, pulled the phone out and listened for a moment to a strange and insistent *beep-beep-beep*. A voice, muffled and small, spoke to him: "Please dial the number you require."

A dark hole opened in the floor in front of him.

"This number cannot be reached..." said the voice. Gantrua ripped the phone clean from the box. Then he tore the phone box clean from the ground and thought for a moment, looking down at the newly revealed hole.

"You," he said to the smallest Fomorian he could see. "Get down there."

"Of course, Your Fearsomeness," said the loyal Legend immediately, dipping a toe into the hole, turning to find the right angle to fit his frame in. Gantrua grabbed his shoulders and pushed him roughly down, and the unfortunate Fomorian dropped in with one leg trailing the rest of his body.

Once Gantrua was satisfied that he had heard the thump of the Fomorian soldier's hard landing, he called after him, "What do you see?"

"Stone," replied the Fomorian, sounding somewhat winded. "Curved corridors. Strange lights stuck to the walls."

"Tunnels," announced Gantrua. "This is where the humans are hiding. That is where they scurried like dungrats." He turned to his army. "Go down there. Find them. Exterminate them. I will remain above ground with a detachment of soldiers and the Hydra. The rest of you, do not return to me until all the humans are dead."

Fomorians began converging, shoving and elbowing their way to get into the hole.

Still furious about Trom, Cryf now began kicking at any object in the street that might possibly be another entrance into the world beneath Darkmouth. Bollards were mangled; a bench was yanked from its foundations; a water hydrant ripped clean away.

"Here," said Cryf, holding the hydrant in his hands. Below it was another hole into the tunnels.

It was not easy to get several Fomorians into spaces

designed for humans with narrow shoulders and wiggly shoulder blades. No part of a Fomorian wiggles. But they made every effort, tearing at the concrete with their hands, pulling and pushing each other into the tunnels below.

"How you spent time with these rodents, I will never know," Gantrua called up to Broonie.

"Sssssssgggssssss," replied Broonie uselessly.

Around them, Legends poured into the tunnels.

At the furthest edge of the town, through the slats of the church's bell tower, with a view that carried over Darkmouth to where the town's only phone box had stood until only moments ago, Finn, Emmie, Hugo and Gerald watched.

"They're going into the tunnels," said Finn.

"They've bought the diversion," said Hugo. "Fair play to those Half-Hunters who acted as decoys. They did what was needed."

"They've guessed the tunnels are a hiding place," said Hugo, a switch mechanism in his hand. "But they obviously haven't guessed they're rigged to flood with Desiccator fluid."

"Don't mess this up," said Gerald.

"You have to stop saying that," Hugo told him. He squinted again through his binoculars.

"I want to desiccate every last one of those Legends,"

said Emmie. Over the hours she had emerged from being mute and dazed to growing more and more furious at the loss of her father, determined to be a part of whatever revenge could be meted out.

Hugo pushed the switch over to her.

"You sure?" she asked, her thumb hovering over the box and its red lever.

Hugo nodded. "When I say so, you flick that on and blow open the vat. We'll hear the Desiccations all the way up here."

"We've to make sure they pay for it, Finn," said Emmie. "Right?"

He hated to see her like this, so full of sadness and revenge. He didn't answer her.

"Just another few moments," Hugo said, his eyes pressed against binoculars jutting through the wooden slats of the bell tower. It was cold up here, the breeze rippling through the cramped space so that the single bell resonated a constant eerie chime that sounded too similar to a groan for Finn's liking.

"Wait until they're all in," Gerald instructed Emmie.

Finn could see his great-grandfather was in pain, and furrowed his brow in sympathy. Gerald glared at him. "Pain tells me I'm still alive, even if we *are* reduced to sitting still, waiting to press a button. We might as well be at an amusement arcade. I *hate* amusement arcades."

"Any moment now," Hugo whispered to Emmie. Across the town, they could see more Legends heading towards the tunnels. From a distance, Finn urged them in. Some were still waiting to enter, or smashing things up. Some had disappeared from view.

"Are they all going in?" Finn asked his dad.

"Most, I think. I can't see every one of them."

From below them, a loud whisper carried up the stairs to the bell tower. "There is some concern that nothing appears to have happened yet," said Estravon's voice. They heard the sound of his boots on the wooden steps grow louder until he himself appeared at the top of the ladder.

"We will trigger the device when the moment is right," said Hugo, half turning to him, "not because someone needs the toilet."

"Actually," said Estravon, "quite a few in there need the toilet at the moment, but that's not the only reason for impatience."

"I'm ready, Hugo," Emmie said.

"Not all the Legends are in the tunnels yet," said Hugo. Finn peered through his binoculars and could just about make out a commotion where the phone box had been ripped from the ground. A Fomorian had become stuck at the shoulders, and Gantrua had motioned for the Hydra to stamp him in.

"We'll be ready when we're ready," said Gerald. "Honestly. These people. They almost make a man regret coming back from the dead."

"One more moment," said Hugo.

"I'm concerned about the health-and-safety aspects of having all those civilians in such close proximity to so many irritable, weapon-bearing Half-Hunters," Estravon said.

"You should be more concerned about the health-and-safety aspects of Fomorians getting in here and ripping everyone's arms off to use as chopsticks," said Hugo.

Grumbling, Estravon retreated.

"I like that image," said Gerald. "At least some of what I taught you clearly rubbed off."

"There *are* a lot of very grumpy people down here," Clara said from the stairs. "Including me."

"Sorry," said Hugo with a sigh. "Thanks," he said to his grandfather.

Gerald looked at him, less impressed.

"Would you prefer to be down there dealing with the

people, or up here dealing with the Fomorians?" Hugo asked him. "Clara has the tougher job, trust me."

Gerald seemed to quietly acknowledge this.

Finn watched the Hydra tromp over and lift a leg, and the unfortunate Fomorian looked up aghast at the gigantic foot being raised above his head, ready to pound him into the tunnel like a cork being pushed into a bottle. The Hydra stamped down hard on the wedged Fomorian, a clomp that sent a tremor through the street.

When the Hydra lifted its leg and stepped back, the Fomorian was still stuck, and utterly dazed.

"OK, we'd better not take any more risks," said Hugo. "There are a lot of Fomorians in there now, and we'll have to mop up whatever's left on the streets." He looked at Emmie. "Ready?" he asked.

"Ready," she confirmed.

"Now."

Emmie pressed the switch.

Nothing seemed to happen.

She pressed it again.

Still nothing happened. The Legends were still at the entrances to the tunnels. The stragglers, plus Gantrua and the Hydra, were still crashing about Darkmouth.

Finn took the device from her, pressed the switch.

"Again," insisted Hugo, concerned.

Nothing was happening, no matter how many times Finn pressed it.

"Let me have a go," said Gerald, grabbing the remote control from Finn and thumping the button aggressively. "You must have rigged this wrong, Hugo."

"*You* rigged it," Hugo said.

"You watched me do it," said Gerald. "If there was a problem, you should have spotted it."

Estravon popped his head into the bell tower again. "Excuse me," he said. "It must be time to activate the device now."

"*We know*," Hugo and Gerald said simultaneously. They stood, Gerald a bit more gingerly, but not wishing to betray any discomfort.

"It didn't work. I'll have to go and trigger it from within the tunnels," said Finn's father, working his way down the creaking wooden steps towards the main body of the church.

"You can't do that," said Clara, waiting with Estravon at the bottom of the stairs. "The people in here need protecting. You can't run out on them."

"She's right," agreed Gerald. "I know those tunnels. I'll have to do it."

"Your body is breaking down. You mightn't make it alone."

"How about I—" started Finn as he and Emmie followed.

"Don't be stubborn, Hugo," said Gerald.

"Don't keep trying to do my job for me," Hugo argued back.

"I could—" said Finn.

Hugo pushed open a door from the bell tower into the church, to reveal the rest of the town, hidden here all evening and terribly annoyed by it. They erupted in protest.

"This is ridiculous," said Mrs Cross.

"There's a town full of people getting on each other's nerves down here," said Clara. "But not nearly as much as they're getting on my nerves." She raised her hands to calm them. "It'll be OK, not much longer."

"That's what you said when I had that tooth out last year," complained a woman.

"I only gave you a scale and polish," said Clara.

"There's an awful smell in here," someone griped.

Manus and Conn Savage sniggered with gleeful guilt.

"We need to keep our voices down," urged Estravon.

"Look, I know this is no fun for anyone—" said Clara.

"Actually, I think it's kind of exciting," squeaked a voice.

"—but we need to remain calm while Hugo sorts this out."

"I don't remember them being this ungrateful," Gerald said to Hugo. "Although, on second thoughts…"

"If you leave, this church is undefended against whatever's out there," said Clara.

"We don't have a choice," said Hugo.

"I will go," Gerald insisted. "I came back to sort out this mess, it's about time I did it."

"There are plenty of Half-Hunters who can do it," Clara said.

"They don't know how the device beneath the obelisk is rigged," Hugo said. "They won't be able to release the fluid. No, this is our town. Our problem."

"You won't have a town left if you leave this church," Clara said.

The whispered arguing continued, the voices melding into one haggled blend of words, watched by the entire town, assistants and visiting Half-Hunters.

Except for Estravon. Who had noticed something.

"Listen to me," he said.

They didn't.

"*Listen. To. Me.*"

That finally hushed everyone.

"Where are Finn and Emmie?"

"We need an entrance as close to the obelisk as possible," said Finn, peeking an eye out from a shopfront to look for danger. "There's a bin on the street very close to it, and beneath it is a hatch. If we can get to that without being found, we can drop in, open the pipe manually and get back out again quickly. Go."

Emmie dashed from the shopfront, up one block between laneways, then ducked into the entrance to the pet shop. Finn followed immediately behind, and together they crouched at the door, unseen by anything but a cockatoo, two gerbils and a disinterested stick insect.

"We've not got much time until Mr Glad comes back," said Emmie. "What if he does and we miss him? What if we miss my dad?"

"We'll make it," said Finn. "Come on."

They left the gazing animals behind, found themselves

further up the street at the bookshop, a chunk of its second floor sitting incongruously on the street, paper and covers everywhere.

"The Legends are in the middle sections of the tunnels," Finn said, his eyes on the quiet, empty street. "We have a few minutes before they reach the section under the obelisk."

"How are we going to get him back?" asked Emmie.

Finn didn't know the answer to that yet. He could only deal with one disaster at a time.

"I don't see any Legends – let's go," Finn said, and dashed along another block of shopfronts, carefully pressing himself against the wall as it curved round towards where the obelisk squatted. He stopped at a grocery store, its door ajar. He slid in through the door for shelter. Emmie followed and they crouched at the open ice-cream freezer, beside a shelf of baked beans and wine, while watching carefully for any activity down the street. Finn's mouth was dry with fear. He swallowed, trying to keep it down. At the same time, he pushed away the nagging thought that bravery would only lead him into the jaws of death. Actual jaws. Crunching, mangling, slicing jaws of...

"Is the tunnel entrance close?" Emmie asked.

"Just around the corner," Finn confirmed, glad for

something else to distract him. "I'll go first, but you'll have to give me a hand just to push it open quickly. Then we get in, trigger the obelisk and get out before we're desiccated ourselves in the flood. You ready?"

Behind him, Emmie grunted.

"There's just one thing worrying me, though," Finn said. "We haven't seen the Hydra since we left the church. It must be up to something."

Emmie didn't respond.

"Just keep an eye out for it, all right?" he said.

Still no answer from Emmie.

"Emmie, did you hear—"

He turned around and saw her pressed back against the wall, a finger at her lips. At the window was an eye.

An enormous eye.

Then the eye moved back a little, became a head. Teeth. It was so close the breath of its nostrils was fogging the window.

Finn and Emmie did not move. They did not breathe. They dared not blink in case the breeze of a fluttering eyelash alerted the Hydra to their presence. They couldn't be sure if it saw them behind the freezer, where they were curled up as tight as possible. Finn felt that old familiar fear rising in him again. Mixed

in with it was that strange lurking energy he couldn't control.

At that point, he decided he would definitely take a thousand Completion Ceremonies, with 10,000 scorpions, over this any day.

Slow moments passed.

Finn and Emmie concentrated on breathing quietly.

Apparently seeing nothing of interest, the Hydra head turned away.

Finn and Emmie watched it draw back from the window and stand in the street. They could see the full scale of the thing now. It was dragging a couple of heads, eyes blank. On the two-headed neck, one looked fully crazed. And high on its back, spindly legs just about visible, was strapped a distressed and exhausted Hogboon, still trying to get a word out from behind its muzzle.

"*Ssssgggggsssssss!*" they heard Broonie say. "*Ssssgggsssss!!*"

The Hydra began to move away from them, down the street, sending a shudder through the shop.

Thud. Thud.

On the shelf above Finn and Emmie, champagne bottles rattled, shook, wobbled. *Pop.* A cork shot from one. *Pop.* Another.

Pop. Pop. Pop.

Finn and Emmie looked at each other, aghast.

The shop's till opened with a *ting*.

The Hydra stopped, whipped a head back to the window and blew so hard it shattered the glass. It sniffed at the air, nostrils quivering, then thrust its head in, teeth snapping.

42

The Hydra's head bit at them, so close that Finn and Emmie could feel its wet breath as they scrambled for an escape out of the rear of the shop. Finn reached the back door first, fighting with its lock while Emmie joined him.

"Hurry, hurry, hurry," she said.

"I am hurrying!"

Another Hydra head smashed through the front window, rushing through the shop, its neck sweeping aside shelves, sending magazines and newspapers flying into the air.

The head filled the space, its fangs taller than either of them.

"Hurry!" Emmie said again.

The lock clicked and the door released them into the yard just as the Hydra head snapped at them. It wedged itself in the doorframe, growling as it struggled to release

itself while Finn and Emmie ran through the small yard towards the back wall. Behind them, the Legend's head withdrew violently, gouging a Hydra-head-shaped chunk through the wall.

Another head came swooping over the shop's low, flat roof, headbutting the wall with a terrifying smack as Finn and Emmie scrambled over it into the back lane.

"*Sssssgggsssssss!*" Broonie was saying as he fought with the restraints pinning him to the creature.

"We need to find another entrance to the tunnels!" shouted Emmie as she and Finn sprinted down the narrow cobbled alley.

"We can't," Finn replied, panting. "We'll run into Legends down there. We need to get to that bin by the obelisk. It's this way." He turned a sharp left, stopping dead at the sight of a double-headed Hydra neck, one head with utterly mad eyes, leading the rest of the Hydra straight for them.

Emmie ran into the back of him.

"Go right!" he instructed, spinning and going on a straight sprint down the laneway, grass growing through its stones. His Desiccator felt like a dead weight in his hands, a hindrance rather than a help against the Hydra. The Hydra was gaining on them.

"Here!" shouted Finn, taking a running jump into a rotting wooden door. It came straight off its hinges, falling flat with Finn spreadeagled on top of it. Emmie followed, dodging the two-headed neck as it ploughed the cobbles behind her in a spray of shattered stone.

She helped Finn up, and they realised they'd escaped into the pre-school. A brightly coloured sign on its wall read: *Little Monsters*.

The Hydra sent three heads after them. Over the wall, Finn could make out Broonie, tossed around like a rubber duck on a stormy sea. But, even in the dark, the whites of his eyes were clear. He looked as scared as Finn felt.

Either side of its back door, the pre-school's two windows were open, probably a result of the town evacuating quickly. Finn and Emmie took one each, climbing awkwardly through them. As he fell into the building, now separated from Emmie by a hallway, Finn caught his boot in the latch and hung, stranded, by one foot.

From the room on the far side of the corridor, he heard Emmie drop from the window, followed by the breaking of glass as a Hydra head followed after her. Through the door, he saw her lean back and fire her Desiccator point-blank at the head. She'd had no choice, but as the blasted neck retreated it was already budding two new heads.

She scrambled from the room. "Where are you, Finn?" she called.

Finn meanwhile was fighting to release his boot, trying to undo the laces to get rid of it. But pulling at them only made the knot tighter. A Hydra head swung from the darkness, smacking against the pane, cracking it but not breaking it. Yet.

Even as his mind worked overtime to imagine all the ways he might die now – well, one way: horribly, by Hydra – a bit of him, some kind of instinct or training or composure, gave him the clarity to reach for his belt, pull out a small knife and slice his bootlace.

Crash.

The window caved in as the Hydra hit it again. It gulped down the boot left behind as Finn crawled away on his hands and knees.

"Come on, Finn!" cried Emmie from the front of the building.

The Hydra reared up, most of its heads especially angry, two of those heads with *extra* heads on them, and it crashed down on the building, children's paintings scattering everywhere, masonry firing in chunks all about them. A piece struck Finn in the back and he fell forward, winded, just as a swinging head passed centimetres over his head.

They were in a playground at the front of the pre-school. Emmie jumped on to a roundabout, turning away from an onrushing head, jumping from the spinning wheel and running up a slide to jump off it as another head snatched at her.

She landed on a small bouncy castle.

Even in this moment of terror, Finn was impressed by that move.

Then it was his turn. He rolled, stood, made it to the other side of a swing. The Hydra thrust a head in towards him, its fierce fangs biting, skin like boiled lava. Out of pure fright, he pulled the swing down hard around its neck, so that the rope snagged the Hydra, becoming more knotted with every attempt it made to break free.

"Broonie!" Finn shouted. "Do something!"

"Ssssgggggssssss!!!" replied Broonie, strapped tight on the creature's back.

The rest of the Hydra was wearing the school like a uniform, one leg outside, three in. Five necks whipping wildly, two still subdued for some reason. Finn didn't understand. Didn't have time to.

He backed away further while he tried to pull the Desiccator canister from his weapon, and press the button that would set the charge on it. He needed to get under that belly.

Emmie was trying to get through a small window at the back of the bouncy castle. There was a bang and a deep hiss as a head bit into the springy structure. The castle quickly deflated, swallowing her in multicoloured rubber. The Hydra head snuffled for her, but she crawled out quickly from the flattened fun, crawling, then running, towards a bulbous climbing frame shaped like an upturned submarine.

Finn, shaking with nerves and adrenalin, struggled with the canister, and finally pulled it free. Then he dropped it.

Get a grip, he thought, trying to literally get a grip on it with his shaking fingers.

His hand stretched…

…and he caught it, just as the Hydra wrenched the swing clean from its bolts, and roared free.

Finn backed up even further against a tall garden wall, canister in one hand, searching for his knife with the other. Maybe if he found that, he could stab the Legend in the eye and distract it enough for him to run under its belly and—

Instead, he found something else. A cufflink. Nils's

cufflink. Silver. Square. A natty design on it. But a cufflink all the same.

He shrank back.

Emmie was trapped in one corner of the playground, stuck in the centre of a climbing frame, a porthole revealing a face of fear. The Hydra was flailing itself free from the walls of the crumbling pre-school, one of the heads already striking the edge of Emmie's hiding place.

And Finn was armed with a cufflink.

Wait.

A cufflink that he now realised had a small button on its side. A small red button. He remembered Nils telling him about this. The Half-Hunter who loved his gadgets talking about wanting something explosive. Now Finn wondered…

"Take this!" he shouted, more confidently than he felt, and pressed the button on the cufflink just as the Hydra broke free of the building.

He wasn't sure what he expected. Something to shoot out of the cufflink perhaps. But instead the small square of metal launched itself into the air, spinning towards the Hydra's back, distracting at least one of its heads as it caught the playground lights. It reached as high as its back, where Broonie looked at it with a little curiosity, and immediate suspicion.

Then the cufflink burst. It was a decent explosion as far as cufflinks go, but not nearly enough to kill a Hydra. Or badly hurt it. Or scratch it at all really.

But it did two things.

First, it bought Finn enough time to scramble away.

And second it left Broonie with a nasty scorch mark across his face. "Be careful!" the Hogboon shouted.

This happened to be the *same* moment Broonie realised the small explosion had blown the muzzle from his mouth. And the restraints from his hands. He jumped away and, as he did, he shouted the word he'd been dying to say for a long time now.

"*Sausages!!*"

The two snoozing, dormant heads awoke. It was as if a switch had turned them on, a hypnosis deactivated by a single word.

The heads launched themselves at the seven heads on the other five necks and instantly the Hydra was at war with itself, a creature in a battle for control of its own body.

Finn didn't know that the Hydra had been hypnotised by an Orthrus, turned against itself by the power of suggestion and a single trigger word. All he knew was that he had his chance. He held the canister, found the button on the side to prime it to explode, steeled himself to press it, run and stick it on the belly of the Hydra.

And, just as he was ready, Emmie skimmed down the slide –"*Wheeeeeee!*" – straight under the belly of the Hydra, and shoved her Desiccator canister into it without even stopping.

Broonie was already on the ground beside them, sweating and babbling in a mix of relief and despair and disbelief and joy at the sight of a Hydra in chaos.

"You said *wheeeee*," Finn said to Emmie.

"Yeah, I know. Not very cool at all, was it?"

"Not cool at all," smiled Finn.

"Can we go, please?" begged Broonie. "I want to bury my face in a bucket of worms and never go anywhere else again."

The three of them bolted from the playground, just in time to feel the air sucked in around them, as the Hydra imploded with a not-so-stifled *whoooooooppp*.

Every night, as the streets of Darkmouth emptied and quietened, the town's street cleaner would emerge from his small cottage at the edge of town, whirr up the rotating brushes on his push-along sweeper and head out to do his job. His name was Dessie and he'd done the same thing for twenty-five years, night after night after night. And tonight he headed out to do the same, a little grumpier than usual, having slept through his alarm. As a result, he'd had to rush his meal, which would be dinner to everyone else, but was both dinner and breakfast to him – meaning that he'd had to shovel down his bowl of Chocky-Flakes and pasta.

As he'd hurried about his house, he thought he'd heard something outside, but, when he pulled up his coat collar and left through the front door, all seemed quiet. He popped on his protective earmuffs, revved up his sweeper and began his nightly route through the town.

He was proud of his work, of the way he could make a filthy cobble gleam.

He moved slowly, deliberately, through the streets, his world shrunk down to the square of road in front of him about to be scrubbed by the rotating brushes, and their muffled sweeping as they turned. At one point, over the hush of his ear defenders, he thought he heard some kind of thudding not too far away. A crash maybe. A gurgle mixed in there. And, as he pulled the large earmuffs away from his ear, and the brushes wound down to a stop, he thought he may possibly have heard a not-so-stifled *whooooooooppp* off across the houses.

But there was nothing else. Just silence.

So he revved up the street sweeper again, once again imagining it was a Formula One racing car, put on his ear defenders and began his long sweep of the street.

Near the obelisk, he spotted a crisp packet. Even at a distance of fifty metres, his instinct, honed by long experience, allowed him to detect and track it as it swirled about a gutter, hopped up on the pavement. He revved the sweeper and, not even realising he was making motorcar noises in his throat, went straight for it. He stopped, picked up the packet and crossed the street to the bin.

Then he stopped.

The bin was at an odd angle, shoved aside a bit, as if it had been knocked or pulled.

It made the street look disorderly. The street cleaner did not like disorderly. So he pulled the bin across again, and twisted the catch at the bottom that secured it to its metal base. *No more disorder*, he thought, and swung the sweeper round towards the curve on to Broken Road, happy that neatness had been returned to Darkmouth.

Then he stood at the end of the street, mouth agape, at the sight of rubble, broken glass, rogue mannequins and disorder on a massive scale.

"Ah now…"

Meanwhile, directly beneath his feet, ten metres down below the street, Finn, Broonie and Emmie were creeping through the tunnels towards the pipes at the base of the obelisk. They were preparing to flood the tunnels with Desiccator fluid, to shrink an army of Legends, all the while completely unaware that their best escape route had just been sealed off.

44

Below Darkmouth, Finn, Emmie and Broonie hurried onwards. Behind them, in the vast network that ran beneath the town's streets, they could hear noises. Growls. Shouts. Yelps. The distant scrape of claw on stone. The crashing of shelves, the smashing of doors, the splintering of wood and metal.

"This is crazy," said Finn.

"You've only just realised that?" Emmie responded, serious but revitalised by their encounter with the Hydra.

"What if someone presses the remote control again and this time it works and releases all that fluid? We'll be desiccated with everything else."

"Ah," said Emmie as if she hadn't thought of that. "Well, they'll have noticed we're gone by now. Surely they'll guess what we're doing?"

"We'd better hope so," said Finn.

"Will someone tell me what's going on?" demanded

Broonie. "Actually, on second thoughts, don't tell me what's going on. I'm better off not knowing what ridiculous misadventure I'm being dragged into."

The sound of the army of Legends in the corridors behind was growing louder.

"I just can't escape them," said Broonie, glancing back fearfully. "Or you, or that fella Mr Glad, or anyone."

They passed a poster that read:

THINK CALMLY OR DIE SCREAMING.

"Mr *Glad?*" said Finn to Broonie.

"Oh yeah, he's over there in my world too, you know. The dust does it, the magic that allows him to appear."

"Did you see him?" asked Emmie as they passed another poster.

SHUSH! BIG BANGS ATTRACT BIG FANGS.

"Saw him. Heard him. It was all 'vengeance this, vengeance that'. He hates you for trapping him. *Really* hates you. Understandable, I suppose. It doesn't look like fun."

"Fantastic," said Finn, not meaning that at all. "Anything else?"

"Yes," said Broonie. "They've promised to save him. I mean Gantrua has, in return for his help. They say they can give him his body back."

Emmie stopped, swung round and pinned Broonie against the wall. "How?" she demanded.

"Oi," complained Broonie, "don't pinch."

"How do they get the Trapped back?"

"Let me see if I can remember," said Broonie, frowning. "Oh yes, they fill the sky with pure dust. At the moment, they kind of mix it up a bit, using a Troll and some gibberish. But douse him in enough pure Coronium and, apparently, no more Ghost Glad. Just him. An ordinary bag of goosebumpy bones like the rest of you humans."

The noise of the ravenous Fomorians down the tunnels was echoing towards them.

"That's why the locket stopped Mr Glad before," realised Finn. "The dust of the crystal inside it. If he'd trapped me, he would have absorbed it. It's not that it would have poisoned him or killed him or anything—"

"He would have become human again," said Emmie, her face brightening.

"Normal. Powerless."

"My dad's not lost. We can get him back!"

The sound of approaching Legends was getting louder.

"I am so happy for you," said Broonie, shaking off Emmie's grip. "But might I suggest that if you want your dad back, you need to *not be dead*."

They started down the tunnels again.

"Although I'm destined to expire in this place, aren't I?" Broonie said. "My lovely skin will be nothing but worm meal in this world."

"You need to stop being so glum about everything," said Finn, reaching a short corridor leading to a door, its ceiling lined with zigzagging pipes. "Don't you trust us by now?"

He opened the door to the storage room, lit blue by the huge vat of sparkling Desiccator liquid. Its level had dropped after they'd siphoned so much off for the bombs that did not work, but there was still a lot in there. More than enough.

"Your idea is to give everyone in this tunnel a bath?" said Broonie, unimpressed.

"That's the device the switch was meant to control," said Finn, pointing to an old-fashioned timer attached to a complex-looking motor running a series of cogs that in turn were attached to a wide tap drooping like an elephant's trunk from the lower part of the vat. "Isn't it?"

"Yeah," said Emmie, looking at it, then him. "At least

I think that's what Gerald said earlier."

"Well, this is not *at all* going to end in disaster," snorted Broonie.

"We probably just put the time on the timer that we need, open the tap and run. Right?" said Finn.

"Or do we turn the tap and then do the timer?" asked Emmie.

"We should have paid more attention when Gerald explained it all," said Finn.

"*You* should have paid more attention," said Emmie. "I'd just lost Dad."

"I sort of assumed the remote control was going to work," admitted Finn.

"Me too," said Emmie.

They both sighed.

"It *is* going to end in disaster, you understand that, yes?" said Broonie. "It always ends in disaster."

The hubbub and clamour of oncoming Fomorians was getting closer, echoing through the tunnels, warning Finn and Emmie that they needed to get this done quickly.

Finn pulled at the teeth of the timer, setting it at three minutes. "Is that enough time? It had better be."

Timer set, Finn grasped the cog whose teeth connected to the wide tap. It didn't budge at first, and needed him to grunt with effort before it turned. Once. Twice. A third time.

"Do you think that's done it?" he asked.

A great ominous gurgle ran through the ceiling, a *blaub* travelling upwards through the obelisk above as the liquid loosened, prepared.

"Sounds like it," said Emmie as they ran.

Back the way they came.

Past the safety posters.

To the ladder to the surface.

Breath rasping in their throats, hearts pounding.

Finn, one foot still missing a boot that the Hydra had eaten, climbed up awkwardly and put his energy into opening the hatch above in one swift movement so they could get out quickly before the Desiccator fluid flooded the tunnels, and them.

There was a problem.

"It's stuck," he said.

From down the tunnel came a gurgle. A *blaup*. The sound of thousands of gallons of Desiccator fluid about to burst from their container and rush through the tunnels.

"What do you mean it's *stuck?*" asked Emmie.

"I told you," said Broonie, having to shout to be heard over the approaching rattle of Fomorian armour and weapons echoing through the tunnels. "Disaster."

"It won't open," said Finn, straining at the handle.

"It has to open," she said.

"It won't. It's like there's a weight on it."

"But we checked the bin," said Emmie, voice strained. "It was clear."

"Well, it's not now."

Finn abandoned his futile attempt to open the hatch and slid back down the ladder, the metal at his kneecaps rattling along the rungs until he reached the ground and stood in the tunnel, deciding which way to go. The clamour of Legends down the tunnels. An echo growing, encroaching.

Blaurrp went the liquid.

"We've only a couple of minutes," Finn said. "We'll have to take another exit."

"But that could bring us right to the Legends," said Emmie.

"We don't have any choice. Or time," Finn said, and started running, epaulettes bouncing on his shoulders, the metal plates of his armour clanking through the tunnel. Emmie followed and Finn was aware of the lightness of her steps and hush of her fighting suit behind him, in contrast with the growing racket of Legends up ahead.

"When did you become so brave?" Emmie shouted.

"When I had no choice," Finn answered.

The obelisk produced a *blurp* that reverberated through the tunnels. The Legends were still going crazy. Both sounded scarily close.

"Tell me we're nearly there," said Broonie, trying to keep up.

Emmie hurriedly looked at her watch as they crashed through the corridor, reached the corner that led to the next hatch to the street. "We've only got half a minute until this whole place gets shrivelled."

They reached the exit just as the Fomorians reached the end of the corridor ahead of them. Finn couldn't hear anything now but the creatures' hungry clamour.

Emmie went up first this time, her weapon lost at the playground after half of it had been used to desiccate the Hydra. Broonie's size and dexterity meant he could climb the edge of the ladder at the same time. Emmie turned the handle and the hatch moved aside easily. She and Broonie were out of it in no time.

Emmie and Broonie disappeared into the street. As Finn scrambled up the ladder behind them, welcoming street lamps burst into sight.

Fomorians reached the hatchway and, realising Finn

was above, they stopped dead, piling up on each other, their claws clamouring for human flesh, bone, blood.

Finn put his arms on the top of the hatch to haul himself out.

Glaurrbbbbb went the obelisk, loud enough to carry through the snarling of the Legends, to send a shudder through the tunnels.

Then a Fomorian grabbed Finn's leg, warty hands wrapping round his calf. Finn jolted downwards.

Desperately, Finn wrapped an elbow round a rung of the ladder while pointing his Desiccator straight down. The Fomorian let go of his leg and grabbed the weapon's nozzle and pulled it so that it rested on a great dark nostril. Finn fired.

The Legend took the blast full in the face, his dismay frozen in place for the merest of moments. But the bright fizzing blue of the shot also raced back up the barrel that Finn was still gripping. He let go just in time for Fomorian and weapon to implode into a leather-lined, metal-streaked ball and drop on to the heads of those vicious invaders following immediately below it.

From above, Emmie thrust a helping hand down to Finn. At the same time, another Fomorian reached for him, grabbing him by his remaining boot and pulling hard enough that Finn thought his leg might be torn off. Ignoring Emmie's outstretched fingers, Finn gripped the

rung with both hands, and held on as tight as he could.

"Give me your hand, Finn!" Emmie screamed.

He couldn't. He was clinging to the ladder while his leg was in danger of being ripped from its socket by a very angry Fomorian. A Fomorian with a grudge. A Fomorian who had lost his closest companion and soulmate in the course of the benighted life that he led as Gantrua's guard.

"I'm going to crush you up for what you did to Trom!" Cryf shouted, his head wedged into a helmet that appeared too tight ever to be removed again, his teeth chipped tombstones, his skin a moonscape of craters and scars, wounds built up over the years.

"I'll take your soft, skinny leg and I'll use it to clean out my ears."

Cryf pulled on Finn's foot and Finn felt the rung dig into the hinge of his elbow, the burning of muscles being yanked from bone. He thought he cried out in pain, but couldn't be sure.

"Give me your hand," Emmie repeated, her eyes bright with alarm.

He couldn't let go of the ladder or he'd be torn to pieces. Below him, the rest of the Legends were piling in, eager to grab a bit of the human. Any bit.

"Your hand!"

All Finn could hear was growling, snarling, shouting.

Until another sound gradually swelled, louder and louder.

It was the deep but distinct *blaaaaauuuuurrrpppppp* as a flood of Desiccator fluid was released into the tunnels.

bove the tunnels, a particularly grumpy Hogboon
stood in the air, one foot facing towards escape,
the other back towards the hatch. All the
while, his brain argued with itself about what he should do.

He looked back at Emmie reaching in to Finn, listened
to the screams and cries, and pushed at the loose tooth
in his jaw as he heard the voice of his tormenter Cryf
declaring a sentence of death on the human boy.

In the tunnel itself, for all the noise echoing through it
– Legends, Desiccator fluid, the general onrush of disaster –
Finn didn't hear very much. His hearing sort of shut down.
Most of his senses really. As if his mind was protecting him,
pulling down shutters and saying to him that he didn't
need to hear all of this, see any of that.

Except for one part that he couldn't escape. The pain
where his hip met his leg, due to a Fomorian pulling on the
latter with the full intention of separating the two for ever.

Which in turn made him aware of the great pain at his arm as he tried to hang on to the rung of the ladder. So that, he realised, it felt like he was *only* pain, and a Desiccation might come as something of a relief.

Cryf roared at him, an eruption of anger.

Finn felt his reserves of strength shredding. One more yank on his leg would do it.

Cryf pulled.

Something crawled swiftly down Finn's body. *Someone.* He recognised the smell first. It was Broonie. The Hogboon jabbed something at the Fomorian and immediately scrambled away again.

Cryf screamed. A high-pitched and piercing scream, quite out of keeping with his fearsome appearance. He clawed at his eye with one hand, where a fat tooth was embedded deep in his pupil.

Finn felt the Fomorian's grip loosen.

The leg-armour of his fighting suit tore away in the giant's hands, and the boot with it. Cryf fell back into the chamber of clamouring Fomorians.

Simultaneously, a flood of blue Desiccator fluid rushed suddenly through the tunnels. An outpouring of destruction washing through the corridors and desiccating everything in its path. Legends. Posters. Doors. Cryf. Broonie's tooth.

Whatever happened to be in its way.

Finn just managed to swing his leg out of the hatch as liquid splashed towards the ladder. He fell to his hands and knees beside Emmie and Broonie and gasped for breath. They watched the icy-blue fluid rush below them, listening to the sound of mass Desiccations, balls of Legends surfing the wave as it rushed past the manhole they'd popped up through.

"What did you do to him?" Finn asked Broonie.

Broonie curled a corner of his mouth, a tooth popping out and resting on his lip. "I had a loose tooth. I pulled it out and stuck it in his eye."

Finn gaped. "Impressive. Thanks."

"I didn't do it just for *you*," said Broonie, and Finn realised the Hogboon was as close to smiling as he'd seen before. "That deflated wartbag's name was Cryf, and he deserved it. He and I have history."

"And now he's history," said Finn. It was the kind of line his dad would have used, the quip of a real Legend Hunter. He felt pleased with himself.

"Good line," said Emmie.

"He'll have a hard life," Finn said, immediately regretting not quitting while he was ahead. "*Hard*. You know, because he's desiccated."

"I'll let you get away with that," she grinned as the Desiccations continued below. "It sounds like popcorn in the microwave."

"It's like one of those kiddy ball pits," said Finn.

"I don't know what kind of play centre you went to," said Emmie. "The ball pits at ours weren't usually made up of frozen Legends."

Finn didn't say anything. He just shifted his eyes.

"Your dad actually *did* make ball pits out of desiccated Legends, didn't he?" said Emmie, amazed.

"Well…"

In the welcoming cool of the air above ground, they began to laugh with relief and a touch of craziness, and the fact that Finn had no boots at all now, and was missing a leg of his fighting suit too, and instead would have to move on in a pair of socks with left and right written on them. But which were on the wrong feet.

"Only problem is I was keeping that tooth for a special occasion," said Broonie.

They laughed even harder.

They would have kept laughing too if a razor-sharp shard from Gantrua's bow hadn't sliced into the ground between them.

47

"You!" Gantrua shouted as he steadily bore down on them.

Finn and Emmie were up and running away.

"Your time is over," Gantrua growled.

Broonie disappeared over a wall into someone's back garden. They heard him grumble as he climbed and yelp as his hands touched whatever nails and broken metal were supposed to keep Legends out.

Gantrua did not bother going after him. He had eyes only for the two young humans.

Finn and Emmie sprinted down a short alleyway off the street. Finn's feet hurt, protected only by socks from the punishing hardness of the concrete. He trod on pebbles, struggled at kerbs. But he ran as fast as he could regardless, fear urging him on.

They couldn't see Gantrua, but they could hear him, the thud of his steps, the sparking scrape of his

337

sword on the concrete.

"Where are we running to?" Emmie asked.

"I don't know," answered Finn.

"The church?" she said. "Back to the others?"

"No," said Finn. "We can't lead him to the hiding place."

"Where then?"

"Just away. Away is always good."

Gantrua followed, relentless, his shoulders simply demolishing the walls either side of the narrow alley. He appeared from it, his long stride worth four of Finn and Emmie's.

"This is my world now," Gantrua said, remorselessly keeping pace with them, without even needing to run.

They turned on to the promenade, ran along the seafront.

Finn felt the tiredness in his limbs, the fatigue in his brain as he realised they weren't going to be able to outrun Gantrua.

"You stole this world from us," the giant Fomorian bellowed at them. "You put up a wall. You left us to rot."

He tore a bin from the ground, pulling it up with a single hand, and flung it towards Finn. It tumbled through the air, striking the ground only a few centimetres from

Finn's feet. He didn't stop running. His fear wouldn't let him.

"We need to get to the stage," Finn called to Emmie, turning to jump down on to the sand of the beach, its softness a relief to his burning feet. Emmie followed just behind. "We can hide there. Maybe."

They were so close now, prompting Gantrua to stop toying with them and make a move. He broke into a longer stride that shook the ground, rattled the scaffolding on which the stage was built.

"We own this world," he said, drawing his sword from his belt. "We are only taking back what is ours."

Finn and Emmie reached the long curtain draped at the bottom of the stage, as Gantrua came at them with his sword raised. He brought it down with massive force, the blow shaking the structure's foundations.

Finn and Emmie had just managed to duck into the shadowy space under the stage in time, the quivering metal ringing through Finn's ears. Finn scampered round thick metal pipes, further into the darkness beneath. Ahead of them, Gantrua pulled hard on the curtain, tearing a section of it free and allowing his bulky silhouette to fill the space.

Finn and Emmie retreated, but with the edges curtained

off behind them there was no sense of how far in they were, how far they had to go, or which way was out.

They couldn't see Gantrua any more. All they could hear was his sword being run along the scaffolding. It carried through the entire structure, louder and louder in its reverberation, sounding like it came from one place, then another, then everywhere at once.

"What are we going to do?" asked Emmie.

"We need to get out," Finn said, but it was all he could suggest. He had to calm his breathing. There was no help for them here. No devastating move he'd learned for this exact scenario. Finn could just about make out the gleam of Emmie's eyes, and it told him she was almost as afraid as he was.

Gantrua stopped rattling the scaffolding. It turned out the silence was just as frightening.

"Where is he?" Emmie whispered.

Still unseen, Gantrua started to strike the floor of the stage instead. *Clang, clang, clang.*

"If the stage comes down, it'll crush us," said Finn.

"And him," said Emmie. "But us more."

They backed further in, the stage's support structure growing more intricate and dense the deeper in they went. Beneath Finn's socked feet was damp grass and weeds. The darkness was almost total now. Finn felt like he was at the bottom of the ocean, the surface far above him, a crushing weight between them and safety.

Gantrua's voice reverberated through the metal. "Niall Blacktongue talked about you. Year after year. He convinced us you were dangerous. He warned us of a prophecy. He told us you would be there at the end of the world."

The ominous clash of sword on metal hurt their ears.

"He was right," snarled Gantrua, his voice echoing about them. "This is the end of *your* world."

Finn's back touched the curtain, the underside of the stage. He grabbed Emmie's arm, pulled her towards him and, without a word to identify where they were, pushed up the heavy fabric and squirmed out from under the stage.

Gantrua was there to meet them.

He loomed over them, almost as wide as he was tall. The terrible gathering of teeth at his helmet, his eyes burning with frustration, resentment and hate.

"All this trouble," Gantrua said. "For someone not much bigger than a death larva."

"You don't scare m—" started Emmie.

But Gantrua whipped out a hand, grabbed her by the

waist with fingers that could crush cars, lifted her and flung her directly backwards.

Finn watched her fly, hands and legs outstretched uselessly. She hit the grassy sand with a thump a good ten metres away, rolling violently a couple of times until she stopped face down.

Finn jolted towards her, but was stopped by Gantrua slamming his sword in his path.

"You are a disappointment," said the Fomorian. "So flimsy. Mostly bone. No muscle." He sniffed the air. "So much fear."

Finn felt heat flood his face. Surge through his body.

"You hear that sound?" Gantrua asked, taking a step towards him, half his face lit by the street lights from the promenade, the other in the shadow of the stage. "That is the sound of my soldiers at the church. We found the humans. They are wiping them out. Clearing out the infestation."

Finn could see Emmie groaning, hurt, unable to get up. He wanted to go to her, wanted to see if she was OK, wanted to get help. But Gantrua was in his way.

"That is the sound of your war being lost." Gantrua pulled the sword from the earth, rubbed his hand along it and looked at the sand in his hands. The sword was upright, ready to be wielded. Properly. One final slash.

Emmie was hurt.

No one hurts Emmie, thought Finn.

Gantrua snarled, the broken teeth of his own mouth visible beneath the serpent's tooth. "You. Are. Finished."

Finn did the only thing he could at that moment. The only thing instinct would let him do.

He stepped forward. Towards Gantrua.

And he roared.

As Finn let his anger loose – a thunderous, throat-scraping roar that surprised even the mighty Gantrua, ruler of the Infested Side – he heard a rattling sound. He wasn't sure at first if it was his fighting suit. Or his knees knocking together. Or something else. Something bigger. Either way, he did not stop his howl until the very last hint of breath had been expelled from his lungs.

Gantrua let the sword drop just a little, a curious expression on his half-lit, half-hidden face. Finn maybe even detected just a hint of respect.

There was a rattle. Finn knew what that was.

He thought of car alarms going off.

He thought of televisions changing channels.

He thought of soaked hamsters.

He concentrated on the tingling in his body, the one that had preceded his explosions on the Infested Side,

the one he had worked so hard to keep a lid on. This time he let it grow, envelop him, flood him; stopped holding it back, stopped trying to control it.

Then he pushed it out of him in a wave, out of him and towards the stage.

He heard a very slight creak.

Gantrua frowned. "Is that all you have? A loud squeak?"

Finn didn't answer. Took a step back.

Gantrua waited for a moment. "Well, no matter," he said. "Legend Hunter tricks and distractions will not save you now." He stepped forward, raised his sword with an air of finality.

The rattle became an avalanche.

The stage collapsed forward. Completely. As one single, falling mass.

The Fomorian leader saw it at the very last moment, turned his head, shocked, just before it hit him. He hardly had time to even raise a hand in defence as the combination of steel, glass and wiring crushed him, bending and twisting as it hit him and the ground instantaneously.

Finn jumped back as it collapsed, pieces of it flying all around him. He threw his hands over his head to protect himself, but looked through his elbows enough to see the

stage envelop Gantrua. It was followed by towering lights and speakers, crashing down on top of the twisted pile of debris under which the mighty Fomorian already lay.

Finn propped himself up where he had dived on a patch of spiky grass, kicked lumps of metal from where they had rolled on to his legs and looked at the scene. Nothing moved but loose pipes and sparking wires.

"Emmie…" Finn ran to her.

She was sitting, coughing, trying to say something, but winded enough that she couldn't get the words out.

"Take your time," Finn said. "Are you hurt? Is anything broken?"

"Th-th-th…"

"Get your breath back."

She coughed. "That." She coughed again. "Was. Awesome."

Finn sat back on the grass beside her, watching the edge of the stage lurch further, adding new tonnes of weight to those under which Gantrua was squashed.

"You made it collapse," Emmie said. "I saw you. You… rippled."

"I think so," said Finn.

"Do you reckon he's dead?" Emmie asked.

"I hope so. I don't think I could do that again."

"That was some scream," she smiled.

"You're the one who said *wheeee* when taking out a Hydra," Finn said. "Don't think I've forgotten that."

They sat a little longer, both getting their breath back. Then Finn remembered something, jumped to his feet.

"It's almost time," he said.

"For what?" asked Emmie, looking up.

He put his hand down to help her to her feet.

"To rescue your dad," Finn said. "I've figured it out."

She looked like she couldn't decide how serious he was being. "How?"

"Broonie told us how we can get the Trapped back," he said, helping her up. "We have dust in the lockets, right? We have rockets too. The fireworks for the ceremony. All we need to do is get Mr Glad here."

"And how are we going to do that?" Emmie asked.

"They said he'll be able to come back at midnight," said Finn. "That's close, but I have a plan. When the time comes, I'm going to give him what he wants. I'm going to give him *me*."

LIECHTENSTEIN:
SIX HOURS EARLIER

TWO WORLDS — ONE VICTOR

*N*ews of the strange events in Darkmouth was passed swiftly through to the Liechtenstein HQ, dispatched through the communications tubes, so that it scooted around the building, before popping out on to Lucien's desk.

Fwhop.

He opened the canister. Read its contents. Knew what he needed to do.

He marched through the corridors, with the piece of paper held aloft in his right hand. Assistants stood aside, while others stuck their heads out from their offices to see what was going on.

"*Follow me,*" Lucien demanded.

He led them to the canteen, which was busy with those getting in just before the teatime rush. Axel was already there, his hand in a bag of crisps. Lucien strode right to where he sat, placed the report beside him, grabbed a chair and used it as a step to clamber up on to the table.

"Give it to me," Lucien told Axel.

Axel handed him the bag of crisps.

"Not that," Lucien said, just about restraining himself from screaming at his friend. "The report."

"Sorry," said Axel, replacing the crisps with the curled paper.

Lucien stood before a canteen that was now entirely still with anticipation, but for the slow chewing of assistants trying not to make any noise for fear of breaking the silence. Assistants wearing suits in every shade of beige kept arriving through the door. Every single person in the building was gathering there, drawn by Lucien's intensity and the knowledge that a crisis was unfolding in Darkmouth.

He lifted the paper in his hand. His glasses slid down his nose. "Events in Darkmouth have become critical," he said. "The situation is grave. Catastrophe looms. But here we are, carrying dinner trays instead of weapons, hunting snacks rather than Legends—"

"The Council of Twelve would struggle without its mid-morning jam tarts," grumbled Axel, a little hurt.

"—and repeating failed experiment after failed experiment on those pulverised crystals, which a mere twelve-year-old boy was able to use to cross between worlds. To cross between years."

A murmur of acknowledgement carried across the room.

Lucien looked out of the window – which, because of the confused nature of the building, faced out on to another window.

"Both my parents were highly decorated Legend Hunters," he said. "My grandmother was awarded the Order of Certain Death for her heroic defence of our village."

He looked out at the crowd, at faces familiar to him. "You, Matilda," he said, pointing to one pasty-faced woman. "Your grandfather defeated a terrifying Cherufe using only a toothpick and a bookshelf."

"In an active volcano," said Matilda.

Lucien sought out another face. "You, George," he said to a short fellow at the dessert section. "Your family invented the intestinal combustion engine."

"It was a messy business," said George.

"But it worked," Lucien told him, with conviction. "It made your family famous. But us? Me? What are our achievements? A well-stocked canned goods shelf? An efficient laundry service? Look at us. Look at us!"

The assistants glanced at each other, heads down in shame, embarrassed by how their biggest daily battle was over which grey tie to wear to work.

"No longer," said Lucien, and a couple of voices shouted in support. "Darkmouth is in crisis. Darkness has taken hold there. It is time that I, we, stepped in and saved the last Blighted Village from those who wish to destroy it."

More voices, maybe half the room now, shouted in agreement.

"It is time we stepped out of the shadows of our ancestors, and became warriors once again."

The shouts and whoops were loud, constant.

"I will go to Darkmouth. I will bring back glory!"

The canteen erupted in cheers.

"You'll need a packed lunch," said Axel, but he was drowned out by the ovation for Lucien.

All was quiet. More or less. What remained of the stage was a crazy mess of wood and jabbing steel, all slumped at an alarming angle. A couple of surviving, but dark, stage lights were bent at a precarious angle, and the banner stretched between them whipped in the wind, straining against its ropes.

CONGRATULATIONS 'FINN THE DEFIANT' LEGEND HUNTER AT LAST!

Sparking light came from a severed wire, pulled free in the collapse and jolting dangerously on the ground. Beyond that was the flat glow of the town, its street lights occasionally matched by the flare of a Desiccator out there where Hugo, Gerald and the Half-Hunters must have been facing the Fomorians.

"I guess that puts paid to any Completion Ceremony," said Emmie.

"I don't know," Finn said. "All they've wanted is for me to become a Legend Hunter at the earliest opportunity. If I don't do it now, my dad'll be so annoyed. He's supposed to join the Council of Twelve after all of this."

"They're going to need him now. They're going to need eleven of him."

"Poor people," said Finn sadly. "Poor Nils. Cedric. Aurora. That man with the strange sayings. All gone."

"Aurora was awesome," said Emmie.

"I wonder how she got that scar on her face."

"I was scared to ask in case it was something really boring, like she was mowing the lawn."

"I think it was probably a better story than that," decided Finn.

There were further flashes of blue, Desiccators firing.

"Did you ever notice that picture in our hall?" he asked

Emmie. "The one of me, Mam and Dad on holiday?"

"The one where you're in the tent?"

"Yeah. Anyway, that picture was taken in Darkmouth. On the cliffs, before they were… well, you know." He watched the skies. "That's the closest we've ever got to a holiday. And it rained heavily. Just, like, normal, everyday, non-life-threatening heavy rain. So we didn't even stay that long. Mam and Dad packed up the tent, we headed home and I ended up camping in the library instead."

"That was your holiday?" said Emmie.

"Yep. We sent a postcard and everything. To ourselves. It arrived two days later, and my mam had written on it, 'Having a great time in Darkmouth!' Except the picture on the front was of a kitten playing with a ball of wool because it wasn't a postcard at all, but a birthday card that had been torn in half. Shops in Darkmouth don't have postcards. Darkmouth doesn't have tourists."

"Until this week," Emmie said.

"I've never had a holiday. Ever. Never been anywhere but here. Unless you count the Infested Side, which wasn't much of a holiday."

"No swimming pools," said Emmie.

"Maybe I'm just meant to stay in Darkmouth. Like my

dad. Like all those people in the portraits."

"I like it here," said Emmie. "This was my holiday. Me and my dad's…" The words got caught in her throat.

Finn picked up a couple of pebbles and knocked them together. He checked his watch. It was almost time for Mr Glad and the Trapped to reappear. If they were going to reappear, that is, now that they had opened the gateway for Gantrua and his army. Finn thought Mr Glad would be back, though. Because the traitor had unfinished business: revenge on Finn, and his family, for trapping him.

Weirdly, he found that he *hoped* Mr Glad would be back, otherwise Steve was going to be lost for ever.

This had better work, he thought.

The breeze ran through his hair, and he felt exposed without his helmet. There were further flashes out in the town.

"I'm hoping those lights and bangs are a good thing, not bad," he said to Emmie.

"There weren't many Legends out of the tunnels," said Emmie reassuringly. "They'll be OK. Anyway, your dad won't give up. I don't know about the other Half-Hunters. Hopefully, they haven't just run away."

"Well, I'd know how they felt."

"You haven't run away this time," said Emmie. "And, you know, thanks for that. I kind of lost it back there for a while after my dad was taken."

"I owed you. All this is my fault," said Finn, running the pebbles through his fingers, looking up to see if there was any action in the sky yet.

"You can't say that," said Emmie. She meant it.

"It's true," insisted Finn. "Mr Glad wouldn't have come back and taken your dad if I hadn't trapped him in the first place."

"I was there when Mr Glad was pushed into a gateway in your library," said Emmie. "We didn't know what it would do. We saw him kind of burst or whatever. He looked pretty much dead to me."

"He came back," said Finn. "The only good thing about that is that we know your dad can too."

In the sky above them, a glimmering of light. There and gone before Finn could even catch exactly where it had appeared from.

They were coming.

Finn didn't want to admit how nervous he was, but couldn't avoid being reminded anyway. The quivering epaulettes on his shoulders gave him away. He hated those epaulettes, cursed the fact that he'd ever agreed to include the stupid things. The whole uniform was intended to be ceremonial, a suit for showing not fighting in. He pulled an epaulette free, threw it to the ground. Tore the other one off, discarded it too.

"They look so stupid," he said. Then he felt a bit guilty about littering, so picked them both up and put them in his pocket.

Another light in the sky. Silent lightning, just as earlier when the Trapped had appeared in the Black Hills.

Finn and Emmie stood, alert now.

The wind pushed a slab of flooring from the pile of the stage.

Finn looked at his watch. "They should be able to appear about now. You hide. I have to face Mr Glad on my own."

"That's just not right," insisted Emmie. "I want to wait with you. I'm not scared."

"I *know*," said Finn. "But we have a plan. And the first part of it relies on Mr Glad seeing me alone. As bait. And the second part relies on you being over there at the fireworks."

Away from the stage, out of sight in the dark, were half a dozen grids of tubes facing skywards, each filled with rockets of various sizes and shapes. A complex network of wires ran to one fat wire and a launch box.

More importantly, the fireworks now carried something very precious. Small packets of the dust, left over from when Finn handed them out to the Half-Hunters. He'd held on to them, and was glad he'd done so.

Emmie smiled. "It should work."

"It should."

"It's totally crazy, though."

"Yes."

She nodded. "OK, let's do it. But are you sure? You can still back out of this."

"I can't," said Finn as light rolled through the unseen clouds above. "I won't. Not now."

He stepped towards the crumpled stage. Emmie turned away.

"Keep out of sight," he told her.

"OK," she said. "But if I have to save you I will. It seems to be all I do." She smiled broadly, cheekily, and then ran off, away from the stage.

Finn watched her go.

He waited.

Clouds built in the sky. Crackled with energy.

Then, behind him, a word on the breeze.

Maybe. He couldn't be sure.

He looked up at the sky, a pink flutter of light. No thunder, but another word on the breeze. But what made Finn's hair prickle was that the word seemed pretty clear to him.

"Boy."

He spun, but saw nothing except for the roll of light in the sky above, the silent approach of a storm.

Finn had done an ever-expanding number of crazy things in his life. Most of them, he had to admit, had happened by accident rather than design. Or because of incompetence. Or because someone made him do them. Or because he had simply done them without thinking. Or some kind of mix of all those things. But this was a foolishness he was entering into of his own free will.

This was his idea. This was his increasingly ill-thought-out idea.

He was alone, except for the nearby presence of a crushed Fomorian, buried underneath a stage that jittered precariously in the breeze. And he hadn't even taken into account the prophecy he'd hoped had been left behind on the Infested Side, but, the more he thought about it, didn't exactly come with an expiry date. All he knew was that Niall Blacktongue had claimed to see him at some point in a fiery cataclysm that ripped the sky apart.

Tonight was probably as good a time as any for such an occasion.

"*Boy.*"

He looked around again, twitching with nerves, realising he had dug a fairly decent hole into the ground with his right foot even without its boot on. He was a mess. An already dented fighting suit missing a leg. A big toe sticking out in the breeze.

Something caught the edge of his vision. A star where there had been none, drifting out of place. Just one, almost imperceptible at first, but Finn could see it begin to drop slowly. And he felt a shiver run through him, his teeth chattering so much that he had to quieten them with a palm under his jaw.

The light brightened, grew, got closer. And Finn felt the dread build within him as it did.

He had wanted Mr Glad to leak into Darkmouth. Right at this spot. And he had come, pouring into reality in the dead air above the collapsed stage.

Finn took a moment to wonder if he should have gone through with this. If he was really that desperate to prove himself, to act the hero. He glanced over at a low nearby wall where he had placed his locket containing the dust that was meant to protect him. He had left it there because he knew the only way to attract Mr Glad was to offer himself as defenceless bait. It had seemed very clever when he first thought of it.

It was not very clever at all, he realised.

It was a really dangerous, stupid, idiotic thing to have done.

It was time to back out.

It was too late.

"Boy."

Mr Glad poured like melting tar into the world.

50

The first thing Finn did when Mr Glad appeared was to dash back, almost falling, so that he could grab the locket from where he'd placed it. He'd been defenceless as bait, but now he needed to hold it out to ward off the phantom presence.

Mr Glad watched curiously. Finn didn't sense him flinch, didn't get any indication that Mr Glad saw him as much of a threat. Then again it was hard to get a full idea because of the way the Trapped man's skin crawled. Up his face. Across his neck. A queasy rippling of a body that existed between spaces.

"Why so disgusted?" said Mr Glad. His voice seemed to come from some other place, reverberated through the air, a thrum across the surface of existence. Finn could feel it in his kidneys. "You made me like this. You should be proud. Are you proud?"

Mr Glad moved forward, and Finn did all he could to

stand his ground, locket held out in front as a shield.

"You pushed me into the jaws of a gateway and locked me between worlds," said Mr Glad. "But something else happened. Every time you opened a gateway after that, I was torn back into this world, and then into their world, put back together a thousand times, through pain a hundred thousand times greater than you can possibly imagine."

Finn took a step back, locket still held out in front of him. He found himself backed up against the stage, had to push himself away from it.

"I have travelled through the skin of the worlds," said Mr Glad. "I have seen its veins. Its gristle. I have *been* all those things."

"It doesn't have to be like this," Finn said.

"And what have I learned?" continued Mr Glad, ignoring him. "That time is a boiling river, sucking you under, throwing you to the surface every now and then. But I have seen into two worlds. I have seen that you are getting older, but no wiser. That you are not *special*. That you have no destiny beyond the certainty of disappointment and defeat."

"I know Gantrua promised to bring you back, to make you human again," Finn told him, backing away round the edge of the crumpled stage. "We could do it too. I know what the dust does."

"I've learned I can control those who I trap. Their thoughts are my thoughts. My movements are their movements."

Finn thought of the voices he had heard in that brief moment when he too was almost trapped. Recalled the feeling of giving in, of falling under the control of Mr Glad. "I can use the dust to bring you back. I know it draws you from between the worlds and that enough of it can bring you back completely, just like you were before," he said. "I can help you. You don't have to be... this way."

Mr Glad stopped moving. It was as if he was letting that idea percolate, run through the roughly formed neurons of his mind. "The dust could give me shape again," he said, and Finn felt a glimmer of hope. Mr Glad was contemplating this idea.

"It could restore your body," said Finn. "Make you normal again. A Hogboon told me. Broonie. He learned about it on the Infested Side. He said the Legends control you and they promised you life. But they're lying – they'll never do it. They only want to keep you as a weapon, keep you Trapped for ever."

Mr Glad looked at Finn, what passed for a head cocked to one side, eyes burning. But Finn sensed the humanity in there, the conflict, the sadness within.

"You will use the dust to bring me back?" asked Mr Glad.

"For good." Finn sensed this was working, that he was softening Mr Glad.

"After all I've done…?"

"It's not too late," Finn assured him. "I'll be the Legend Hunter here. I'll make sure you're OK."

Finn was sure he could see the turmoil in Mr Glad, not just in the shifting of his body, but in his thoughts.

Mr Glad surveyed the scene, as if taking in the view of Darkmouth. The place that was once his home. That could be his home again. "This town has had so many strong Legend Hunters, for generations. I know now that with you as this town's Legend Hunter…" he looked deep into Finn's soul, a scowl floating to the top of his writhing mouth, "…Darkmouth will *die*."

He moved towards Finn again. Finn stumbled back, knowing that his gambit had failed. He held the locket out in front of him again, a defence that suddenly seemed far weaker than it had before. He knew he was failing. The other Trapped were still missing. Steve was still missing. But Mr Glad was still here. And he was steadily pushing Finn back into a corner.

"You see, boy," boomed Mr Glad, flowing towards him, "you are so naive. You have no idea of what I am now. No idea what power I have gained. No idea how much stronger the Legends have made me. They think they control me. Yet every time I have been torn into this world, or *that* world..." He pushed out his right arm as if pointing, but his hand was missing behind the curtain of the air, perhaps in the Infested Side. "...I have grown stronger. Gantrua had no idea what he was creating. You think I am trapped here? You think *they* are deceiving *me*? Wrong. I am in control of them. I am more powerful than I have ever been. And there is so much more to come."

Finn waved the locket at him.

"Do you really think that can protect you?" Mr Glad asked him.

"Yes," said Finn, locket dangling from the end of the chain. "Because otherwise you would have killed me already."

Mr Glad laughed, a hideous sound. "Maybe you are cleverer than you look. Tell me, boy, what do you plan to do? You must know that one day you will forget that trinket, and I will be there. Waiting."

"That's why I want to make a deal with you," said Finn. His heart was a jackhammer in his chest.

Mr Glad didn't laugh. No, it was nothing so straightforward as an evil cackle, or anything that Finn might have understood. The response was deeper, a derisory grunt that sent a minor quake through the air, shook his fighting suit.

"What could you possibly offer?" asked Mr Glad, floating still, every part of him in constant motion.

"Me," answered Finn. Once again, his brain tried to shut down and replace all this bravery with more normal thoughts about soft furry animals, his mammy and just getting the hell out of there. "I'll put the locket away, let you take me. On certain conditions."

Electricity sparked on the ground beside the collapsed stage, making it even harder to focus on the shifting form of Mr Glad as he hovered above the rubble and debris. He seemed closer all of a sudden, as if he had leaked forward. Finn took a step back, his cold feet uncertain on the rough ground.

"The dust in the locket can be for Steve," Finn said. "Just let me use it on him. Bring him back and I'll use it to save him, bring him into this world again, and then you can have me. I'll take his place."

His brain had shut everything down so that his vision was limited, his thinking stifled, his entire energy diverted into preventing himself just collapsing, jabbering with fear. And he was trying to make a deal with a demon.

"*You* trapped me, but now you want to strike a bargain." Mr Glad's words trembled through the ether. Finn gripped harder on the chain, drew the locket closer through his fingers.

"Y-yes," he said.

Finn stood back again. He had a sense that Mr Glad was more powerful now than he had been when they met before, fuelled perhaps by anger, or revenge, or dust, or something Finn had yet to even contemplate. He felt so out of his depth.

"I can see you have no idea if the dust will work," sneered Mr Glad. "It may return your friend Steve, or maybe just parts of him. It may destroy him. But you are willing to take that chance, because of your noble sacrifice. Right?"

Finn blinked. "Erm…"

"I thought as much. So I have a better deal for you."

Mr Glad raised a hand. Three stars appeared above, a flare of light flickering round each of them. "You drop the locket and come with me. Or I will manipulate one of *them* so that they open a gateway in you."

In the sky above them came the flickering of lightning in a sky empty of cloud. A single star floated down from its moorings in the night sky. Mr Glad had a black, charred hand raised towards it, summoning it. As it neared the ground, it very slowly began to find form. Nose. Eyes. A mouth gasping for mercy.

Kenzo.

Above, the remaining two lights grew into faces stretched in agony, bodies being sculpted out of sheer anguish.

Douglas.

Steve.

The Trapped.

51

Kenzo was closest to Finn, and getting closer, though Finn could see he was acting very differently from Mr Glad. He was being pushed towards him, a puppet under Mr Glad's control. It was hard to know how much of the old Kenzo was still there, but this version of him was a tormented, controlled phantom. Coming straight for Finn.

Kenzo flowed towards Finn, reaching out to open a gateway in him.

Finn realised he was clutching the locket at his chest now, tight against the fighting suit's painting of a Minotaur's gaping jaws. His knuckles were white from gripping so tightly. His mouth was dry. His vision was filled with the howling visions of the Trapped, led by an entity so molten it was hard to focus properly on him. And all he could hear were the bells ringing out a simple rhythm.

"I…" he said.

Mr Glad had moved closer, the Trapped now forming a crescent above Finn, their howling silent but visceral.

Church bells rang out.

Finn swallowed hard, found clarity in his mind. "I've just remembered something," he said. Mr Glad's face showed the tiniest quiver of curiosity. Kenzo paused, frozen in torment.

"The bells," said Finn. "It means it's after midnight. It's my birthday. And, if it's my birthday, then there have to be fireworks. RIGHT, EMMIE?!"

That was the moment. They had a secret plan, a brilliant one worked out quickly between the two of them in the minutes before Mr Glad appeared. A truly brilliant plan.

Which wasn't actually happening right now.

"ISN'T THAT RIGHT, EMMIE?" Finn shouted, louder, a squeak of desperation in his voice as he did his best not to be intimidated by the hovering phantom of a half-dead man hellbent on revenge.

But still nothing happened.

Out there, hidden away in the dark, Emmie was at the control box of the fireworks, smacking a button while staring in horror at the rockets strapped with packets of dust. They were supposed to have risen majestically in the air, to burst and spray dust over Mr Glad and the others, to return the Trapped, to restore Mr Glad to his human form and take away his powers, to end this madness.

But they had failed to launch.

Mr Glad smiled venomously, floating above the ruined stage. At least, Finn *thought* it was a smile. It was hard to tell through a shifting mass of molten features.

But it was enough to make Finn step back instinctively, scramble up on to the ruins of the stage, where he put a foot on a loose piece of scaffolding, and fell on to a pile of rubble.

The locket spilled from his grasp, slipping away through the cracks.

Finn looked at Mr Glad. Who was definitely smiling now.

52

In the dark bowels of the crumpled stage, beneath toppled pylons, heavy steel, right at the bottom where no human could survive, someone stirred.

It was no human.

Gantrua's face was pressed into the trampled grass and soft earth of the Promised Side. It smelled extraordinary to him. This dirt contained such life. The sound of microscopic creatures mulching the soil filled his cavernous ears. The scent filled his equally cavernous nostrils.

He assessed the pain in his bones, allowed the torture in his head to build, urged it to turn into rage. Rage gave him strength. Strength was what he needed right now.

Something dropped against the back of his skull, *tinked* against his helmet and landed by his hand. He pawed it closer, held it in his palm, a small object on a chain. It smelled of human. It smelled of that human boy.

Gantrua found his rage.

He pressed at the ground, pushed up at his back, tried to feel movement in this collapsed structure. He felt it give a little at his right shoulder. Just enough for him to gain a bit more room, to plant a foot a little deeper into the ground, to push again.

Another nudge, more give, the other leg finding space.

One more effort. One more summoning of his anger and he would be free.

The debris shook as he threw the great weight from his shoulder, bursting through into the clear air.

53

It was not often Finn would have welcomed the sudden appearance of a furious Fomorian conqueror. But this was turning into a night of firsts.

Gantrua emerged out of the debris between him and the oncoming Mr Glad, and immediately thrust his sword out so that its tip rested on Finn's nose.

But Mr Glad was still moving and, when he reached Gantrua, he touched the Fomorian's back.

Gantrua dropped the sword, as the heat of the tiny gateway Mr Glad was making bored into him. He howled in agony.

Seemingly operating on pure instinct, Gantrua turned and thrust the locket into Mr Glad.

Mr Glad recoiled, a splash through his liquid form reacting to the dust in the locket. Behind him, for an instant, Steve, Kenzo and Douglas shifted in form too.

Hand still plunged into the writhing Mr Glad, Gantrua

lifted his sword again. He held it once more to Finn's neck.

The cold dark steel of the sword remained steady on Finn's skin, stretching away from him until it met with the hilt in the grasp of the furious Fomorian. Finn looked along its length, trying not to move, not to trigger even the slightest push. That would be enough to end it all. To end him.

But Gantrua did not strike. Not yet. Instead, he examined Finn, assessed him. Finn stared back, at eyes boring into his mind. He couldn't hold his glare so averted it to the grille with its now shattered serpent's tooth. All those other teeth and fangs there too. One looked human. He was not to know it had once belonged to his grandfather, Niall Blacktongue, many, many years ago.

Finn wanted to find that anger within him, that energy he had drawn on to topple the stage. To use whatever power he had against Gantrua. But when he searched for it he found only fear.

Through the spectral shimmer of Mr Glad's body, Finn saw his locket dangling from Gantrua's fist.

With the locket still inside him, Mr Glad was spasming, seemingly on the edge of some final change. To return. Or to rupture. In the sky, Steve's face buckled, distorted.

It was the same with Kenzo and Douglas. Their pain filling the night.

"I never trust humans," sighed Gantrua. "Even the half-dead ones. You are only useful dead."

There was a rumble at the remnants of the stage. A judder. Finn and Gantrua each looked to its source.

Emmie had her hands on a long piece of metal propping up a corner of the stage. She yanked it free.

The debris jolted, Gantrua briefly lost his footing, dropping to one knee as the pile slumped beneath him. This released his hand from Mr Glad's chest, allowing him to surge away. Finn took his chance to escape. He rolled back, then crawled away over the wreckage, sharp steel sticking into his knees and hands.

Gantrua steadied himself and followed, feet mashing through steel and wood. He kicked up detritus that landed loudly and dangerously close to Finn's head.

Finn reached the grass, stumbled. Gantrua kicked a pipe at his feet. He hit the ground on his shoulder, but spun, got up, kept going round the edge of the stage. A large slab of wooden flooring thudded in front of him, sticking upright in the ground, forcing him to a halt.

Gantrua followed it, great strides eating up the ground

and reaching Finn where he was backed against the obstacle.

Gantrua held his fist steady, and his sword straight at Finn's nose. Finn felt like he was being swallowed by the darkness of the Legend's shadow, which grew larger as the grotesque broken wings rose unfolded on his back. They were lit by the strobing of the snapped, sparking wire.

Finn had no defence. No weapon. He had a penknife and a torch; he had a compass. He had a belt with a ridiculous buckle on it. None of it was much use right now.

Gantrua raised his sword to strike.

54

A voice interrupted. An already familiar one, laced with the usual layers of disappointment. "Is this the best the Infested Side can send here these days?" asked Gerald the Disappointed as he appeared on the beach, slightly out of breath.

Gantrua hesitated.

Finn grabbed a stake from the ground, a splintered length of wood hardly enough to even graze this formidable Legend. But he had to try. He stabbed forward and struck Gantrua hard on the side. The Fomorian's wings sprang open. Finn backed away quickly.

"Was that intended to hurt me?" asked Gantrua and started to follow. Then he grunted in irritation. He couldn't move. His wings had wedged him into the broken pieces of stage around him.

"Finn!" shouted Hugo, running up behind Gerald, catching something from him and, while running,

throwing a small egg-shaped object in Finn's direction.

Finn caught it one-handed.

Gantrua was using his blade to cut away at the straps attaching the wings to his torso. Finn jumped in, shoved the egg on to the broken serpent's tooth on Gantrua's grille and retreated immediately.

The egg leaked. Burst. Purple plasma splashed all over the Fomorian.

Deep in the helmet, Gantrua's eyes widened with hatred. Crackling flumes of plasma ran over him, through him. Teeth cracked and burst on his grille. His wings shattered as if glass.

Schlloop.

An instant later, the mighty Gantrua was roughly the size and shape of a biscuit tin.

Gerald and Hugo reached Finn.

"Why can't you be more like Finn, Hugo?" asked Gerald. "That was superb work from the boy."

"Do you have to ruin even our last moments together?" responded Hugo.

"How old are you again?" Gerald asked, still more interested in Finn. "Fourteen, fifteen? That's impressive stuff."

"Mr Glad's coming back!" Emmie shouted.

Mr Glad had recovered even as the gallery of the Trapped remained in agony around him. He appeared renewed, re-energised, ready again to strike.

"What now?" he asked in his spectral voice. "You have lost Steve and the others. You will never get them back."

Under his control, the Trapped began to move in, to converge on Finn, Emmie, Gerald and Hugo.

"Desiccate them!" Finn said.

"We used up the ammo fighting off the Fomorians at the church," said Hugo as they backed away.

"Hugo used his last shot to take out three in one go," said Gerald. "I'd have got four, of course, but it was still impressive."

Loose electricity fizzed and hissed behind them as they edged back from the phantoms flowing towards them – a cable that had been split in two so that each end thrashed, spitting sparks.

"*Stop*," said Gerald. "We'll be electrocuted."

They were cornered.

"The dust will not protect you," Mr Glad said, remaining where he was as Douglas, Kenzo and Steve separated to surround those on the ground. "Nothing will protect you."

The electricity sparked, the snapped cable cutting

them off, hemming them into a circle of descending Trapped.

"The wire," said Finn, an idea hitting him hard.

"We'll have to jump it," said Hugo.

"No, it can *save* us," said Finn. "The split wire is the reason why the fireworks won't ignite. Emmie strapped dust to the rockets, but they wouldn't fire."

"Of course," said Emmie. "The switch was hooked up to the wire."

"So all we have to do is reconnect it," said Finn.

"*All* we have to do?" said Hugo, looking at the two sparking ends of the cable whipping on the ground, trailing electric fire.

"Just trust us," said Finn and started to bolt for the wire, but Gerald reacted quicker, grabbing him and shoving him out of the way.

"I trust you," he said, "but this is a job for a dead man."

The Trapped were converging on them, fast, zombified spectres. Kenzo flowed towards Finn. Douglas towards Hugo. Steve's spectral hand reached out to grab Emmie.

Each was on a collision course with destruction.

Only Gerald was free. He threw himself at the loose electric cable, and turned on to his back as he grabbed either end and slammed them together. He held on even as the electricity shot through him, fixed in a union of sparks and lethal power, until he could hold on no longer and was shot violently away, rolling on to his front.

The Trapped stopped.

Above them all, Mr Glad poured through the back of his head to see what had shot into the sky.

A streak of light rose into the night. Then: *crack*. There was a green sparkle of a flowering firework. Another followed.

Crack.

Two more. This time a boom shook the air. The sky began to fill with fireworks. A blossoming display of colour and noise and sparkles and, most importantly, dust, drifting down, sparkling red in the light.

Kenzo had got so close that Finn would have been able to smell his breath, if he had been breathing in the first place.

He was certainly close enough that Finn saw the change immediately. The hardening in his face. The anguish taking hold, clear and painful. In the continuing firework display, the dust tied to the rockets had blown through the sky and was now drifting all across the Trapped. The fabric of the air about them pinched and twisted. To Finn it was like they were being hauled into the world, pulled from where they had been stuck.

"Dad!" Emmie shouted. Finn turned to see Steve, his mouth widening, and widening, and widening yet more until it enveloped the face, such as it was. He was being turned inside out, the rest of him being pushed up and through his mouth, pouring forward until…

Steve was there.

Collapsed on his hands and knees on the grass beside Emmie.

The same was happening to Kenzo, his mouth stretching in the most grotesque, repulsive way as he solidified. Finn rolled away as Kenzo dropped to the ground, leaving the dissipated remains of his own phantom.

Douglas was last, so that he too was left exhausted and gasping on the grass. Hugo stood over him, cautious, hands raised in anticipation of trouble. But none came.

"What's happening to Mr Glad?" Finn asked, and Hugo and Emmie turned their attentions skywards. Where the others were turned inside out, Mr Glad was spreading, growing as he fought the dust that fell in a curtain around them. He flowed across the sky in the storm of the fireworks, like oil thinning on water.

The last firework launched upwards, a blur of bright light exploding into a golden palm tree that cut through the smudge of the shimmering veil of red dust.

It was followed immediately by a thunderous boom.

The dust settled, a scarlet snowfall. And when it was finally done, and the curtain had fallen, Finn searched for one person alone.

"He's gone," said Finn. "Mr Glad is gone."

Steve was on his hands and knees, gasping for air.

Emmie was hugging him round the waist, laughing through tears. Then she started pounding him in the side. "Don't be so stupid again!" she ordered him. "Don't scare me like that."

Hand on his head, he wobbled to his feet while Emmie tried to support him. "The strangest thing…" he said, then patted himself down and appeared relieved to find his legs there. Then his face. Then the hands themselves. "Just the strangest thing."

Kenzo stayed down, mumbling one word only. "Nibbles…"

Meanwhile, Douglas sat on the grass, looking around. "Did a' miss anythin'?"

"He's gone, Dad," Finn repeated, finding his father in the settling dust. "Mr Glad is gone. Or not here. He should be here too. Why?"

But Hugo didn't seem to hear him, and as Finn got through the cloud he saw why. His father was leaning over Gerald, who was lying on the ground looking broken and blackened and barely alive.

"Stay awake," Hugo was telling him. "Stay with us, come on."

Gerald mouthed something through a cracked mouth.

"Save your strength," Hugo said to him. But Gerald

just about summoned the energy to beckon Finn towards him, urging him closer. Finn leaned in, his dad close too.

Gerald gripped Finn's arm with surprising strength and fixed him with eyes that were burning their last.

"You… brought them back."

"It's OK," Hugo said to him gently. "Save your strength."

"It's what the dust does," Finn told him, Gerald's grip digging into his wrist. "We figured it out."

Gerald's look of disappointment, which had seemed so firmly frozen on to his face, melted away for the first time. His face was softer than Finn realised. Kindly almost.

"You… did well," said Gerald. He went quiet, his head lolling back, his grip releasing.

Hugo and Finn stayed by him in silence.

Gerald spluttered again. "Something… I…" he said, struggling to get the words out.

"Yes?" said Hugo, reassuring him, calming him.

"…always… wanted…"

Gerald coughed again, dark flecks jumping from his throat, coating his lips. His eyes darted from Finn to Hugo, back again. The urgency of a dying man's last words. His last will and testament. Finn felt that grip dig into his arm, even through the fighting suit.

"Build a statue…" he pulled Finn so close he could smell the burning of his skin, "…of… me."

Gerald flopped back, his final words carried on his last breath. "Big statue…"

And, with that, he was dead. This time, there was no coming back.

56

Hugo placed Gerald's head gently on the ground. "*Unbelievable,*" he said, letting out a semi-stunned laugh. "Actually, come to think of it, it's not unbelievable at all. It's exactly what I should have expected of him. Finn, if I'm like that on my deathbed, and even if that deathbed has been shot out of a cannon or something, just tell me to zip it."

Finn stood over the lifeless Gerald, tendrils of smoke still rising from his electrocuted fighting suit. Hugo rose too and squared up to Finn, placing his hands on either shoulder. "For someone who never wanted any of this," he said, "you've become a magnet for trouble."

He squeezed Finn's shoulders and it felt to Finn like his collarbone might pop with the strength of it. But it was a squeeze of appreciation and respect and relief, and a heap of other things.

There was such a creak and groan from the collapsed

stage, it felt like a settling butterfly could tip the rest of it over. Beyond the buildings was the glow of a couple of fires in Darkmouth. The aftermath of battle.

"Happy birthday, Finn," Hugo remembered.

"Yeah," said Finn. "Suppose."

He looked around. At the devastation. At the death. At Emmie with her father. At Kenzo and Douglas back from their half-death. At the reddened sky. At Darkmouth. A thought occurred to him. And he spoke before he had a chance to push it away.

"Is it too late?" he asked his father.

"Too late for what?" Hugo replied.

"For a Completion Ceremony. Or just to be made Complete. Maybe not even a ceremony. Just something that gets it done."

"Really?" Hugo asked.

"You sure you want to do that?" asked Emmie, overhearing. This was not what anyone would have expected from Finn. It wasn't what Finn would have expected from himself a few weeks ago. Or even a few hours ago.

"Yeah," said Finn. He meant it. Right now anyway.

He felt so pummelled and weary from everything that had happened, he didn't have the energy to fight this realisation. He had come so close to losing Darkmouth, to losing everything, to earning nothing for those journeys to the Infested Side. He had faced up to so much he never wanted to have to face. He had survived so much he never thought he could. And, besides, he had been through all this with his father. If he didn't do this now, they would both lose a great deal.

"I suppose we don't need a stage…" said Hugo, thoughtful. "We could do it here tonight," he said, growing more enthusiastic. "Maybe in the morning at the latest."

"OK," said Finn.

"You don't need to worry about the state of your fighting suit." Hugo was almost giddy now.

"But he'll have to get new boots," said Emmie.

"Right. Boots," said Finn, wiggling his toes.

The last of the dust settled. They heard a commotion arriving from Darkmouth's streets. Pouring from alleyways, they could see figures taking shape. Finn began to pick them out. Clara. Estravon. Assistants. Most of the population of Darkmouth too, it seemed.

"Thankfully, Stumm survived the battle, so, as long as we have a member of the Council of Twelve present, it'll be official," said Hugo.

"Great," said Finn, not sure if it was actually great, but ready to see it through anyway.

At the head of the approaching crowd was someone Finn didn't recognise. He was an assistant perhaps, but his suit was cleaner than anyone else's, as if he had just stepped into the town. He was a man with very large glasses that he appeared to have difficulty keeping on his very small nose.

He was the first to arrive.

"Hello, Hugo," he said. "My name is Lucien. We should talk."

"Q uick," Lucien said, motioning to a couple of the assistants. "Give those people medical help."

He hovered over Gerald. "He died gloriously? There is no need to answer that. Of course he did. We must do something to remember him. A statue perhaps."

"Who are you?" Hugo asked him.

"I have been tracking the events at Darkmouth for some time," said Lucien as Gerald's body was covered respectfully. "Investigating you, reporting on you—"

"Did you just get here?" Finn asked.

"—and *assessing* you," Lucien concluded, polite but determined not to be interrupted. "How is everyone over there?" he said to those who'd been Trapped. Steve was waving away the medical attention. Emmie was still with him, but looked uncertain as to what was happening. "Not good, I'm sure. You've all been through a lot. There

will need to be some kind of compensation. Medals or something. Everyone likes medals."

Lucien glanced behind at Estravon, who made a note. It was the first time that Finn realised Estravon had yet to say anything at all, to even make an observation or quote a rule.

"We stopped him," said Finn, stepping forward. "We stopped Mr Glad. The Fomorian is there, in the box. Well, he *is* the box. And we got the Trapped back. Except for Mr Glad."

"Except Mr Glad," Lucien echoed. It was not a question, but a statement. As if confirming something. That struck Finn as odd and worrying.

Hugo hadn't said anything either. No one else had. It was as if they were trying to work out just what was going on.

"You're also forgetting the Twelve," Lucien said, and bowed his head momentarily. "Apart from our esteemed Stumm the Eleventh, they have been taken from us. I suggested they take Stumm away for a rest. The shock has left him quite tired."

"Sorry," said Finn, "I didn't mean to…"

Clara arrived with a couple of dozen townspeople to see what the fuss was about. She pushed through the crowd, running through the dust to get straight to

Finn. "This is getting ridiculous," she said, checking him over. "This is getting out of control. This *has to stop*, Hugo. He's too young for this."

"Technically, he's exactly the right age now," said Hugo.

"I'm fine, Mam," Finn said, unhappy at being shown up like this. "I'm fine. We sorted it."

"You sorted it?" Clara responded, looking at the catastrophe surrounding them. "I'm pretty sure it wasn't as straightforward as that."

"Listen to your mother, Finn," said Lucien. "Her instincts are correct."

"You're from the Liechtenstein HQ, right?" Hugo guessed.

"Yes, as it happens," said Lucien, and smiled. "You probably think we're a little soft-edged? Too many biscuits and breaks. Well, perhaps. But I can assure you, while my main weapon has been my desk, trust me when I say it gives me power greater than anyone else's here."

Lucien's face straightened at that, the smile put away like it had been only used as a prop. To Finn, this was all building up to something. He could almost hear it, like a distant onrushing train. He felt a little like he was tied to the tracks.

"What happened to the Twelve?" asked Steve.

"Desiccated at the battle on that hill, most of them," Lucien informed him. "Smothered by a Desiccation bomb. Nine Council members. One big mess. Quite impossible to reanimate them, of course, even briefly." He was trying to make his voice sound sad, Finn thought, but his eyes didn't look sad at all.

"A hill..." said Steve, searching for the memory. "The battle..."

"Quite a glorious end, at least it would seem," said Lucien. "You were there, though, I believe. In a manner of speaking. Can you remember much?"

Steve shook his head.

"Why are you here?" Hugo asked Lucien.

"For the Completion Ceremony," Lucien explained. "Quite a moment in our history. I was concerned I would miss it."

"It's not happening *now* surely," Clara exclaimed. That was met by a silence from Finn and Hugo that translated as only one thing. "Oh, come on. You're not really thinking of going through with it?"

"We need to," Hugo told her, a little sheepishly.

"I want to," said Finn. "If it doesn't happen now, it'll be another year at least."

"It's true," said Lucien. "What rule is that, Estravon?"

Estravon jerked forward. "Section 6b of the Protocols Tradition, governing the exact age at which—"

"You see," said Lucien, cutting him off. "Anyway, I would have given you warning of my arrival, but you were a little distracted, Hugo. What with the Completion, the disappearing Half-Hunters, the..." he paused, "...the *everything*. We felt it best to conduct our work quietly. Especially given the sensitivity of my investigation. And its conclusions."

The Half-Hunters were watchful. Estravon remained almost sheepish. The locals who had gathered seemed afraid to make so much as a whimper in case someone shooed them away. They hemmed in Finn, made him feel almost claustrophobic.

"What conclusions?" Finn asked, not sure he wanted the answer.

"Excuse me?" said Lucien.

"You said you'd come to conclusions, but you haven't told us what they are."

"Just get to the point," said Hugo. "We've a Completion to get on with."

"No, Hugo," complained Clara.

"We're all here," said Hugo, waving his hand around. "The invasion is dealt with. We'll get some kind of stage

401

together from the scraps. There's no need for the animals or any of that stuff. We'll keep it simple. Like that Legend Hunter who became Complete in that really bare ceremony. What was his name?" He clicked his fingers, searching for it.

"Jacques the Naked," said Estravon.

"Him. We don't need any ceremony or trappings and fuss. We can do this."

The stage clanked and slumped as he said it, a crunch and a puff of dust rising from its centre.

Lucien coughed. "Actually, I don't think there's any need for a Completion Ceremony," he said, adjusting his spectacles.

Once upon a time, Finn would have punched the air at those words. Not this time. He just wanted a certificate, something that said he'd done it. Then he could get on with the rest of his life as a Legend Hunter. His father could be one of the Twelve. Emmie would get her chance to become Complete next. Everything would fall into place.

"Why?" said Hugo.

"Finn won't need to bother with a ceremony," said Lucien, "because he is not going to become a Legend Hunter at all now."

58

Finn's heart dropped through his chest. Even Clara, who didn't want this to happen anyway, looked taken aback.

"What are you saying?" Hugo said, challenging this upstart arrival.

"Young Finn, how was Mr Glad trapped in the first place?" Lucien asked.

"I pushed him into a gateway in the library," answered Finn, feeling a growing incredulity.

"Right," said Lucien.

Estravon made a note. Behind him, the crowd craned to see what he was writing, to get a better look at what was going on.

"But you've spoken to Mr Glad since?" continued Lucien.

"Yes," said Finn, "after he appeared to me."

"What's this about?" Hugo asked, increasingly tetchy.

"That seems quite the coincidence," observed Lucien.

"But I stopped him too," Finn maintained.

"*Have* you stopped him, though?" asked Lucien. Estravon made a note. "I don't see him here. I see these three Half-Hunters, returned to this world. I see Gerald there, returned to the dead. But Mr Glad?" Lucien looked around him, for effect. Shrugged his shoulders. "Nowhere to be seen."

Estravon made another note. The crowd was almost on top of them at this stage.

"Finn's done nothing wrong," said Emmie, moving away from her father. "I've been with him all this time. I know that."

"You were with him when he met the traitor Niall Blacktongue on the Infested Side?" Lucien asked.

"Yes," said Emmie. "Well, no—"

"You were there for every conversation he had in that world of the Legends?" asked Lucien, moving closer to her. "Every encounter? You were there when he became a human weapon, able to explode at will?"

"No, but—" Emmie began.

"You were there the entire time Hugo was in the mountains with the Legend resistance?"

"Be careful with what you're saying," Hugo warned.

Lucien stepped back, beckoned to someone behind. "Bring the Legend to us."

A wriggling, complaining figure was dragged through the thick crowd by assistants who looked like they had already had enough of the Hogboon they'd been asked to restrain. Broonie's mouth was taped over and he was once again trying very hard to roar from behind it. The tape was pulled clear and he yelped in pain.

"Mind my warts!" Broonie protested. "I won some of those in a wager."

"We found this Hogboon wandering around the town with a mouthful of worms," said Lucien.

"I wasn't finished when you grabbed me," said Broonie. "Help me, Finn. I thought I had developed a tolerance for every type of torture and forbearance, but I was wrong. I just want some grubs and a sleep. A proper sleep. Not one of those sleeps that follows being frozen in the agony of time. Just a lovely, long, cosy kip."

"Has Finn helped you before?" Lucien enquired.

"If you can call it help," answered Broonie, then reconsidered. "He let me escape, didn't he? He saved me. He was good to me when the rest of you wanted to turn me to stone and stick me in a bottle. I've met many humans. He and Emmie are about the best of the lot of you."

Finn realised immediately that this was not helping.

"Thank you," said Lucien.

The assistants started to tape up Broonie's mouth again, and the last words he squeezed out were loud, clear and pierced the night. "You've all got ridiculous ears, you know. I hope they drop off!" He was bundled away.

"You're stitching us up," said Hugo. "That's what's going on, right?"

Lucien displayed shock. "We're just trying to understand what is going on. Nothing more. Nothing less."

"There's nothing going on," said Finn.

"Wrong, Finn. There's something going on here all right," said Hugo, eyes narrowing. "I can see it."

"You want an explanation," Lucien said. "We all do."

He half turned to address the crowd behind him as much as Finn and Hugo. "Finn not only rescued Legends, as we have just heard from the mouth of that Hogboon, but he found a way into their world to collaborate with them and help them invade Darkmouth. Explain that."

"I saved this town," insisted Finn.

"Hugo, you spent two weeks on the Infested Side," continued Lucien, "among the Legends, protected by them, just like your father, Niall Blacktongue. Explain that."

"Those Legends were rebels," Hugo argued. "They want peace, not war."

"And Finn did not stop Mr Glad when he had the chance, but instead trapped him so he could become even more powerful. Explain *that*," said Lucien.

"No," said Finn.

"Mr Glad returned, and helped bring the Legend army you betrayed us to." Lucien took a step forward, determined.

"Not true!" said Emmie.

"Their aim was to kill the Council of Twelve. To wipe out the Half-Hunters. To conquer Darkmouth."

"Look around," said Hugo. "Darkmouth was saved."

"All we see is destruction, death and a man poised to join the Council of Twelve when almost everyone else has been wiped out," said Lucien. "And beside him the boy who was meant to become the only new Legend Hunter in years."

"You are twisting this," Hugo accused him.

Finn felt like his life was being stolen from him, piece by piece. And he was helpless to stop it.

"Together, you planned to keep Darkmouth at the centre of the world," said Lucien with unwavering certainty. "To keep us at war. To control the Legend Hunter world."

"It's a lie," Finn said. "All a lie." The crowd had come right in now, closed the circle, a wave of murmurs and whispers and gasps rising within it.

Lucien gestured to the assembled Half-Hunters and townspeople. "Well then, if you have someone who can back up your version of events, then by all means point them out."

"Estravon," suggested Emmie, standing by Finn.

"Yes," agreed Finn, seeing their chance to be saved. "Estravon will back us up."

"Tell them," Emmie said. "You were on the Infested Side with us. Tell them what happened."

But Estravon remained quiet, pensive.

Hugo shook his head, knuckles once more scraping on stubble, his anger barely suppressed.

Lucien pushed up his glasses, turned to Estravon. "That seems fair." He beckoned the administrator forward. "You were with Finn on the Infested Side. You saw what happened?"

"Yes, I saw it," said Estravon.

"Thank you," said Finn, relieved.

"But not all of it," added Estravon.

Finn was struggling to breathe. He felt his world closing in on him. So many eyes were on him now. Half-Hunters. Townspeople. Their stares bored into his skin.

"I'm afraid I can't support everything Finn says," continued Estravon, turning to him. "Not that I'm accusing you of anything, it's just, well, it is possible, from a certain angle, that, well, Lucien has a point."

Finn flicked his gaze from person to person, mouth open in disbelief. It was like being pulled along by a tide, dragged out to sea without anything to cling to.

"This is not right," said Hugo.

"I was not there when Finn met Niall Blacktongue," said Estravon. "I was not in the mountains of the Infested Side as Hugo spent time with the Legends. I do not know for sure why Niall Blacktongue destroyed the cave. I don't know what Finn and Mr Glad may or may not have talked about before he was trapped, or since."

"You're calling me a traitor!" shouted Finn. "I've done nothing wrong."

"Let us be clear, Estravon," said Lucien. "Do you think it is safe and proper for this Blighted Village to be left in the hands of Hugo the Great who spent two weeks on the Infested Side in the company of the enemy?"

"You know that's not how it was," hissed Hugo.

"And do you believe, Estravon, that we should leave Darkmouth to Finn, who might have deliberately created a super-powered Mr Glad, who opened a gateway to the Infested Side and made allies there, returned with a Hogboon, conversed with the traitor Niall Blacktongue, collaborated with him to destroy the crystals at the Cave at the Beginning of the World, and who came dangerously close to assuming the powers of the Trapped?"

"That's a lie!" shouted Finn.

"That's as clear as day," said Clara.

"Don't do this, Estravon," Hugo said.

Finn felt heat rising within him, a volcanic torrent of dread bubbling up from the very deepest reaches of his soul.

"Well, Estravon," Lucien repeated. "Do you think Darkmouth is safe in their hands?"

Estravon raised his head. Thrust out his chin. Pulled the sleeves of his suit down, straightened his collar.

"No," he said. "Darkmouth is not safe in their hands."

"And what do you recommend be done?" Lucien asked him.

"That they be removed as Legend Hunters." Estravon couldn't look at them as he spoke. "Darkmouth should be taken away from them."

It felt unreal to Finn. As unreal as anything that happened that day. In his life so far. It was as if his whole world had been shredded and thrown into the breeze.

Behind them, the huge celebratory banner finally lost its mooring, fell and draped itself across the wreckage of the stage.

LIECHTENSTEIN:
THE VERY SAME MOMENT

*I*n the dim basement of a dull building hiding off the street in Liechtenstein, two people stared at dust made of materials they could not fully understand.

One was a chief scientist to what had been the Council of Twelve, and she looked baffled. The other was her deputy chief scientist, and his moustache now stretched beyond his earlobes. Both had thick, steel-mesh gloves on as they continued their so far futile attempts to make the dust open a gateway.

A third person arrived. It was Axel of the Office of Snacks. At this point, he was yet to realise that almost the entire Council of Twelve was gone, bound together during a terrible fight at Darkmouth. Which meant he was also unaware that an order of jam tarts for Cedric the Ninth would be entirely wasted.

Axel was eating sherbet dip, but as its candy stick was already munched he had taken to poking his finger into the bag and using his wet, blackened fingernail to pull out the fizzy treat within.

"Stumm the Eleventh eats this," he told the scientists, neither of whom were paying him much attention. "It's about the only thing that keeps him awake. Or less sleepy anyway." He dabbed his finger in and sucked on more sherbet.

Meanwhile, the scientists were attempting to open a gateway in the lab, for the 1,521st time. The chief scientist gathered some dust from where it was piled on silver weighing scales, lifted it on the end of two gloved fingers, tried to push it against some invisible wall between worlds that might be there, but couldn't find it.

And, as the dust for attempt number 1,521 fell away, having resolutely failed to burrow towards the Infested Side, she sighed and her deputy made some brief notes on his clipboard.

"I just don't understand," she said. "We've tried everything, but nothing works. We simply can't open any gateways."

They went to a desk in the corner to examine the computer there. Axel watched them point at some numbers, drag fingers across charts, discuss what they should do next. As they did, he wandered over to the pile of red dust on the silver weighing scales, leaned over for a closer look at this substance that had become so vital to them, which had caused so much trouble.

As he did, a thin stream of sherbet poured from the packet he was holding on to the dust.

Panicked, he looked around at the scientists. They were still huddled over a chart on the screen. So Axel mushed up the red sherbet with the dust before stepping away quickly.

The scientists returned to find him leaning casually against the furthest wall, sucking on his finger as if he'd not moved.

"Right," said the chief scientist. "Let's try it raw again. Just dust, no mixing agent, but this time using 9.3 mils."

The other scientist measured out some dust, then scooped it on to his gloved hand. Axel watched, wincing at the thought of how much he'd ruined their experiment.

The scientist carefully angled his hand so as not to drop any dust, and waved it across the air. Nothing happened. Axel turned to leave.

Phwooooack!

The room lit up, a sunset glow in the corner of Axel's vision. He whipped round and saw it. A small sparkling smear in the air, but flowing from the outside in, quickly collapsing until, with a phoap, it was gone.

But it had been a gateway to the Infested Side. Here, in this room. And Axel knew it meant two very important things.

First, they had found a way to open up a path between the world of humans and the Legends.

And second he was going to have to order a lot of sherbet.

59

Finn tried to close the door of the house. Its lock didn't catch, so he had to go back and push it shut. But it still wouldn't so he slammed it hard enough that the lock swung free.

"I'll fix that later," said Hugo, with a sigh of frustration. "Unless Lucien has decided I can't touch anything here either."

Finn stood in the hall, such as it was. It felt strange walking into the house Emmie had stayed in for so long, but this time knowing that he wouldn't be leaving. Not for now.

"It's so small," said Clara, looking at the way the front porch led straight to the living room. She pulled a large suitcase behind her. Hugo carried a larger bag in one hand and two fighting suits on hangers in the other. Finn had a backpack filled with almost everything he owned. A leg of his cuddly toy peeked out of the base of the zip. He still

held on to it. He didn't know why.

"I was born to be a Legend Hunter," said Hugo, staring at the blotchy green wallpaper. "It's all my family have ever done. I've never not had a job to do. I'm not going to start sitting around now."

"I didn't think you would," said Clara, upset and sadness tightening her voice. "Anyway, no one's going to do my job for me so I'll go to the surgery. I'd better not crack anyone's tooth today. You two get us settled here. Finn, fetch your school uniform out of that bag before it gets too scrunched up. You've missed a lot of homework."

She started out of the door, ignoring his groans, but seemed to remember something and returned while pulling an object from her work bag. She handed a book to Finn.

"The bookshop was doing a damaged-goods sale after the, well, after the you-know-what smashed into it. I saw this and thought you'd like it."

Finn read the title. *How to Become a Veterinarian: A Complete Guide from Aardvark to Zebra.*

That had been his dream: to leave the Legend Hunter world behind and look after animals.

Things had changed now his destiny had been taken away from him.

He forced himself to smile, though. "Thanks, Mam."

Clara headed out, the door flapping behind her.

Finn put the book down on the back of the sofa. "I'll read it later."

His father had his head tilted right back and was now inspecting something on the ceiling. "That's damp, I think. Do you see it? Or maybe it's an old bloodstain. That'll be fix-it job number two."

The choice of who would take over, Lucien had said by the collapsed stage, was clear.

"We must do what is right," he had said. "We must give the house to someone else."

"I won't do it," said Steve.

"Excuse me?" asked Lucien.

"I won't take Hugo and Finn's house. I won't take what is rightfully theirs. Not now. Not after everything. I'll admit it's what I wanted at times. Still do, I suppose. But not like this. Myself and Emmie won't do it."

Lucien had been puzzled. "I wasn't going to ask you. You have been compromised too, Steve. By where you've just been, how you've been trapped. That will need a full report. Proper investigation."

Steve had looked utterly crushed. He was obviously sincere in not wanting to take the house. But he had wanted to be *asked* at least.

"No," said Lucien, turning to Estravon. "The person who will take over Darkmouth is standing right here."

Estravon had pulled at the cuffs of his jacket in anticipation.

"It is me," said Lucien.

And that was that.

"The town is not going to be safe in his hands," Finn said now, pulling at a thread on the sofa in this small house. "He's spent so little time here."

"I don't doubt that at all," said Hugo.

"We can't be sure Mr Glad is gone. He told me that every time he travelled between worlds he became more powerful. He didn't come back like Steve and the others. He's still out there. I know it. If he comes back…"

"They're playing with fire and at some point very soon it's all going to go up in flames," agreed Hugo. "And you and me will have to be the fire brigade."

"You're being very calm about this," said Finn. "How can you be very calm about this?"

"Because I know things."

"Like what?" asked Finn.

"For a start," said Hugo, "I know that the last thing I did before leaving our house was to arrange for it to become the temporary pre-school while they fix the one demolished by the Hydra."

Finn couldn't help but smile at the thought of Lucien being overrun by little monsters. Then again, their own new living arrangements were not exactly ideal. "But we can't stay here too long, Dad. It's too small for all of us. You and Steve are going to be a nightmare to live with."

A key rattled in the door, but the door swung open anyway and Steve and Emmie stood on the step, looking at the broken lock.

"I'm not exactly delighted Lucien's demanded that we stay in Darkmouth until further notice," said Steve. "But if we're going to live together, you'll need to understand how a door works."

"Hey-ya, Finn," said Emmie, holding out a clear plastic bag with a goldfish sloshing around inside.

"Hey," he replied. "You're holding a goldfish."

"For you. For the house. While we're all living together, I thought we should have a pet. We can take it for walks."

Finn smiled. "We'll get a fish tank with wheels on it and pull it along."

Emmie took the fish to the kitchen.

"You're holding sticky notes," Hugo said to Steve. "You're going to label the food so we don't get it mixed up, aren't you?"

"It's the only way," Steve said, following Emmie into the kitchen. "It'll stop us arguing."

"No," said Hugo. "I don't think anything is going to stop us arguing."

Finn and Hugo were left alone again in the sitting room of their new home.

"I'm sorry," said Finn.

"What for?" his father said. "Did you break my Legend Apprentice of the Year trophy on the way? I asked you to be careful with it."

"Not that," said Finn. "Although I did crack it, I think. Just a little bit. But that's not what I'm apologising for. I'm sorry for everything. For causing this mess."

"Listen to me," said Hugo, stooping to stare at Finn with such intensity he was pressed back against the sofa and worried he'd have to backflip over it to escape.

"This is not your fault. You earned the right to protect Darkmouth. That was stolen from you. Don't you ever forget that."

He straightened up again, releasing Finn from where he had been pinned against the sofa. Together they moved around and sat on it, in front of a square TV with a wilted potted plant on top.

"We'll get Darkmouth back, won't we, Dad?" Finn asked.

"We have to," Hugo replied. "But *you* have to remember that this conspiracy will go deep. Lucien has convinced the rest of Headquarters to remove us. Do you know how often that's happened to any Legend Hunter family in the past? Of course you don't. It's happened only twice. And that's counting us."

"Did the others end up getting their Blighted Village back?" asked Finn, hopeful.

"No," said Hugo. He grinned. "But that's what makes this all the more of a challenge."

From the kitchen, they could hear Steve telling Emmie what sticky notes should go on what cereal.

"But, before that, I think it's about time I took a trip," said Hugo.

"Really?" exclaimed Finn. It hadn't even occurred to

him that they had freedom now. No expectations. No pressure. No need to stick around. He felt delight and anticipation flood through him. "Where? I mean, there are so many places I want to go to. Spain. Portugal. France. I've always wanted to go to France."

"Possibly," said Hugo.

"Or Italy. Greece. Brazil. Germany. Australia. It's Australia, isn't it? New Zealand on the way. America on the way back."

"None of those."

Finn looked at his dad. They had never been on a holiday. Never run along a soft sandy beach in some tropical part of the world. Never kicked back by a sun-heated swimming pool. Never been *in* a sun-heated swimming pool. But it was dawning on him that this plan didn't involve palm trees or suntan lotion.

"You're going to get Darkmouth back, aren't you?" Finn said.

"Absolutely," Hugo said.

"You're going to Liechtenstein."

"We're going to go wherever we need to," his father said, with relish. "I still have a few friends out there."

Finn thought about it. Thought about the life now open to him in a town where he was no longer expected

425

to be the Legend Hunter. No Legends. No ceremonies. No prophecies. Just an ordinary life, in which he could do whatever he wanted, *become* whatever he wanted.

But he also thought about Mr Glad's threat, and about how Darkmouth remained the last place on Earth where Legends still invaded. He thought about the destiny he'd always been told was his.

"Want to come along?" asked Hugo, with a smile.

Finn didn't need to think twice before answering.

THANK YOUS

Thanks to my legendary editors Nick Lake and Samantha Swinnerton.

Thanks to James De La Rue for the illustrations that so bring Darkmouth to life.

At HarperCollins, thank you to interiors designer Elorine Grant and cover designers Kate Clarke and Matt Kelly, who make these books jump off the shelf. (Not literally, although we're working on that.) I'm also grateful to Geraldine Stroud, Mary Byrne, Ann-Marie Dolan, Simon Armstrong and Nicola Carthy in publicity, Nicola Way and Hannah Bourne in marketing, Brigid Nelson and JP Hunting in sales, Amy Knight for production, and to Tony Purdue in HarperCollins Ireland.

Continued thanks to Ann-Janine Murtagh, head of children's books at HarperCollins.

As always, I'm indebted to my wonderful agent Marianne Gunn O'Connor for all her remarkable work.

Particular love and thanks go to Maeve and our children Oisín, Caoimhe, Aisling and Laoise for sharing the adventure. (And in case you're wondering, Caoimhe is pronounced Kwee-va. The Irish language is a magnificent thing.)

And, of course, thanks to all you fantastic readers. Now, you may want to jump out of the way because this book will self-destruct in 5… 4…

SHANE HEGARTY